Born to a single mother in Dust Bowl-era Nebraska, Roy Manger learns to deny his true self from an early age. The rural Midwest is no place for a boy who wears girls' clothes for fun—let alone for one who suffers gruesome hallucinations. It is only when he leaves home that he can embrace his true identity, spending his days as Roy and his nights as Raina, working as an escort in a ritzy Chicago bordello. But after a run-in with the law, Roy is torn between extremes: to live as a man or as a woman; to ignore his grief or struggle to accept it; to suppress his visions or seek to understand them. With the support of Woodrow, a convict with a murky past, Roy will have to come to terms with the fact that, in life, all of the greatest joys must come from within—and the greatest dangers, too.

I0679770

Published by
NineStar Press
PO Box 91792
Albuquerque, New Mexico, 87199
www.ninestarpress.com

Warning: This book contains sexually explicit content which is only suitable for mature readers.

Print ISBN # 978-1-911153-84-9
Cover by Natasha Snow
Edited by Sasha Vorun

A DECADE OF VISIONS

Cameron Ramses

Dedication

To my mother

BOOK ONE

Chapter One

First, she noticed the twine was gone. Then the shears. And when Inez pried open the icebox—the dust on the lid cascading off in streams—she noticed the milk was no longer where she had put it. She stood there a moment, scratching her scalp through her red bandana. She shook her head, slammed the icebox shut, and started down the hall.

The dust in the air made way for Inez, parting around her hips and thick calves, sticking to the blond hairs of her arms still moist with the day's sweat. It dusted her hair with beige. Whether her nose was freckled or her pores were merely clogged with dust, it was hard to tell.

The cloud reformed behind her and hung in the bloodstained light of evening. In the hall, the light became a muted yellow, filtering through the newspapers they used to seal the front windows and keep out the tiny pieces of dust. Streaks of light caught in the hairs the bandana failed to keep down, illuminating her round face, haloing her head. She turned the corner and entered Roy's room.

Here, too, the dust clung, thickening the air into ochre. The dust turned the column of light traveling from the window to the floor into sparkling molasses, a statue of amber. In this room, the windows bore no newspapers, since no matter how many times she taped them up, Roy would always tear them down.

Roy was where she expected him to be: hunched over beside his bed. Around the bottom of the wrought-iron frame were tied hundreds of husks of corn, a jungle of dried yellow and brown, as if the whole bed were a corn-husk doll wearing a skirt. The skirt was thickest around the bed posts, where the longest husks brushed the ground; as they traveled toward the center, the husks grew shorter, creating an opening into the space under the bed, like a dry curtain opening onto a stage.

Roy hadn't heard her come in. She watched his hunched head—black-haired like his father—sway as he measured out a length of twine. She heard the snip of the shears. Curled up like this, resting on his heels, his little body was a bean. A bean like before he was born, a bean like when he curled up in her arms at night, crying or screaming or staring into the dark after a nightmare. From this distance she could have picked up her beloved, black-headed bean and swallowed him like a pill. Then he would have been safe.

The bean leaned forward and wrapped the twine around the bed post, slipping a husk under the string before tightening it. From under the bed peeked the edge of a saucer.

Briefly she considered leaving. If she said nothing, he would never know she had seen him at his work. By tomorrow morning, the twine, shears, and milk would be returned to their places like magic, and the saucer would stand in the cabinet—washed, no less. He was good about those kinds of things. Besides, she could find some other way to tie the legs of the chicken together, another way to sever the neck. She could just step back and return to the kitchen and make dinner without a word.

But at that moment he turned. The look of shock on his face was complete; his shame and surprise sucked the last bit of color from his cheeks, draining his thin lips. He paused with the scissors in his hand, the twine hanging from his fingers. Limp-jawed and silent, he sat as still as a hurricane lamp and as rigid as a clapboard.

Before Inez could say a word, her son bolted under the bed.

She rushed forward and swung her arms closed, nabbing only air as his legs curled out of sight, rustling the husks like wind. She heard him jostle the saucer and watched as a thin dribble of milk crept out from under the bed—bringing to mind a crying eye—and turned beige as it absorbed the dust. She immediately pulled the dish rag off her shoulder and slapped it onto the spill.

Squatting on her haunches was no easy feat for a woman her age, especially after a day in the field. Her knees in particular protested at being bent. She knew that tomorrow, when she squatted to sit on the dairy stool, she would regret this.

Crouching, she asked, "Roy? Honey?"

The mouth of the cave was silent. The hundred flimsy snaggle-teeth stuck out in defiance.

"Honey, come on out." She picked up the twine and wound it around her hand, resting her elbows on her knees. She stuck the bundle in her apron pocket. "Can't you come on out?"

Inez rubbed her eyes with the heels of her hands and then rubbed her palms together. The friction caused the film of dust and sweat to form tiny pellets, which she brushed off onto the floor. She wondered if she should go ahead and pull the bed from the wall to force him out. Or she could return to the kitchen and make dinner and wait for him to be drawn out by the smell of roast meat. Or she could threaten him, say he could no longer sleep with a candle if he didn't come out right this minute.

Or she could wait.

So she rocked slowly on the balls of her feet. The printed squares of the window inched up her back as the sun moved faster and faster toward the horizon. The dust swirled around her head, in every vacant inch of the room, and the milk soaked into the dish rag. Two minutes waiting, and she could hear her own heart. Four minutes, and she worried she would not have enough time to butcher the chicken. Seven minutes, and she was perfectly still, listening to the mouse's breath coming up from under the bed. Sometimes he took this long to un-scare. Sometimes he just needed a little patience.

She ran her tongue over her teeth, checking a sore spot on her gums. She deepened her breathing and listened to her heart rate slow down. She planned the finances for the next week and wondered whether it was such a good idea, after all, to kill a chicken tonight. Maybe she should wait and see if the old hen really couldn't lay another egg. Maybe she was just taking a break. She planned for when the vet, Mr. James, would come, either tomorrow or the next day. She would have a lot to explain to Roy, then. She rehearsed.

Son, you know how the flowers disappear when the weather gets hot? Well, sometimes living things go away and don't ever come back.

She scrapped it. Too morbid. Besides, he was twelve. He already knew the basics.

Your cat is dead.

No, that would not work either. Might set him off. He was a very sensitive boy, she knew.

Your cat is with your father.

Well...no. She didn't like the sound of that.

She rested her elbows on her knees and interlaced her fingers. She decided she would just play it by ear. She closed her eyes and raised her brow, thinking, *I may be crouched in this very same spot tomorrow, waiting for him to crawl out, waiting to console the poor dear for the passing of his old, sick cat.*

She hefted herself up, brushing fresh dust off her skirt. Knees righted and spine straightened, she heaved a sigh of relief.

"Roy," she said, clearly and slowly, "I'm gonna fix dinner, but you better bring back the twine and the shears after you've washed up."

She cast a last glance at the silent maw of the bed-cave, thinking, *There will be no cat to come live in your cave, honey. No cat to lap up that milk.*

She passed through the hallway, dim now. Past the framed

postcards of Vermont and Ohio, past the raccoon skull that Roy found and wanted mounted on the wall. Past the old bouquet hanging upside down from the lintel, strung up and hung there at Roy's insistence. No, she wouldn't kill the chicken tonight. She would just make some biscuits and hash. It is wiser to spare the chicken for later. As a consolation for Roy.

Chapter Two

"Veterinarian" was a loose term. The man who went by that title was more of a Jack-of-all-trades than a true vet. Animals were just one of his many areas of expertise. He changed the oil on tractors and birthed a lamb with the same deft hand, the same no-nonsense concentration. Because of his skill and his straightforward and upright business manner, he had been in constant high demand since he was sixteen, the greatest entrepreneur of his Baltimore neighborhood. Despite his packed schedule he somehow found the time to get married, have three kids, and move out West. Since he could not wash his accent of its Eastern European tone, to survive unmolested in this new, flat land, he jettisoned his family name and insisted everyone simply call him Mr. James.

Mr. James wore a black hat over thinning, blond hair, kept a tin of snuff in his pocket, and drove a black Ford with the two right hubcaps missing. Even with this unbalanced car and his odor of old tobacco, Mr. James was popular with women, who seemed to assume that, since his own wife had tuberculosis, he was necessarily in the market for another woman. Besides, there was some irresistible allure to a man who could repair a deck in a forenoon and reduce a dead raccoon to a pelt and a skeleton.

Adrian resembled his father at that age. Boasting blond hair and a strong jaw, he was blessed with handsome, square fingers that manipulated the world however he desired. Mr. James noticed with relish that the shrinking of his own body was not in vain, for it contributed, by the law of inversion, to the filling out of his son's chest and to the general broadening and thickening that was youth.

So this man and his eldest son, Adrian, rocketed down the roads of Furnas toward the Mangers'. Mr. James, in a genius move of generational economy, had split his greatest talents evenly, cleanly, between his three children. His youngest son, Jacob, could dismantle and reconstruct a threshing machine with his eyes closed. His daughter, Lidia, was a master carpenter, even though her father had to insist that he built her beautiful cabinets himself, or else the men in town refused to buy them. His eldest son, Adrian, knew more about animals than his own father even, having been inspired when he saw the miraculous calving of triplets. In this way, Mr. James ensured that each skill was attended to by the next generation, and even added to by the accumulated insurance of monomania. He knew he ran the risk of losing a whole third of his knowledge should one of his children die. But Mr. James was a hopeful man. He rarely, if ever, let this thought cross his mind.

The one thing he mourned about his kids was that they had never learned Polish. So while he and Adrian drove across the gray landscape, there were very few words exchanged. The factors for this were twofold: the first being that, whenever Adrian spoke aloud, the English words struck his ear as coarse and unfamiliar. But on top of this, they were discouraging in their implication—they could not be English without being not-Polish. So the father did not respond when his son spoke, in part because he did not understand and in part because he chose not to.

Besides the equal division of his skills among his progeny, another thing Mr. James believed in firmly was that one should never cut corners. So when Adrian gestured to his father, saying, "It's easier to drive across this field; it saves us having to go around the whole of the Roberts' property," his father continued driving straight. Mr. James knew that, when Adrian was alone or with his siblings, he drove off-road, traversing ravines and powering through areas of dangerously sharp rocks. Of course he knew this. No matter how fast Jacob could replace the fender or mend a tire, Mr. James could detect an axel misaligned by mere centimeters or a headlight whose glass was scratched by a branch. He did not reprimand them for this deceit. He knew they would eventually realize that uprightness was the only means to earn a spot for yourself in the world. They would, the three of them, come back home after sowing their wild oats, ready to assume their father's moral staunchness. They would stand up for justice, even if, today, all they cared about was fun. He knew they would come around, because he had done the very same, twenty years prior.

Mr. James silently refused the shortcut and drove all the way to the cross-streets before turning onto the road to the Mangers' while Adrian stared out the window and guarded his silence like glass.

Chapter Three

For Roy, mornings began with a gasp. As dreams flowed away and the details dimmed and ebbed like the tide, he felt himself find his footing in the here and now. Reality was not a liquid, as he had believed while asleep, but rather a firm and enveloping solid. He did not wonder, "Do I really *feel* the sheets on me? Does the crack in my ceiling seem *real*?" since there was no doubt that the sheets were there, and there was no doubt the ceiling was cracked. The affirmation of having awoken was this: no longer did anything change just because you asked whether it was real. Once you were awake, things were real whether you wanted them to be or not.

The day was so fine that even the cows were in a good mood. They greeted Roy with a low, thoughtful, "moo," and he mooed in response to let them know he was happy to see them. Their milk was not a gift, according to his mom, since it was not given freely. It was something you had to earn, through kindness and attention.

Since the dust storms had started, the cows' eyes always seemed irritated. Each morning he would clear out the brown crust from the corners of their eyelids, careful not to poke them in the eye. Their water, too, had grown so silty that his mom had had to cover it with canvas and only unveil it at night, when the dust was the most settled.

Milking was not a chore for Roy. He enjoyed the rhythm, the warmth of the cow's flank as he rested his cheek against it. He murmured to Zeeda and kissed Skye's cheek, and carried the pail back inside without spilling any. If he wanted to keep the cream for Dolly, then he could not afford to spare a drop.

The house was already filled with the smell of baking biscuits. The gravy on the stove already bubbled with the excitement of a new day. His mother was already churning butter while he poured the milk into jars. There was already a scrim of sweat and dust on her brow.

"Roy, honey, could you bring me the water?"

Roy, setting down the pail, brought his mother the covered pitcher of water.

"Thank you, honey."

Roy finished pouring the milk and moved the gravy off the heat, checking with his thumb whether it was warm enough.

Inez, churning butter, stared at her son with amazement. It was not the exact same gesture as his father, since Roy Manger the Elder preferred to use his index finger, while Roy Jr. chose the thumb. But the similarity was striking enough to pause the piston of Inez's arms and force her to wonder: had he seen his father do that very thing? Or was this action inborn?

The question beat on her head like a beggar at the door of a church. *Did he see him do that? Did he see him do that?*

Her son dribbled water from a clay cup into the pot of a small plant on the windowsill—a tiny, vibrant vine that had shot forth seemingly overnight from the tin can in which it was planted. Hearing the churn stop, he turned. His mother smiled just in time. Her thoughts turned from the difficult and fraught question of inherited traits toward her son's physical form. Namely, how his slender arms showed through the dirty sleeves of his shirt, the narrow waist, the fingers, long and thin, and the voice, thin too, and lilting.

None of these traits were shared with his father. For years the older Roy had held the title of Strongest Man Around. Where he grew up in Vermont, there was still a hatchet stuck in a tree where he had thrown it fourteen years ago, since no one, not man nor mule nor machine, could extract it without destroying the hatchet, the tree, or both. His had been a clean brand of strength. Harvesting wheat or chopping wood, he would sweat through his thin, white shirts in mere moments, his body steaming on cold mornings. The dark jaw, the black hair. The Strongest Man Around.

She churned on, telling Roy Jr. to remove the biscuits. She thought, *Maybe if Roy didn't inherit anything physical from his father, then the other things skipped over him as well.*

The biscuits were laid on the table, still hot, and the butter served in a bowl. They drank milk with breakfast. They switched between pouring gravy and spreading butter on the steaming biscuits.

"Ma?" asked Roy.

"Yes?"

"When is the vet gonna come?"

"He may come today, dear. And please don't talk with your mouth full."

He shut his mouth with a snap and chewed, washing the mouthful down with milk before continuing. "What if he doesn't come today?"

"Then he will come tomorrow."

"What if he doesn't come tomorrow?"

"Then... Well, he will probably come tomorrow."

"I want him to come today."

"Me too, honey. But you know, looks like tomorrow will be nice and sunny."

"Yeah?"

Inez licked a spot of butter off her lip. "So we could head into town and maybe have a picnic."

Roy thought about it for a moment. He licked the dollop of jam off his plate. He looked up at his mother from underneath his bangs and then looked back down. "I don't know about that."

"No?"

"I think Dolly and I will...have a lot to catch up on. She's been gone so long," he said. His legs, which did not yet touch the ground, swung back and forth in the air. "I have a lot to tell her."

"Oh. All right. Well, you should ask her when you see her, and let me know what she says. I'd like to go if you're willing."

"May I be excused?"

"You may."

He darted up and placed his plate in the basin and ran back outside to finish his chores. When the door slammed shut behind him, Inez let out a long sigh. Once, when he was a baby, she had promised to protect him from all suffering. Now she would just settle for most.

Chapter Four

If Mr. James was known to be scrupulously clean, then his son Adrian was known to always smell a little rank. To his father, this was the ultimate insult; the puerile and deliberate rule-breaking practiced by his children could only be borne with dignity so long as no one else—clients, clerks, or extended family members—suffered because of it. Bungling the Ford's muffler on an off-road adventure was one thing. Offending the sensibilities of a lady of the town was another.

So, despite his father's entreaties, young Adrian had refused to bathe all week, agreeing to wash his face, at least, or else be left at home. In the car the oniony, brown smell of human body wafted over the odors of gasoline and baking dust. As they turned onto the street that would lead them to the Mangers', Mr. James cracked open a window.

His brother had studied music in Warsaw. There, he had learned that, whenever Liszt grew frustrated trying to explain a certain movement, he would ask his orchestra to play certain colors instead of notes. Mr. James was sure that if sounds could be colors, then smells could, too. He had lived his whole life hiding this quirk of perception. It felt good to learn he was not alone.

Now in the car with his son, Mr. James tried to nudge out the brown from the register of his senses and replace it with something less offensive. Gradually Mr. James began to perceive dark green and, hidden behind that, black.

The open window supplied the green. The smell of baking vegetation swirled around the cabin of the car, of dew sizzling off of leaves, of young sprouts seared into eternal adolescence by the sun and the blistering dust. It had been the worst summer in decades. Rain evaporated before it could reach the ground. Even if the corn did flower, then the kernels would still end up small and hard as chunks of sand. That is assuming, of course, that the corn could stay rooted for another month. This was the vision of deep green: plants burning up and having the soil pulled out from under them like a rug.

He did not know where the black came from. Absently he lifted one hand from the steering wheel and sniffed it. Usually his fingers smelled black after he had changed a tractor's oil or strapped a new fan belt in the Ford. It went without saying that his younger son, Jacob, usually represented the black smell, while Adrian wore not only his personal odor, but also the deep purple and red stench of animal. And when his daughter, Lidia, brushed the sawdust from her arms and shook the stray nails out of the folds of her skirt, he saw rich orange.

Where is the smell coming from? he wondered. Mr. James rolled up the window. The dark green vanished, but the black grew more intense.

18

Adrian, who had been leaning with his head against the window pane, looked at his father.

Mr. James did not look his way. Both men found themselves wishing it were Jacob and not Adrian in the car.

Gradually the smell dissipated, or, at least, Adrian's body odor overtook it. They were only a half-mile to the Mangers' anyway. Adrian, respecting his father's silence, assumed that he knew best and would deal with the smell in due time. So he laid his head back on the window and watched the corn go by in silence.

Chapter Five

Mid-morning was spent inside. Inez Manger fought the urge to lie down, even though every flat surface beckoned to her. The couch, the armchair, the rocker —even the kitchen table seemed as smooth and inviting as a feather bed. Sometimes she let herself rest after lunch. But according to her father's watch, wound daily and guarded in an inner pocket, it was barely ten a.m.

So she decided to sweep. Removing the bandana from her head and wrapping it bandito-style around her nose and mouth, she plucked the broom from the corner and set to work. With brisk motions she swept the dust toward the door, the pile fattening as it went, like a snowball. Not counting the dust on the rugs, which she pulled up and hung outside, she kicked a pound's worth of dirt out her front door onto the porch, where Roy Jr., with a scaled-down broom, whisked it out onto the ground.

This done, she opened the windows to let the brown cloud filling the house dissipate. It was still early enough that all the moisture from the night had not yet evaporated. In a few hours, the wind would pick up the tiny grains from the fields and carry them for miles. But for the moment, thank God, the breeze was clear.

Exchanging her broom for a carpet beater, Inez navigated the front steps with her skirts hitched up. Her knees creaked, sore from crouching the day before. Roy sat on the porch swing, gazing out at the road.

"Honey, come on, help me with this carpet."

He stared at the road for a minute longer.

Inez called, more firmly, "Honey."

Roy snapped out of it. He stood and leaped off the edge of the porch, narrowly outstripping the ring of nettles that clung to the base of their house. He landed without a second thought, as if it wasn't a miracle to jump that far or from that height without being hurt. Inez thought something wistful about youth, and picked up the carpet-beater.

Roy turned and looked at the cruel weeds behind him and the musty, dark cavern under the porch. If he was taken by some thought at that moment, it passed quickly. A moment later he joined his mother at the clothesline, grabbed a cane, and joined her in beating the rugs.

He went at it blind, his eyes screwed shut and his lips clamped like a vise. He swung and smacked with verve, nearly hitting his mother. She recoiled from the whiz of the cane and laughed.

"Honey! Watch out! I know I'm dirty too, but I don't need a beatin'."

He opened his eyes, smiling. Before he spoke he shot a glance at the porch. His gaze stuck there.

Inez said, "Hon?"

He snapped his head back to her. "Sorry, Ma." And beat the rug again.

Eyes closed, he whipped the cane into the puffs of brown air rising from the rug the way a soul might leave a body. He was terrified to be blinded. He must be vigilant. What he had seen so vividly just now, and from which he had to flex every muscle in his neck to avert his gaze, was a peculiar quality of the nettles under the porch. A sort of shimmer he had learned to fear. Normally oily and thorny, just now the weeds seemed even more malignant than usual; from the corner of his eye he thought he saw the waist-high weeds weep with poison, the dribbling rivulets coating each needled leaf as they flowed from the stem and dripped down the tips. The serrated edges seemed to buzz with malevolent energy— seemed to vibrate and whirr like the blades of a saw—while the tops of the plants, the four-fronded eyes, tilted toward him and leered with dark intent. With his back to the porch and with eyes and nose clogged, he knew he was vulnerable. He saw what was going on behind him as surely as he saw the sun. He saw the vines rushing through the dried grass like slick, green snakes, seeking the paper-thin skin around his wrists and his ankles. Wherever the nettles would touch would erupt in sores and weep clean pus, the slipperiness forcing the vines to wind tighter and even tighter. He would die on the lawn, torn to shreds by the monstrous weeds without ever knowing whether his cat had survived, all because he hadn't been looking when he should have.

* ~ * ~ *

"Roy?"

His head snapped back around to her, shocked. He immediately turned to the porch. When he looked back at her again, he seemed relieved.

"Roy," she said, "I think this one's done."

The other rugs were smaller. The few cushion-covers that they bothered to clean only took a few minutes more. By ten forty-five, they were done. Roy offered to get them each a glass of water while she replaced the upholstery. But as he leaped up the steps, shooting a wary glance at the weeds, Inez turned around, sure that she heard something on the road. He froze on the porch and turned, too.

There was what appeared to be a gargantuan, tan-colored snake speeding toward their property. Its hide was made of dust, and its length lay along the road. Its head was a black dot, and one of its nostrils blew smoke. As it approached she saw that the dot was a car—a car whose hood was fuming black. Roy gasped and jumped in the air, waving his hands toward the dust-cloud.

"He's here!" he yelled. "The vet!"

Inez said, "Now, hold on, Roy—"

But he was already out of earshot, running down the road, toward the mouth of the snake.

Chapter Six

Even Adrian could tell that there was something wrong with the car. Besides the deafening sound of rattling, the cabin reeked of oil, and the hood spewed heavy smoke. He wanted to tell his dad to stop, to pull over and examine the engine. But Mr. James drove with stony resolve. Adrian knew better than to say something now. So he sat bolt-upright, his thighs flexing under his overalls. His arm reached out of the window and grasped the hood of the car, the tension in his muscles sparing his body the worst of the shock from the road. Like this, they rode in silence toward the wooden house whose roof bent in at the middle, whose porch beams were rotting, and whose windows were buffeted opaque by the dust.

A little boy ran toward them. His arms flailed desperately as he ran, his pale legs pumping beneath him. At this distance he seemed to be running in place.

Adrian wiped the sweat from his brow. The smoke was choking him. Not wanting his dad to think him weak, he turned his head demurely toward the open window instead of shoving it all the way out. He prayed they would get there soon. Otherwise, one of them would have to bend to the pressure and admit there was a problem. And Adrian doubted it would be his father.

Mr. James had once gone a week without shaving cream because he was too embarrassed to tell anyone he had broken his shaving mug. It wasn't until Jacob commented on his red and bumpy skin that he was forced to admit what had happened and had gone into town to buy a new one from Hardt's. He suffered for the pleasure of not ever admitting to suffering. He was nothing if not proud.

The car slowed down. Adrian watched his father's foot go wild, slamming on the gas and receiving nothing in response but a dull, defeated whirr. Adrian smiled with a tinge of malice. He would have to acknowledge it now. He looked at him with quiet triumph. It was not that he wanted his father to suffer. But, if his father were to suffer anyway, it may as well have been the fault of his own infuriating stubbornness.

After setting the emergency brake and removing the key, Mr. James hopped out of the car and lifted the hood. Adrian, who was just getting out, watched his father be engulfed by black smoke and turn away to cough and wipe the greasy soot from his eyes. Adrian smiled and pulled the bag of tools out from the footwell. Beyond the hunched, handkerchief-blowing form of his father, the little boy ran toward them, waving a hand and yelling something incomprehensible.

Chapter Seven

Mr. James identified the problem before Roy reached them. He stopped ten feet from the car, bent over and panting. Adrian, too young still to have perfected the affectionate, condescending manner that wise adults take with children, decided to ignore him altogether. He stood behind the open door of the Ford with the sack of tools resting on the seat beside him, handing his father a wrench, a hammer, and then a rag through the open window. Meanwhile, Mr. James had become part of the machine. He probed and twisted in the grease-streaked cavern, unaware of Roy standing, breathless, behind him.

They stood like this for a while—Roy too shy to say anything, Adrian not willing to act, and Mr. James too engrossed in the work at hand to think of anyone but himself or his failure at having brought the wrong son.

It was almost eleven now, and the sun had stripped the land of all moisture. Even the breeze was weighed down with dirt. Cicadas screamed. The moos of the cows in the barn came slowly, lazily. Roy was still catching his breath, wiping his nose on the back of his hand, shooting glances at Adrian, who busied himself with the tools, and Mr. James, whose rear end stuck out of the hood of the car like a Jack-in-the-box. There they stood: three strangers.

Roy worried the car troubles were caused by Dolly herself. If she could find her way into Roy's bed after his mother had locked her outside, then it stood to reason that she could have found her way into the guts of the car, and there been killed. The black oil that coated the inside of the hood looked like Dolly's fur. Roy began to panic. But he trusted Mr. James, the man with the stinking tobacco, who could snatch a fly from the air and let it gently out the window. Roy calmed himself. He was resolved to be strong. To wait for the prognosis.

Mr. James knew he was missing a part. But to admit this now would mean admitting he had failed to make sure the car was in working order before they drove the ten miles to the Mangers'. Which would have meant admitting his own mistake. Which, for Mr. James, was worse than death. But so long as he did not reveal that it was his own mistake that caused the breakdown, then he could blame the whole catastrophe on the car and, by extension, Jacob. If he was crafty, he could even hint that the issues arose from Adrian's joyrides. He could absolve himself of guilt and buy himself enough time to borrow a horse from Mrs. Manger, ride to town, buy the part, bring it back, and install it, all before first light tomorrow. Yes, that's what he would have to do. If he played his cards right, he could get out unscathed.

* ~ * ~ *

Meanwhile, Adrian rooted through the tools. He had always felt it was frivolous to name one's animals, and so never took the time to learn those of his clients' pets. But he had seen the collar on Roy's cat and the letters carved into the circle of pounded copper in the hand of a boy obviously unused to writing. Now he could not help but remember the five letters that jumped and clung to each other as if scrambled in a pan: DOLLY. Dolly, who seemed sick enough to die when they picked her up and put her in the padded cage in the back. Whose ailment resembled that of a dozen different cats they had saved: emaciated, unresponsive, and languid, with blood in their stool. Adrian cared little for the lives of individual animals. He did this job because humans could not survive without animals. They were a resource, like water or clay or wood.

He stared into the bag of tools, greasy and rough, and wondered whether he hadn't worked just a little harder for the cat with the nametag, hadn't given her a little more attention and care than she deserved, being an old housecat and a lazy mouse killer. *But I tried my best*, he thought. Whatever special care he had given this animal in particular felt like a form of weakness, like a sprout that sprung too early and was doomed to die in frost. He listened to his father rummage around under the hood. He set his fingers around the tiny sprout and plucked it from its roots. All for utility's sake. The cat was worthless anyhow.

* ~ * ~ *

Mrs. Manger, who had been plodding down the road for two minutes, finally arrived at the car and let go of her hitched-up skirts. "Roy," she said, "Roy, mind what I say. Don't go runnin' off when there's a car in the road."

She stopped a step behind her son. He turned to her with his head downcast.

"Now, Roy, don't go doing that again."

He nodded. She turned to Mr. James's raised backside.

"Good mornin', Mr. James."

The only reason the vet took the trouble to respond was that he stood to lose money by being rude. So he turned around and wiped his hands on a rag, ignorant of the streaks on his face.

"Hello, Mrs. Manger. How do you do?"

"Fine, Mr. James, just fine."

Roy stood in front of her, still staring at the vet.

Inez spoke up before Mr. James could return to the engine. "Car trouble?"

"Yes, ma'am. The engine went and took a vacation."

"Aw, what, without us? That's awfully rude of it."

"Yes, well, sometimes machines have a mind of their own."

"An easy fix?"

"Not sure yet. Gotta wait and see."

Adrian clinked the tools in the bag, not saying hello. Inez forgave his shyness. She chalked it up to self-consciousness.

Having a son as sensitive as Roy bred sympathy. Not only could she spot such a boy from a mile away, but she treated them all with the utmost maternal respect, that for a boy Adrian's age meant stepping back and giving him space. Meanwhile, Roy turned to her, grabbing her apron and tugging.

"Mr. James, I think Roy here is eager for some news."

"Hm?" replied Mr. James from deep within the mouth of the Ford.

"I said, Roy wants to know about his cat."

"Oh. Yes. Well," he said, pulling himself out, "we did all we could, but the cat passed away last night. We have the body in the back. We would be happy to dispose of it for you."

The strap of Inez's apron grew so tight that it pinched the back of her neck. Words came automatically. "Oh, thank you, doctor, but I think we can bury her ourselves. I appreciate all you've done."

"Our pleasure. Adrian will give you the body. If you please, that will be three dollars."

It felt as if Dr. James had opened up her chest and plucked a key vertebra from her spine. Three dollars? It was exorbitant. It was inflated. It was criminal. But an automaton arm reached into her pocket and pulled out a crisp five dollar bill. Mr. James was stuck back under the hood of the car.

Adrian, to save her embarrassment, rushed forward and grabbed the money, making change from his back pocket. He thanked her and wrote up a quick receipt, forging his father's signature with ease. He would not even give Roy a smile for his loss.

"Thank you, Adrian," she said.

Roy detached from her skirts and plodded through the field toward the barn. She watched him and wished the men were not here. Even if they were stiff and unpleasant guests, she still had to entertain them, which meant she could not talk to Roy about what had just happened. She could not ask him how he felt. She could not ask him where he wanted Dolly to be buried. All she could do was watch him shrink into the sunlit field of blazing, brown fronds, growing smaller with each step, until he was just one sharp shadow among many.

Chapter Eight

"If you all would like, you could come inside for some water," said Inez.

Mr. James did not reply, and Adrian was rearranging the tools again.

"Or," continued Inez, "I could bring it out here for you."

"No, thank you, ma'am," said Mr. James.

Inez uncrossed her arms and set her fists on her hips. She had a long history of hiring Mr. James; almost everything on this property still worked thanks to his expertise or that of one of his children. She had worked with their family since before her husband died. Come to think of it, it was Roy Sr. himself who recommended him. She had trusted his opinion, never thinking to shop around, never wondering whether there was someone out there who could do what Mr. James did without the brusqueness, without the masculine, businesslike ice. Or maybe there was a handyman around here with kids who weren't totally inverted, who could play with and talk to Roy. *Maybe,* she thought, *I will never hire him again.*

Mr. James called his son over and handed him a curved length of pipe. The son held it in front of him, its shape a subtle U. Mr.

James told him to rotate it so he could see in one end. He measured a ring of metal against the lip of the pipe. *They could be playacting this whole thing, and I would be none the wiser,* thought Inez. In measuring the end, he tilted the pipe upward. Suddenly the far end released a stream of black oil right onto Adrian's shirt, soaking him from the neck all the way down the front of his pants.

Inez gasped. Mr. James said nothing and pulled the pipe from Adrian's hand as if he was a kid playing with something he was not supposed to. Adrian instinctively pulled the fabric away from his skin. But the oil had already seeped through, and when he let the shirt fall back, it stuck to the ridges of his abdomen like a second, painted skin.

"Oh, my," said Inez. "Come on honey, we have a pump in the back. Come on, this way." She grabbed his hand and pulled him away. She did not know what was going on between this boy and his father. She did not know why he had made his son hold that piece of pipe like that, or why Adrian stared at his father's bent form so intently that she had to yank him to snap him out of it. Having witnessed the grief of her own son so recently, she was especially disturbed by this conflict. What was it that made this boy hate his father? What corrupted the father into playing a cruel joke on his son?

Whatever it is, she thought, *it can wait until he's clean.*

Chapter Nine

Being near the cows calmed Roy. With his nose crunched against Zeeda's hip, he could let the hot sobs come out of him like lava, the tears and the snot muffling the moans of a boy who had lost everything.

He sat on the ground and wrapped his arms around Zeeda's leg. He heaved and wept until he felt he had nothing left inside him—nothing but the dregs of salt, the very stock of bitterness. He fell flat on his back and looked up.

The barn may not have been the best place to seek refuge. He remembered playing with Dolly by this very stool one year ago. Over there, he had pushed her with his foot to keep her out of the milk, earning the nod of his mother. (But when his mother had left, he had kneeled beside Dolly and lapped up cream from the pail right with her.) Over there he had set up a rig to hoist her up into the loft where he liked to nap and where he had a secret space all of his own. Skye and Zeeda mooed as if to ask, "Where is she? Where is your friend, the cat?" He turned away from them, toward the void of the barn.

Those familiar with cathedrals will know what he saw. The cracks in the ceiling sharpened the sunlight into spears, which grew heavy with dust as they traveled at their special, divine angle toward the hay-strewn floor. He lay down there, arms akimbo. He let the ground come up beneath him and soak up his sadness. He closed his eyes and breathed, sending his pain down to the earth's core like a root, hoping it would be obliterated by the heat and the pressure down there.

Slowly the sun reached its zenith. The ray that had been warming Roy's belly had crawled up his throat and was now teasing the bottoms of his eyes. It no longer felt like the sun's warmth was filling the hole in his chest. Now it just felt hot.

The cows checked on him as he passed. He told them he was feeling better. He headed up the ladder.

A whole corner of the loft was his, separated from the rest of the space by a semicircle of dried cornstalks. Up here was where he kept his treasures: a large piece of glass suspended from the rafters by two lengths of twine, his old high chair, the piled bones of a raccoon (minus the skull, which hung in the main house), a book about sewing, a rusted candlestick he found in a ditch, and a sliding-top box containing two real matches, a pencil stub, and a rhinestone that had fallen from the costume of a beauty pageant contestant at the carnival the year before. He looked through his loot, laying them out on the boards, stacking them, touching them gently. He placed the rhinestone in the pages of the book, closed it, then opened it to make the stone clatter to the ground, as if he had been casually reading when—whoops!—a diamond just *happened* to fall out. He mimed striking a match, and lighting a candle, and waved his hands through it. If he was going to imagine a candle, it had to be huge. Setting the candlestick on the ground, he mock-lit the match and stretched his arm up as far as he could, stretching to the tips of his toes too to light the super-tall, super-thick, milky white candle that smelled like sugar as it burned.

With this established, he moved on to the meal. He brought out the glass pane from its holster of twine and placed it flat on the ground.

This is our plate, he thought.

For dinner he served a piquant, sautéed pencil stub and a hearty leg bone of raccoon. Dessert was a surprise; he hinted, however, that the dish, whatever it was, would be brilliant.

Usually this was the part where he would climb back down the stairs, place Dolly in a rusted pail, and haul her up the pulley to join him in the loft. From there he would set her in the seat across from him where she would bat at the flapping pages of the sewing book while he explained the courses. Finally, he would set the lazy beast upright. She would look at the candlestick, pass her yellow eyes over the stub, sniff the bone, and then lie back down. She would raise her head when he dropped the rhinestone onto the glass serving plate, only to lay it down once more for her after-dinner nap.

Roy sat at the table, in his finest evening attire, waiting for his date to arrive.

He looked out the window. He tied a dry reed around his wrist to serve as a watch, and then he checked the time. She had stood him up. The tears grew thick in his eyes. But his coming sobs halted: there was something walking toward him.

Heart pounding, he ran toward the window, eager to greet this dark blip crossing the field...but something was off. The proportions were wrong. It was too big to be a cat, it seemed, but it was not a person either, since it waddled as it walked. Roy squinted and noticed the figure was carrying something bulky. *Oh,* he thought. *It's just a boy with a basin.*

It was Adrian James, the vet's son. Roy watched as he turned around and shouted something back to Roy's mom, who seemed to be providing instructions from the porch.

Roy knew what was happening. His mom had sent Adrian to collect him and bring him home for lunch. But he was not ready. He needed more time.

He slipped the glass back into the twine and returned the other treasures to their hidey-holes. In the distant corner of the loft stood a little nook where he could hide.

Curled up there, he remembered again what had brought him to the loft. He said a prayer for Dolly's soul, quietly and under his breath, the same prayer his mother had taught him to say every night. When he heard Adrian walk into the barn, he held his breath. If he could have assured his invisibility by stopping his heart, he would have done that too.

Adrian lost some water when he set the basin down. Roy could see him through the crack in the floorboard. The water slipped out and steamed on the ground, running over the hard-packed soil.

Roy saw that his shirt was covered in black, with a powdering of brown where the dust stuck. He also noticed his mom had given Adrian a towel, a rag, and a bar of soap.

Adrian's shirt peeled off his chest. It made the sound of skin tearing. For a moment, Roy thought it had yanked off all his chest hair. Then he realized Adrian didn't have any chest hair to begin with. The oil left the same mark on his torso as it had on the shirt, the same upside-down "V." Adrian's body reminded Roy of his own father's, except scaled-down and smoother. When he was five or so, before his dad died, Roy would shriek with glee when given the opportunity to climb up his strong back or hang like a monkey from an outstretched arm. Adrian turned around to fold up his shirt. His back was not as broad as Roy's father's, but was a close approximation. The arms, too, presented—as they moved through space—some of the same balled-up muscle, the upper-arm bulge with the tiny snake of a vein lying across it.

Adrian turned back around now, undoing his belt, and Roy stared at him silently, marveling at the sensation of something being pulled up through dark water. He did not feel what he remembered feeling with his father. He did not want to run toward him and be lifted up with the ease of an unstoppable machine. What he was looking at now was inapproachable. The open air gaped between them. There was something terrible afoot. His heart beat faster.

Adrian removed his pants and his drawers at the same time, kicking up his heels one by one to pull off his socks. Roy covered his eyes with his hands. He felt like his body was a thin membrane of glass, shattering and re-forming just to be shattered once more, his mind scrambling to reconcile the sense of recognition and the sense of difference—the unreal aspect and the unwavering, naked figure before him. He spread his fingers just wide enough to peek through.

Adrian put a toe in the water and found it too hot. So he stood there dumb for a moment side-eyeing the cows, who stared at his body as if he was a bush or a rock. He refolded his pants, making sure not to let the sticky part touch the clean part, then brushed off a piece of straw that clung to the sole of his foot, stumbling a little on one leg. Roy trained his gaze on the blond hairs that grew on Adrian's lower back and which clung to his sweat like a spider web to dew. He would have laughed at how awkward this body in front of him was, if he hadn't found it marvelous.

Finally, Adrian managed to put a foot in. He held it there for a moment. Roy could hear him breathing heavier. Adrian pulled his foot from the hot water and kicked it in the air until its lobster-redness dulled to pink. Roy watched as he dipped the rag in the water, rubbing the block of soap into a lather. With this, he scrubbed at the oil stain, starting at his collar and running down his chest, ending finally with the border of his pubic hair. The oil came off easily enough, revealing smooth skin beneath. Roy curled his knees to his chest even tighter now as Adrian stepped into the basin and rubbed the rest of his body, too. He rinsed his collar bones, then his lower back, then the length of his thighs.

Something in Roy's brain grew warm and orange. He decided he could watch this all day.

After a few minutes, Adrian grew wary of the gaze of the cows and stepped out of the basin, patting his degreased skin dry. Just as he wrapped the towel around his waist, Roy's mom arrived with a clean set of clothes. She stopped in her tracks at the door and sputtered out an apology to Adrian and walked away red-faced. She left the pile by the door.

Roy did not watch Adrian dressing. He stood and looked out the far window of the barn, tracing his mother as she reentered the house. Suddenly, a shadow crossed his face. The borders of his mind curled in like injured hands. As Adrian, freshly clean, left the barn, Roy stood trembling with what felt like a railroad stake pinning him to the wall. What had his mother meant? Why was she so embarrassed?

He asked himself, *Have I done something wrong?*

Chapter Ten

The fourth plate in the set had been shattered years ago. Inez still knew where her husband had buried its shards in a fit of guilty mania, as if, by hiding the evidence of a fight, he could undo its occurrence. So while the roots of some vile weed silently nudged the pieces of that fourth plate deeper underground, the leftover three, the survivors, remained her best china. Inez only unwrapped them from their burlap on special occasions, such as when the pastor visited them, or when her sister, Terry, came from Lincoln. By some arithmetic miracle, she had never needed more than three.

The table was set. She asked if the men could help her out in the kitchen. Mr. James held the frustrated, far-off look of a man confronted with a mechanical impossibility. He had devoted hours to the engine to no avail. He would have to try again tomorrow. Adrian hovered in the periphery of the room, still wet behind the ears. Her husband's clothes did not find a second life on Adrian's shoulders: though he was strapping for his age, the shirt swallowed him up like a turtle shell.

She put Mr. James to work peeling potatoes. His stony silence gradually wore away. His son sat across from him in the living room husking corn. For tonight, Inez had arranged for the couch to serve as a bed, and she offered the other half of her conjugal mattress to whichever of them was the least offended by the prospect of sleeping beside a widow. While her sheets were shabby, and the pillows would not hold shape, Inez felt grateful that she had remembered to beat the rugs, at least.

Mr. James had been kind enough to bring the bag with the cat's body out to the springhouse, where it could keep cool "until I ask Roy what he wants done with it." As soon as she said it, she noticed Adrian grinning at his corn. She paused for a moment, her knife halfway through a beet, and asked herself whether it wouldn't be better in the long run to just turn the other cheek.

The words were out of her before she could think twice.

"Somethin's funny, Adrian?"

Mr. James, to his credit as a father, turned to Inez before looking at his son. This was paternal instinct: the impulse to defend. But his eyes darted back to Adrian. Inez remarked how quickly the defender became the disciplinarian.

Adrian did not look up, just kept grinning at his corn like it was a blonde-haired sweetheart. "Nothin', just thinking about somethin' funny I heard the other day."

Inez now had another opportunity to drop the whole matter and continue with dinner as planned. But the goddess of collusion was present, for at that moment, Mr. James and Inez looked at each other. The shared thought was clear: his excuse was not going to cut it. Adrian smelled a plot and looked up to the two grave faces before him, his mouth slightly open, his eyebrows beginning to draw together.

"What?" he asked.

Inez said, "I don't know whether you've ever had to raise a kid like Roy, young man." She surprised herself with the hardness of her own voice. "But I personally don't think there's anythin' funny about a young boy lovin' a cat that much."

"I mean," said Adrian, laughing nervously. "It's just an old cat."

Inez tilted her head to one side. "Now, Adrian, do you think I'm wrong to think that?"

His fingers froze, unsure whether it would be more insulting to keep husking or to put the task aside. She watched the will to fight her rise in him, the color flooding under the huge collar of her husband's old shirt, his eyes sharp, staring at the floor.

Despite all his years of taking care of animals, at the end of the day, Adrian held no illusions that they were as important as humans, or that the life of one animal had any serious bearing on the well-being of the species. He did not believe that even the most beloved family pet deserved to be mourned or even buried, outside of what was required to keep the body from stinking. Loving pets and dolls and dresses belonged to the domain of girls. For a boy of Roy's age, Adrian thought, to keep such notions was to handicap himself socially and to risk being known as a Nancy.

Adrian knew he could fight her on this. But whatever small victory he could wrest from this widow's hands would be revisited back upon him tenfold when back home with his father. The burning gaze of Mr. James promised as much. So he made a calculation and said, quietly, "No, ma'am."

She sighed and resumed chopping. "I thought not."

Mr. James was pleased. Pleased enough to provide a pleasantry.

"Mrs. Manger, I must tell you that Lidia, my daughter, just completed a rather strange job."

"Oh, did she?"

"Yes, she did. A woman in Ponka sent a letter asking her to make a casket small enough for a child."

"Oh, dear me."

"But on return post... I mean, when she wrote a letter back—"

Adrian interceded. "Can I tell the story, Dad?" Not impetuous, just aware of the gap between his father's thoughts and the English language. Mr. James gestured to his son in acquiescence.

Adrian continued. "So when she wrote back asking what was his name and how old was he and all this long letter of condolences, this woman writes back and tells her, 'Thanks for your well wishes, but they are not needed now.'"

Inez stared at him, rapt.

"Because—" Adrian smiled, pinching the bridge of his nose with the thumb and index finger of his left hand. "—Because she said it was part of a prank, you see? That she planned to scare her two-timing husband when he came back from Lincoln. She said she was going to have their son's casket right there and guilt her husband into leaving his mistress. Once he pledged to return to her, and once he signed an agreement she had her lawyer draw up, then—" Adrian choked out the last words between laughs. "—then she would have her son *leap* out of the casket and yell"—his face was red, he was heaving with laughter, and the ear of corn he was holding fell to the ground—"surprise!'"

Inez looked down and chuckled at the cutting-board. Even Mr. James smiled.

In the blood of the beets, Inez confronted an impulse. She had a question that beat against her lips, as if she had swallowed a fly that suddenly wanted out.

Without looking up, she asked, "And what if the father didn't go along with it?"

Adrian, wiping a tear from his eye, asked, "Huh?"

"What if he wanted to stay with the other woman? What then?"

Mr. James replied, "She planned for that, too. She said, 'Even if he leaves, he will always feel bad. Thinking that his actions killed his son.'"

"'Negligence,' I think she said," added Adrian.

"Hm." Inez scooped the chunks of beet onto the flat of her knife and dropped them into boiling water. "That's quite a story you got there." She tried to keep her eyes on her work, but they turned to the table anyway at the spot where the fourth plate should have been.

Mr. James stood and wiped some flecks of potato skin off his pants. He asked if he could use the latrine. Inez said of course, but warned him that the door didn't like to stay shut.

During periods of intense awkwardness, such as when two acquaintances are stuck in a room together without the presence of the intermediary friend, one may feel an almost compulsory urge toward efficiency. While Mr. James was gone, Inez prepared everything necessary for the rest of the stew and even began slicing the potatoes. Adrian, having husked all the corn available, and being too shy to ask for another job, began revisiting the cobs he had already peeled, carefully plucking off the strands of silk wedged between the kernels. These occupations were carried out in complete silence.

When Inez did finally speak, it was not because she felt some sympathy for this uncomfortable, over-muscled young man sitting before her, but rather because she realized she would one day have to interact with Roy when he was sixteen. And if Roy was already a painfully shy, backward, solitary, quiet, and thin boy, then she could only assume that with time he would grow even more shy, more backward, more solitary, and even thinner. She shuddered as she imagined the arms and legs of her already stick-thin son being stretched into a slenderness and paleness she had only ever seen in fish bones.

She had already sacrificed so much for him. Only one son and a weak one at that. It had proved impossible to continue working the farm as they were used to. She had to sell off half their land. On top of that, she had suffered the indignity of charity. She had had no other choice. The fields would never have been plowed if not for the help of their neighbors; the well would never have been dug without the kindness of those who pitied her. Meanwhile, Roy tried his best to help. He was skilled at harnessing the animals, and he loved to pluck the weeds from the field. He helped with milking the cows and with cooking. But even if she trusted him with the axe she could not bring herself to make him try to chop wood. Even if he could manage to raise the tool overhead, there was no way he could bring it down with the force and accuracy necessary to split the hard wood that they bought in bulk from town. The days of Manger men and sharp objects were over, and the legend of the hatchet was past—though she was sure it still held fast in a tree some 1,500 miles from here. Roy Sr. used to effortlessly slice through cord after cord of wood and then bundle them up with twine tied in a little bow, as if every winter day was her birthday. The logs were cut so clean it looked like God had grown them like that. *But everyone has their strengths,* she thought. *And things tend to skip generations.*

She stared at Adrian's profile wondering, when—or if—Roy would grow as big as him, he would be able to cut wood with any skill. Looking at the tan and focused hands of Adrian, she felt hopeful. She thought now would be a good time to speak.

"So, Adrian, how's Lidia? Jacob?"

His Adam's apple bobbed before he responded. "Oh, them? They're just fine, thanks."

"Your brother working on anythin' interesting?"

"Nope, nothin' really."

Inez stirred the soup. *Well*, she thought. *I tried.*

*

When Mr. James returned, Adrian was helping Inez slice the kernels off the cob onto a large plate. Mr. James pulled the bowls from the cupboard and ladled each one full of stew and then plopped in some steamed potato. She took the bowls and piled on the fresh corn herself.

Mr. James was in a better mood. While he would not describe the smell of an outhouse as pleasant, he could appreciate the overpowering quality of the odor, its ability to clear out the cloud of colors that had fogged his brain all afternoon. The smell of refuse was simple and strong—a mix of green and brown—the same as good mulch. He was free from the black smell of oil that clung to his hands and the dull, yellow smell of woman and boy-flesh that pervaded the Manger property. His palate was cleansed. He could see clearly at last.

As he entered the room he stared at Mrs. Manger's elbows, dry and cracked. He watched how a whole kernel of corn, hitching a ride on her hand, stuck to the back of her neck as she wiped it of sweat. He noticed how she watched what Adrian was doing, as if she was riveted by his water-pouring technique, as if there was something special in how he rolled up his sleeves to eat.

These observations were made in the period of calm before a meal when no conversation is required. But as they sat down and said grace, Mr. James realized he would have to speak in a moment. So he prepared his boilerplate subjects and held them at the ready like a ring of keys.

He thought about his own bed at home, the cot that he had slept on for ten years. When the kids were still young, he'd decided he didn't want to trouble his sick wife with his comings and goings in the night. It was better for her to have the room to herself. The smell as gray as stagnant water which tinged the rest of his life with the same soggy grief. Even if he clung onto every vibrant detail of smell. Even if he fought for pride and forthrightness in his work. Living in the same room as a waking corpse forced him to wonder whether all these facets of life could ever be arranged in a way that meant something, arranged to prove there was, after all, some single point of truth. He knew he was doomed to bear this cancerous pallor the rest of his life. And he knew he would pass it on to his children, like a venereal disease. Watching Inez Manger suck on her teeth before eating, he thought these two things: that grief is the death of the mind, and that things have no center. For Mr. James, who held very little to be true outside the realm of the technical, this was the closest thing he had to religion.

But over these plates of steaming, shining food, he could ignore that sullen bed for an evening, could ignore the gray smell that attached to the back of his mind. He could eat the fresh corn and the stew. He could stare at his son and at Mrs. Manger and listen to their talk. He could sleep easy tonight, hoping that youth would be spared the pain of the father. *We will find out soon enough*, he thought, looking at Adrian. *But first, we will eat.*

Chapter Eleven

Roy sat in the loft like a spider in a web, waiting until sunset. His hunger scooped deeper and deeper into his stomach. Whenever he was racked with sobs for Dolly, the pain was less. But when his mind turned to Adrian he felt a deeper, vaguer yearning, which hollowed out his whole chest as well as his stomach.

Their family was not big on candles. Inez allowed Roy a small lamp flame through the night for his nightmares, but she never indulged in them herself. At the Manger's, night was absolute. There were no questions in a darkness like that. In blackness he could be alone.

He did not want to think about what had happened. Dolly's death and Adrian. Both of these events stood monolithic in his memory, polar opposites in terms of sensation, but both accumulating a galaxy of related thoughts, feelings, and sensations, which always led, by some magnetic certainty, back to the main thought itself. Just as all comets and planets were eventually drawn in and consumed by a star, all of Roy's thoughts were drawn in to either one memory or the other.

The ladder creaked as he made his way down. He whispered to the cows, "Till tomorrow."

The crickets were already humming their evening song as he walked through the tall, dry grass. He began to plan his break-in.

He knew the door squeaked if it swung past a certain point; he opened it just wide enough to slip through sideways. He made sure to guide the screen as it swung back so that it didn't slam. The house was filled with the pale light of the half moon. Shapes stood out in grays and blues, smooth textures without depth.

His mother's hair peeked out from the end of a blanket on the couch. He had miscalculated. Adrian and Mr. James must have decided to share his mother's bed, forcing her out here.

Should he turn around and go through the other door? Should he continue to his room walking as quietly as he could? Should he try and sneak a cracker from the cupboard or just chew on the hunk of jerky he kept hidden in his room? *Or did I give that jerky to Dolly?* he wondered. *Dolly, who is dead.*

If he went the other way, he ran the risk of waking Adrian. He saw it in his mind's eye: Adrian standing in front of him wearing dad's old clothes, furious at him for doing something wrong. The mere thought filled him with dread, as if the bells in a cathedral all rang at once. No, he decided. He could not go by the master bedroom. If Adrian so much as looked at him, he knew he would turn to dust.

So he slunk through the living room, absorbing the shock of each step in his knees, hunched over like a goblin. He froze in his tracks. On the table, a bowl laden with food, shielded from the dust by a dishcloth. Leftover stew and corn. His salivary glands squirted painfully. He was not supposed to eat in his room. Everyone, including Dolly, ate in the dining room. (*Dolly, who is dead.*) But today he felt his mother would make an exception. Especially because he always returned things to their rightful places by morning.

The bowl scraped the table as he pulled it onto his hand. His steps hastened now, because stealth was exhausting, and because he was hungry.

The latch of his door was loud, so he did not bother trying to close it. His mother had remembered to light the lamp by his bed. He set the bowl of food on the ground and ate with his hands, slurping up the stew quietly. He draped the dishcloth back over the bowl when he was done, pushing it toward his bed so he wouldn't forget it in the morning.

In the corn-husk cave under his bed, the saucer of milk still sat, beige from the dust in the air and half empty from yesterday's spill. It had started to smell.

Roy replaced a husk that had fallen out of place before creeping onto his bed. He sat up against the wall and stared at the shadows in the far corner, pulling them apart from the deeper shadows that gaped in the hall door. The shadows formed faint shapes, hinting at the faces of animals and people. In this position, he was at ease and began to process some of the events of the day— to chip away at the monoliths, to drain some of the seas.

The spot in his memory from which Dolly had been torn was still raw and bleeding. Any thought of her caused a fresh pang of agony. But he prodded the spot anyway. He was used to shoving his tongue into the socket where a baby tooth had fallen out, just to taste the blood and feel the pain, pure and bright as snow. In many ways, this felt the same. Dolly had been in this family since before Roy was born. His mom told him that, when his dad was still building the house, Dolly would balance atop the highest beams and would not move unless bribed with meat. Dolly had been there when Roy cut open his hand on a piece of barbed wire that had latched onto their car, back when they still had a car. And he remembered Dolly's sleeping ball of a body being removed with great care from the armchair when they sold it to the man with the glasses.

Roy was crying. The memory of Dolly made his own flesh feel cold.

Dolly, who had warmed up the bed on Christmas Eve. Dolly, who had left two murdered voles on their doorstep—two little eyebrow-marks. Dolly, whose meowing let Roy's mother know that she was stuck in the icebox, imprisoned there by Roy Sr. for a crime he refused to explain. Dolly, whose claw marks still streaked Roy's bedposts, and whose cave spread out unused beneath Roy's bed, like a grave someone forgot to fill.

The wound was throbbing. The blood flowed freely now, and Roy could barely keep his sobs quiet. If the lamp hadn't had a hurricane shade on it, his breath would have extinguished the flame.

Amidst the ruined and wet flesh where the tooth of Dolly had been, Roy found something solid. The events in the loft. The edge of the next tooth.

Since the shadows on the far wall had begun to leer at him, Roy shut his eyes and eased back into the memory, pulling his knees up to his chest. He played the whole thing through in his mind, slowly. Then he revisited his favorite parts: when Adrian's shirt stuck to the ripples of his chest, when the shirt was being pulled overhead and the shoulders tensed to bulging, when the drawers came off, and the creature between Adrian's legs perked up minutely, sensing the fresh air. But his favorite moment by far was when the soaped rag traveled and scrubbed under his arm; the one arm stuck upright and bent acutely, showing the pale bulge of muscle like a gorgeous, subterranean serpent; the other arm bent at a right angle across his body, showing the same muscle's counterpart, but from the front. This contrast—of tan and pale, of inside and outside, of sameness and discreteness— enraptured Roy.

During this process he opened his eyes periodically just to make sure the figure of his mother was not standing in the doorway, her forehead creased, knowing everything he was thinking, disgusted by it all. But no; the doorway stood empty. He closed his eyes again.

Another wave of excitement rippled through Roy. He watched in wonder as his mind's eye replayed the images he cherished, the ones of dark blond body hairs clinging to the soap bubbles like terrycloth; how his chest has expanded as warm rinse-water rippled over it; how roughly Adrian scrubbed himself.

The image of his shamefaced mother stamped itself onto Roy's brain. He should not have been thinking about this, he knew. There was a reason she had been so embarrassed to see Adrian nearly naked. Roy shut his mouth tight, clenched his eyes, tensing every muscle in his face to keep the thought locked out. He would not think about this dirty and vile thing anymore. He would push this appalling tooth back into the gum until it went away for good.

His features all fell flat at once. He stared at the doorway. His breath caught in his throat.

Yes. There was something in the doorway. But his mother could not see in the dark and would knock her toe on every table leg in the house. *So it must be Adrian*, he realized. *Adrian, angry for what I did. He must know I saw him. He must know what I've been thinking. There must be some way to tell if someone's been having evil thoughts about you and now Adrian is here to punish me, oh God he's going to beat me up until I'm all bloody and he's going to choke me until I die and Ma will know what I did and she will know that it was wrong. Oh God I think I see him please oh please God don't let him kill me.*

Roy stared at the figure for too long, and it dissolved back into shadow. Only after he looked at the ceiling and looked back down again was he able to recognize Dolly, sitting in the doorway, staring right at him. She sat at attention in the threshold, her eyes more luminous than the candle. Roy welled up with joy. He had to cover his mouth to prevent a cry from escaping. After a moment,

Dolly walked across the floor and, as if by instinct, entered her cave. There, he knew, she curled up under the bed, like she always did. *She doesn't have to say hi right now*, he thought. *She's probably tired. She's had a rough day.* Slowly, Roy cried tears of relief.

He did not revisit his feelings about Adrian. There were more important things to think about. Tonight, he felt blessed. In celebration of her return, before he laid his head to sleep, Roy lifted the glass vent around the lamp and, with a tiny puff of breath, blew out the night-light.

BOOK TWO

Chapter One

The Alabaman businessman slash up-and-coming lumber entrepreneur, Darren Deer, watched as the landscape matured into a cityscape, luggage rumbling in the overhead compartment as the train swayed slightly. His hand held a piece of paper with three things scribbled on it, and his legs were spread so wide that no one could sit next to him. He was thirty-five or so, of average height and looks, in a gray hat and suit, sporting a brown belt and matching shoes with a little padding in the heels for height. Chicago stood before him. He felt a wave of excitement. He looked down at the paper—at the three tasks he set for himself. The rubric for a city's worth.

First, he would visit the library. Mr. Deer believed this revealed a lot about a place. Cities where public education was a priority were more valuable than their counterparts, since they recognized how smart an investment it was to empower the populace. For a city to have good libraries also indicated a more liberal, cultivated, European sensibility—something Darren Deer considered himself an expert on.

The second thing was to dine at the best French restaurant in town. For him, French cuisine represented the acme of world gastronomy—the best there was—the, as he liked to say, *crème de la crème*. For a city to insist on the quality of its "native" cuisine was to prove what Europe had been saying for two hundred years: that Americans were impetuous and were blind when it came to quality.

The third task was to hire a prostitute. She, more than anything else, would reveal the true face of a city. The best cities provided the best prostitutes and the best conditions for their work. According to men of his father's generation, America used to pride itself in its brothels, having modeled them after those of European capitals, where women were treated like princesses, beds were canopied in silk, and a bottle of wine cost an arm and a leg. These were the sophisticated years of America, before the biddies in the temperance movement strangled all the charm out of cities, and before the government decided to stifle the economic liberty that had made the nation great.

The next day at noon he had scheduled a meeting with one of the largest shippers of fruitwood in North America, providing himself ample time to get a feel for the city. The moment Darren Deer disembarked, he set to work on his tasks. En route to the library, he could not help but notice a few things: firstly, that the women of Chicago were preternaturally beautiful; secondly, that the streetcars all looked like huge, sleek beetles; and thirdly, that the buildings here were massive. Just an hour ago, he had believed St. Louis to be the most impressive city in the Midwest; now, staring at the beautiful buildings lined up against the water, he shook his head and smiled. Chicago made St. Louis look like an armpit.

Once at the Walker branch library he was committed to checking certain things: first, that the library itself was clean and well lit. Check. Second, that the library did not attract (or, even better, did not permit) any homeless people into the premises. Walking past the new authors display, he stopped in his tracks and eyed a bearded, hatless man sitting in an armchair reading a newspaper. His clothes were shabby and brown. Mr. Deer never wore his glasses in public; they threw off the balance of his face and made him look just like his sister. So he turned on his heel in order to pass by this man and give him a sniff. But a little boy beat him there, asking the older man in his best library whisper, "Grandpa, what does 'trench warfare' mean?'" Passing by the charming scene, Mr. Deer heaved a sigh of relief.

The third library requirement was that they had a good copy of Mr. Deer's favorite book. He ambled along the stacks, counting off the Rs and the Ss as he approached the Ts—and was pleased to see not one, but two good copies of *War and Peace*. Check.

Having verified that the library was up-to-snuff, Mr. Deer moved on to the next thing. He pulled his train ticket out of his pocket. On the back, he had written "Café Dantès," the restaurant his old boss, an Illinois native, recommended. The concierge had given him good directions. He arrived with no issue and got a table for one.

The décor was a little shabby, he had to admit. There was a

crooked painting of the Eiffel Tower on the back wall near the kitchen. This would have been a gaudy feature even if it had been painted well. He was even more put off by the salt shaker, which was obnoxiously labeled "sel." Not very promising. He sat like a child in a doctor's waiting room, eager for the ugly ordeal to be over.

He was heartened at the sight of his server, a blonde woman whose physical attributes sent a frisson through Mr. Deer's skin and whose phony French accent was blessed and exculpated by her beautiful, shapely mouth. She flipped open her notepad and asked, "What would you like, m'sieur?"

Mr. Deer smiled at her. "Well, seems I've already been given everything I could want."

She smiled and rolled her eyes. "Merci beaucoup. Can I g—"

"Pinot noir for me," he said. "Thank you."

Without writing anything, she left. He had proven that not only was he a kind man, but also that he did not waste time. He scribbled something in his notebook about the library and the mix-up with the not-quite-homeless man. He also expressed his views of the city and the restaurant. *Still, it's no New York*, he wrote, though he had never been to New York.

The wine was better than he expected and was made even better by the whiff of the waitress's perfume as she leaned over to pour it. He ordered a croque madame and called the waitress "chouchou."

Unlike the wine, the food proved just as bad as expected. He considered having it taken back to the kitchen. If he did, then he would have more time to spend talking to the busty waitress and he would have even more time to let his erection press against his thigh or to put a hand in his pocket and stroke himself idly with a finger. But it was already half-past eight. He decided to cut his losses. So he stomached the awful food, downed the wine, and left without tipping.

He was back on the streets with more than enough time to address the third task. The road to the Levee District was graced with the same streetlamps as even the busiest thoroughfare. Mr. Deer thought this boded well. If the former red-light district was treated with the same respect as the main street, then perhaps the people of Chicago understood the finer things in life better than their food suggested. Between the two completed criteria, Chicago had one victory and one loss. The final test would be the tie breaker.

As the sun set, his meal flopped uncomfortably in his stomach. The wine reacted with the greasy cheese to create a bitter froth that burned the back of his throat as it clawed its way out of his stomach. Lake Michigan kicked the light of the sunset back into his eyes, making it hard to read the names of the cabarets and nightclubs. The name on the back of his ticket read "the Columbia."

He was forced to ask a passerby for directions. This man's head was striped with the strands of a comb-over, and he kept playing with something in his pocket that rattled. In asking him,

Mr. Deer employed the deep, gruff voice of a man asking another man something of importance. In this masculine posture he was not allowed to flinch or react when the other man told him that the Columbia had been shut down by police raids a month ago. Deer tried not to betray too much disappointment or anxiety in asking where else he could find a club "like that."

The stranger rattled the whatever-it-was in his pocket and looked around. They waited for a group of young men to pass. Finally he said, "There's always the Pineapple."

Mr. Deer blushed. He had to hold back his anger, hold back his impulse to tell this man that he was not, in fact, a fool. But before he could say anything, the man spoke, reassuring him that the club, though unusually named, was the only club "like that" still in business. The only disclaimer offered was the price; it catered, he said, to high rollers, fat cats, and what have you. Mr. Deer smiled. "Then it's perfect." Before they parted ways, the man told him to ask for Mr. Batson. He thanked him, and the stranger rattled the thing in his pocket, as if to say good-bye.

A block down the road, he turned around and watched where the man went. He wanted to make sure he was not being duped by a police officer in disguise. The stranger, too, looked around with a self-conscious turn of the head, before stepping into a seedy bar whose name was too far away for Mr. Deer to read. He felt reassured. At least he was not being had.

Something in the late summer air gave Mr. Deer hope. For the first time, he admired how relaxed the city made him feel, how the brutally smooth face of the lake made the land feel so much more precious. He smoked one cigarette, then another. After twisting down a side street that smelled of garbage and oil, he arrived at a door set into a larger building with a metal plaque beside it showing a pineapple perched above the curved word "Welcome." *This must be the place.* He knocked, feeling his stomach rumble once more in protest before settling down at last.

Chapter Two

He thought it was a joke after all. The girl who opened the door looked nine years old and had lipstick smeared on like a clown. Her bangs were uneven, her mascara clumped, and the dress she wore hung askew, one-strapped, swallowing her skinny chest and trailing on the floor. When he was a boy, Mr. Deer's sister had liked to dress him in drag. The girl in front of him brought this to mind.

She did not speak. For whole moments they stared at each other in silence, nothing in between them but the sound of a piano playing in the other room.

His impulse was to turn heel and run. *If I leave now,* he thought, *I could still find somewhere else before it gets too late.* As if letting him off the hook, the girl turned and vanished into the next room. He stared after her into the open foyer, wondering whether to follow.

After a moment, a woman entered from a different room, stopping in her tracks at the sight of him. She was heavyset and had a fleshy, jovial face between pearl earrings the size of cherries. Her hands were heavy with red jewels. She smiled at him and shuffled to the door.

"Hello, sir. Can I help you?"

He dumbly mumbled some greeting and almost asked for a prostitute; he stopped himself just in time, cleared his throat, and asked for Mr. Batson.

Her face lit up like a teacher's at a star student. "Well, hello, sir, how do you do this evening? Hello and welcome to the Pineapple. Come this way, please. My name is Hattie. Care for a drink?"

He stepped up into the foyer and was pleased at the décor. The rug was oriental and, from what he could tell, genuine. The air smelled strongly of some earthen, exotic incense. He was instructed to take off his shoes.

So it seems the great era of Chicago brothels lives on, he thought. The room he was led into was more lavish than the last: a divan wrapped around the whole perimeter, with huge, tasseled pillows propped up along the seat, and all of this upholstered in ornate, gold brocade. The walls were hung with silk. A censer on the mantle exhaled the scent he had noticed in the foyer: cloves, he decided, and nutmeg. Two massive teak doors leaked piano music. Over the mantle hung a huge, gilded mirror that reflected his face and spurred him to brush the hair off his forehead. He could not manage, however, to wipe the smile of relief off his face.

There were three other men in the room. Each of them wore a suit and tie, and each sat separately, minding his own business. The one closest to the big doors, a Black man, tapped the rhythm of the piano music onto his cigarette case. The man near the mantle read a newspaper and sipped a brown drink. The one closest to the entrance just stared at the bustling body of his hostess.

"'Scuse me, dear," she said, brushing past him. "It feels a little stuffy in here."

Mr. Deer was feeling hot. He thought it had just been him.

The woman took a long pole that was leaning against the mantle and hooked open the windows near the ceiling. The silks shifted in the breeze, and the oppressive scent of the censer lessened.

"Sorry, sir, it's almost time for the girls to come out. I'm afraid I'll have to ask you to sit with the other gentlemen for just a few moments longer. Again, my name is Hattie. If you need anything, anything at *all*, just ask for me, and I'll help you out." She motioned toward the spot on the divan furthest from the other men. "Won't you sit, dear?" He did. "Would you like a drink or a newspaper?" He shook his head no. He noticed how she flipped her hands while she talked, as if her wrists were putty, or perhaps as if her rings were too heavy for her muscles to lift. He smiled at her rings and then up at her. She said, "Hold tight just a few minutes, okay, dear?" And shuffled toward the big double doors.

As she passed into the next room, Mr. Deer craned his neck to see inside. He saw a sea of fabric, greens and reds, velvets and silks, gems, and a leg lifted in dance. Music flooded out in this brief moment. It wasn't until the door slammed shut and the music returned to its muffled state did he realize that that little peek had piqued his penis.

Chapter Three

The divan was higher than Mr. Deer had anticipated. When he set his feet on the ground, he began to slide off the velvet. But with his rear tucked into the fold, his feet dangled an inch above the carpet like a child's. Unwilling to settle, he alternated between the two configurations, checking his watch every minute, uncomfortable.

The piano music impressed him. It was not the thin, entertaining ditty that he usually heard in bordellos, nor was it the languid, loose blues of New Orleans. It wasn't classical exactly, but it had a classical tone. The notes came out as clean as flecks of pepper. The Black man near the double doors seemed enthusiastic about it as well. Between the taps on his cigarette case, he bobbed his head to the beat.

Mr. Deer adjusted himself on the divan. He grabbed a big, red pillow and stuck it behind him. It was more comfortable and allowed his feet to rest firmly on the ground. He commended himself for his ingenuity.

The man with the newspaper folded it up, set it down, and walked out the door. Mr. Deer wondered if he was fed up and wanted to leave. Or if maybe he was just headed to the restroom.

The last man, the one who had been staring at Hattie earlier, was bent over now, his fingers laced between his knees, watching the double doors like a dog watches a foxhole. He was the oldest man here, at least fifty, but with such a clean face and such strong features that one could imagine him living forever, like a rock or a fine piece of iron. Mr. Deer noticed the gold watch chain dangling from his pocket, the fashionable cut of his suit. His tie was silk, though ugly. Deer's heart beat faster as he felt the prickling sensation of inferiority. He wished he had worn his better suit.

The newspaper man returned. And suddenly the music stopped. All heads turned toward the doors. At that moment, the barefooted girl from before darted in from the foyer, zoomed across the room, and slipped through the double doors. Mr. Deer felt embarrassed. He had flinched.

One door eased open to let Hattie's ample form pass through. Her hands were clasped in front of her, and she smiled so hard she squinted.

"Hello and good evening, gentlemen. Hope you haven't been waiting long. We are just so excited to have you all here tonight."

Mr. Deer noticed all the other men were standing. He stood. The pillow toppled forward, forcing him to set it back upright.

Hattie continued, "Well, I know our girls have just been dying to meet you all. I hope you all get along; they have just been so darn *lonely* all day. So without further ado, please meet the ladies of the Pineapple!"

The first thing that struck him was that the women stood in a perfect line. In the brothels of Omaha and Montgomery, the lineups were so casual that they looked almost accidental; as if the women had just happened to find themselves, during the course of their evening, standing before a group of male strangers. Like it was the most natural thing in the world. But here, the women stood in a ramrod-straight line, staring dead forward as if they were a row of mannequins. He had a brief fear that whichever women he didn't pick would be pulverized and melted down to be cast into a better form. Despite the allure of efficiency, he could not help but feel this configuration flew in the face of the laissez-faire, European sentiment he loved.

He stopped in his tracks. *There, in the middle*, he thought, craning his neck around Hattie's retreating form, squinting to pull her out of the mist of myopia. The men ambled toward the doors as Mr. Deer stared, thinking, *There she is.*

And there she was. She wore a black gown of simple silk cinched around the waist, with smooth black jewels laid on her neck. Her black hair was looped in two glossy, thick curls on either side of her head. Her jaw was strong, her eyebrows firm and precise as a military tactic, and her red lips were arched perfectly, cruelly. She looked a cool nineteen. Her arms were smooth and supple, ending in long, black nails. It was hard to tell whether she was attending a gala or someone's funeral.

She was the most macabre, the most solemn, and the most European woman in the room. Such inky beauty rarely thrived in the U.S., but he had it on good authority that the most renowned prostitutes of Paris had the same slender muscles, the same tall, bony frame. She was exactly what he wanted, both as a symbol and as a woman.

Hattie herded the men into a line perpendicular to that of the women, with Mr. Deer, the tardiest, sent to the back. He set his hand on his glasses case in his pocket, almost willing to make a fool of himself to get a better look at her. But no. He decided it was a fool's game, picking favorites before anyone had even made their choice. He would take a moment to assess the other women and, from among them, pick a runner-up.

He counted eight women of varying heights, colors, and ages. They all were beautiful. So beautiful, in fact, that Mr. Deer tried to remember how much cash he had on him and wondered whether he would need to write a check. All the women were outfitted in slim and vibrant sleeveless dresses which hid their feet.

The line alternated in height, with a Black woman and an Asian woman tacked on at one end. They all smiled; some were coquettish, some were bold, some were busty, one was redheaded. He caught another glimpse of the tall one around the ear of the man in front of him. He smiled impulsively and then forced it off his face. As he evaluated the other women, he could not help but notice that all their jewelry was either silver or black, as if they had plucked them off a movie screen.

Hattie said to the man in front, "Now, I believe you were first, weren't you?"

The older man nodded. "Yes, ma'am."

"Would you like to get to know any of these lovely ladies any better this evening?"

Mr. Deer's heart sped up, the prayer whirring around his head: *Don't pick her. Don't pick her. Don't pick her.*

"That one."

Mr. Deer exhaled slowly as the Black girl in a yellow, silk dress stepped forward. She extended her hand to him. "Hello, sir," she spoke in a drawl Mr. Deer pegged as Georgian. "My name is Alexandria. It's a pleasure to meet you." She stepped forward and led him over to one of the tables at the far end of the room.

Hattie clapped once. "Wonderful! I'm sure you two will get along." She walked behind the next man and set her hand on his shoulders. He was the Black one who had tapped out the rhythm of the piano. "And as for you, sir?"

He looked over his shoulder at her and stammered, "Oh—I—I, I thought I—sent ahead a letter? Did you—?"

She burst out with an "Oh!" and clasped her hands. "I'm so sorry, sir, I forgot all about your kind note. Yes, you wanted to see Deirdre, didn't you? Come on forward, Deirdre." The shortest woman stepped forward, her white dress highlighting her tan skin and pinned-up, blonde hair. She looked no older than sixteen. "Sorry for the mix-up, sir. Hopefully she is to your liking." He nodded. Deirdre walked over to him and introduced herself. He blinked hard and said hello.

The newspaper man chose the redhead, Connie.

Now it was Mr. Deer's turn. Five women stood before him. In

the center was the tall one, whose eyes were as shiny as a doll's, whose alabaster neck fell somewhere between the David and the Venus De Milo. Mr. Deer looked up and down the line to make sure he didn't seem too eager. But his eyes swung back to the center and the apparition standing there.

After a moment he was ready. He pointed and said, "Her."

Chapter Four

Her elbow rested on the table. Mr. Deer's eyes followed the upward slant of her arm to the question mark of a hand whose end bore the thorns of her sleek, black nails. He imagined a candle with a black flame.

He knew he did not have to talk. He could have followed the lead of the newspaper man and taken his chosen woman right upstairs after a single drink. Wham-bam-thank-you-ma'am. But that was not how the French did it. They treated their prostitutes like real ladies. Wine, flowers. Dinner, even. A kind of sophistication much lacking in America, signed away in the Constitution, almost. Mutual respect for worker and client. When they arrived at the restaurant, and he pulled back her chair, he was more than a little surprised when she failed to say, "Thank you."

The waiter had to ask twice before Mr. Deer could look away from her face. He had been transfixed by the way she lit her cigarette, how she let the flame burn without the cup of her hand as if she lived in a world without wind. He stammered out, "Pinot Grigio." He wiped his mouth and thought of a question to ask her.

"So." The sound made her look up from the menu. "You said your name was Raina?"

"Yes."

"That's a nice name. But that's not your...real name, is it?"

He immediately felt awful. Not only was it insipid and boring, but it was intrusive. She shifted in her seat and crossed her legs the other way. He was further disheartened that he had unwittingly brought them to a steakhouse. This was not the place to bring a woman. Someone like Raina deserved better. Even if she was a prostitute.

"Well," she said, "actually, it *is* my real name."

"Oh, really? It's beautiful."

The conversation wobbled and toppled. He reprimanded himself and wondered what it was that men usually spoke to these women about. He had the sudden urge to wash his hands, and he tried to examine why. He must have felt dirty, because on the walk to the restaurant, they had seen a bunched-up homeless man on the street, who, in Mr. Deer's blurry sight, looked dead. Raina, for her part, seemed interested in this hobo. Her head had stayed locked on him until they turned the next corner. That, then, was why he wanted to wash his hands—because he had been forced to look at the possibly dead body of a homeless man for longer than was necessary.

Forcing this neurosis from his mind, he decided to tell her a story.

"You know, I'm in the lumber business. I just started a company that buys lumber wholesale from the manufacturer and sells it at a discounted rate. Big returns. You'd be shocked."

Her eyebrows hitched up a millimeter.

"Anyway, I get a lot of my lumber from the Appalachian forests. Couple thousand logs, nothing major. So I often find myself in Harrisburg. You know, Pennsylvania."

She nodded slowly. Mr. Deer could not tell if she was being unfriendly or was flirting.

"So anyway, I have a lot of people working for me, cutting the lumber in the mills, loading it up on the railway, et cetera, et cetera."

She stared blankly. He felt he had overdone it with the difficult words. In a lower, gentle voice, he added, "'Et cetera' means 'and so on.'"

"I know what 'et cetera' means," she said.

At that moment, the wine arrived. For all the ice he was experiencing at the table, the Grigio still arrived lukewarm.

"Yes," he said as the wine was poured, "of course. I'm sorry." He breathed in. "Anyway, I have a lot of these guys working for me, and, well, I guess it's safe to say they aren't all the most up-to-date people, that is to say, in matters of global politics." He slowed down his speaking to better engage her. "So I was talking to their boss, this high-up guy in the lumber industry, one of my good friends, and we were just jawing it up about the state of Europe and all that. We were talking about whether we should try to curb Hitler's invasions or if we should just let him be satisfied with the Eastern European nations that no one really wants anyway."

Raina put out her cigarette. Mr. Deer figured that girls as

pretty as her did not have to be interesting or smart to get what they wanted out of men. *Sure*, he thought, *whatever. That's fine. I just can't imagine this attitude is good for business.*

"So we're talking about this political stuff and we mention Berlin. And one of the worker guys nearly drops his lunch pail and turns around and says, 'What? D'ya just say Hitler's in Berlin?'"

Raina smiled to match his laugh. It seemed genuine.

"So we look at each other and say, 'Yeah, of course. Where else would he be?' And this worker guy, gosh, I really feel bad for him, he says, 'Why, in Germany, of course!' My friend starts laughing up a storm, and I don't really get it, so he tells me that there's a town further north called—"

He baited her. All she mustered was an expectant eyebrow raise.

"New Berlin, Pennsylvania!"

He took a sip of wine, noticing as he exhaled in the glass that his breath was hot from nerves.

"Now," he continued, "he and I just bust a gut imagining this worker running home to New Berlin and telling Billy Bob and Jimbo and Betty Sue and Mayeula May that Hitler was hiding out somewhere in town." He wiped a tear from his eye. "Gosh," he said. "You get all kinds of people."

Raina ran her finger around the rim of her wine glass, smiling. Placid. Looking at the fine curve of that Tonka-bean fingernail made him feel embarrassed of his brutish story. His anecdote fit in with the steakhouse décor, but Raina deserved better. He knew he could cut this date short and take her back to her room at the bordello any time he wanted. But to give up now and just have sex with her would mean admitting that there was nothing more to him than a roll of bills and a pair of balls. See, Mr. Deer's philosophy was this: women in the real world were two-faced. They gave you confidence and compliments, they lied about liking you, they flattered you and promised you all the comfort in the world, and then they squeezed out whatever money and attention they could before moving on to the next sucker in line. There was a grace to the exchange of the prostitute. She was not obliged to give you anything but sex. If she complimented you, you knew she really meant it. She had no incentive to lie. She did not earn overtime for being swept off her feet.

He ordered a steak with mashed potatoes for himself and a shrimp salad for her. He realized he should have asked before ordering something like shellfish, which more and more people were allergic to, it seemed. But she did not protest. She silently sipped the wine.

He leaned forward on his elbows. He was glad the table had no centerpiece.

"I think you're very beautiful," he said.

"Thank you," she replied.

He leaned back and tried the wine. Not only was it lukewarm, but it was cheap. He considered packing up and going to a different restaurant. He even wondered if there were tables left at the budget French place where he took lunch. But the idea of a steak was appealing. Besides, he did not want to wander too far from the bordello in the event he really could not salvage the date.

Raina, thank God, excused herself from the table to go powder her nose. This gave him time to think. He stared at the man behind the bar who wore white shirtsleeves and poured whiskey. A set sequence of ingredients: ice, syrup, lemon juice, whiskey. Methodical, precise. Effective. *Of course*, he thought. *The reason this isn't working is because I'm not thinking about it rationally enough.*

He knew every woman had a pet project, be it children's literacy or veterans or orphans. He could go about it in one of two ways: he could either ask her outright what she cared about, or he could mention the major ones sequentially, in order of probability, until she bit. Divining her pet project would prove difficult. He had been told that beautiful women tended to become invested in things distant from their own lives, such as poverty or relief for African children. On the other hand, in his experience, prostitutes tended to care about things closer to their own lives, such as protections against drunken husbands and shelters for women and children. Raina, being both beautiful and a prostitute, could go either way. Most likely, he figured, she was invested in some wild card of a cause, like animal rights or socialism. It was better not to guess.

He stared at her as she minced her way back to the table. Leaning back, he asked, "So, Raina, what are you interested in? What kinds of causes do you believe in?"

She seemed more receptive since her trip to the restroom. "What, you mean like fire safety, poverty...etcetera?"

Mr. Deer laughed. It was important to make them feel their jokes were worthwhile. "Exactly. Do you have any projects like that?"

"Oh, I wish I had that kind of time. And money."

"You don't?" He lifted the wine and took a sip, holding it in his mouth, willing it to taste better.

"Have any money? No," she said as she brought the glass to her lips. "That's why I have to sleep with you."

The spray of wine that erupted from his mouth flew to her left, missing her by inches before splattering to the floor.

Mr. Deer choked and sputtered, turning red under the scrutiny of the other patrons. He had never been insulted like that by a woman. But despite the slight, he was seized by uncontrollable laughter, partially as a tactic to write off the insult and partially because he found the sass refreshing. He did note that she had evaded the answer. But he was too busy trying to breathe to care.

When he had himself under control, he was able to appreciate how the smile of triumph lit up her face. Her shoulders were set further back, accentuating the tasteful flatness of her chest. Her arms, which had been folded or contorted to some degree for the whole meal, were now set plainly and evenly on the table. The only thing that moved was her left index finger, the nail of which traced the pad of her thumb.

He said, "You got me there. You really got me there." He had to keep the conversation aloft while the waiter mopped up the spill. "Most women just say 'orphans.'"

"Well, I do care about orphans. I would say I care deeply about orphans and animals and the homeless. I just don't have time to act on them."

"Yes, that makes sense." Mr. Deer wondered if his indifference to the possibly dead homeless man they saw earlier had cast him in a bad light. "I'm used to talking to rich men's wives who can spend all day planning fundraisers for some Godforsaken nation's children or some silly social cause."

"Exactly. I don't have those resources. It doesn't mean I care any less about the issues. Just that my contribution is in spirit, not effect."

"Very well put, Raina. I feel the same way."

The food was laid out in front of him. The garlic aioli on the steak was the consistency of baby vomit. He wished he had gotten something lighter and fresher, like the shrimp salad, for example.

Without waiting for him to start, Raina speared a shrimp and ate it in one bite, tail and all. It was either ignorance of proper eating habits or a demonstration of indifference. Either way, he could not tear his eyes away.

She swallowed and asked, "What do you mean, you feel the same way?"

"Hm," he said, indicating he would reply once he was finished chewing.

She looked over his shoulder and waited.

"What I mean," he started, wiping his lips, "is that I am too busy a man to bother with charities *per se*. But I agree with you that, in many ways... Well, it's the *thought* that counts in these issues, is what I'm trying to say. Changing people's minds is a lot more important than giving some money to some socialite who would probably pilfer it all anyway." She was still staring over his shoulder. "Hello? Raina, dear?"

She had gone pale. Her hand drifted to rest in her lap, as still and rigid as steel, her lips lightly parted.

"Raina? Hello?" He touched her hand. She jumped and turned back to him.

"Sorry," she said, picking up her knife and fork and cutting the tail off a shrimp. "I thought I saw someone I knew." She turned to him and smiled a full-frontal, toothy smile for the first time that night. He smiled back, transfixed.

At this point, there was little Mr. Deer could do to resist her. He decided that Raina was the most enigmatic, stunning, and old-world woman he had ever met. He scarfed down half of his steak, tipped the waiter handsomely, and led her by the arm out of the restaurant.

Chapter Five

It had started to rain. Mr. Darren Deer carefully guided himself and Raina from one awning to another. They did not return the same way they came, so he had no way of knowing whether the homeless man was indeed dead or just lounging. The water relieved the street of caked-in dust, manure, and oil. The city exuded a scent so rich and so warm that Mr. Deer felt he was inhaling the breath of the earth itself.

They did not talk as they approached the brothel. There was no more need for speech, for coaxing or goading or vetting. It was a hefty investment, sure. But prostitutes were just like pens or shoes: it was always worthwhile to splurge for higher quality.

She led him by the hand through the antechamber. In it, the newspaper man sat on the divan, his redheaded lover curled up beside him, pulling his tie playfully, begging him not to go. They turned to look at Raina and Mr. Deer. The newspaper man bobbed his head at him once in recognition, as though they were old friends. Mr. Deer smiled sheepishly and followed Raina.

The photos on the stairs showed the Madam, Hattie, as she grew up. Judging from the sequence of pictures, this brothel used to belong to her father. The stately and mustachioed man stood behind her when she was smaller and then one day, between the twentieth and twenty-second step, disappeared.

The name "Raina" was carved on a brass plaque on her door. Inside, the bed spread its silky plain under a sheer canopy. The walls were intricately papered. While there were no windows, the electric chandelier overhead cast sparkling disks on the silk pillows. The back wall was devoted to a mammoth bookcase, as colorful as it was strictly organized. He watched her reflection in the vanity as she slipped into the bathroom. She closed the door behind her.

Alone in the room, he checked the smell of his breath. Traces of steak and wine. Nothing too serious. His thoughts were coming in short, sharp bursts. He looked in the mirror and tried to concentrate, telling himself, *I cannot believe my luck. Such a beautiful woman in such a lavish room. Dainty and all mine.* Chicago, he decided, was the closest thing to Europe that America could offer.

He heard bottles shifting on a counter in the bathroom. The faucet flowed. He sat on the edge of the bed and looked at himself in the mirror. Realizing he looked foolish he sat up and took off his coat, attempting a more relaxed posture. But then he realized he wanted *her* to take off his coat for him and so put it back on. And waited.

The click of the bathroom door caused his head to snap toward it. He willed his eyes back onto his watch to not make it seem like he was too interested. He waited for her to call to him, to pull his eyes from his obviously demanding schedule. But she said nothing. So, as to not make a huge farce of his indifference, he turned to her unprompted.

Light spilled from the bathroom, the hum of light wrapped around the black silhouette. His eyes slid down the black, silk slip that opened up at her collarbones and ran in folded rivulets over her chest. It hung straight as a plumb line down to the floor and, in the front, parted to reveal a knee, like a bit of alabaster sticking out of a tar pit. The jewels, gone; the hair, brushed. She stood with one arm on the door frame, sending two black arrows right through his skull.

He could barely bring his eyes up to meet hers. He spoke a line he had only used once before.

"Are you sure you don't want to put on something...*more* comfortable?"

Her body buckled as she laughed. She drew one foot in front of the other like she was about to start a dance.

"Do you like to read, Mister?" Her voice was suddenly languid.

"Me? I rarely have the time." He added, "Though I would, of course, like to read...your lips."

She curved one half of her mouth into a smile, a shape not from any language he could read—something more Sanskrit than English. She made to walk toward him before turning away, unleashing a puff of air tinged by a spritz of perfume.

"But I do have some favorites from school," he amended.

She plucked a thick, green volume from the shelf. "Oh?"

His vision was shattered. He thought this whole "indifferent scholar" thing was too put-upon. He tried to send the message to her telepathically: *I am not paying you to read to me, bitch.*

His voice came out stilted, strained by the effort of the telepathy. "Yes, I read *War and Peace* in college. Twice."

"Twice?" She turned, her hair bobbing, her finger holding her place on a page of dense text. All that was missing was a pair of tiny glasses balancing on the tip of her nose.

"Yes," he said, "twice." He knew it was an interesting story. He would use it to lure her out of this pretentious drama. He sat on the edge of the bed.

But the question never came. Instead, she finished reading her page, closed the book, and returned it to the shelf. She faced the bookcase, staring up at its heights, with her head cocked at an arrogant angle. He wanted to grab her hand and whip her around, to force her to acknowledge that she was here for him and him alone.

Instead, he cleared his throat. It was getting late, and her antics were wearing thin. Say what you would about the body hair of the French prostitute, but every cultured man knew that she, at least, would not waste your time.

With this in mind, he stood and reached out to her, whether she was ready or not.

Chapter Six

She was so white that he found himself surprised her shoulders were warm. He was also surprised by how quickly, after his touch, she turned around and kissed him—hard and deep. *The French way*, he thought with a smile. The book thing was an act all along. She wanted this as much as he did.

He pulled on the strings of her nightgown, not undoing the bow yet but using them to pull her toward the bed where he sat on the slick silk duvet.

She cradled his head, his chin scraping the silk against her sternum. Looking down at him gave her a double chin. Still, he decided, she was beautiful. Even if he noticed where the makeup ended on her jawline, he could not dream of pushing her away, not now when his ear rested against her chest and her fingers combed through his hair. His hands traveled up her supernaturally smooth thighs, teasing the edges of lace. How could he begrudge her the hushed rumble of her stomach, or the tiny burp she tried to hide as a moan? *No one is flawless,* he thought.

Her hands traveled down his neck to his shoulders. He began to part the mussel-shell halves of her negligée, revealing pearly skin, glimmering as if underwater. He kissed it but could not really feel it; he was too far within his own cinema of pornographic anticipation to think of anything but the areas on her chest and pelvis he was deliberately avoiding. The ones he was saving for later.

Now he peeled apart the petals, revealing white skin—even more raw fish flesh. Coordinating his hands and mouth was difficult, and sometimes he kissed only silk. Still, he managed to trace a line with his mouth down her taut stomach to her navel. There, he looked up, set his chin on her stomach, and parted the curtain.

He watched both nipples emerge from their black cocoon. He licked his thumbs and began to rub them, while her hands ran through his hair. He worried his dandruff would begin to show and then pushed the thought from his mind and rubbed harder. She did not react. He rubbed harder and harder, pinching the nipples, squeezing them like bits of rubber. Her hands grew still on his head. At that moment, he realized his chin was pressing into her stomach in a way she must have found uncomfortable. He gave up on her nipples, disappointed that this trick fell flat, especially since his old boss once told him how well it worked on the whores of Milan.

So he tried it with his mouth. He licked the nipples, relieved to feel her hands moving in his hair again. But it was uncomfortable to lick her that high up her chest, since her breasts were tiny, and to lick them meant lifting his rear end an inch or so off the bed, a suspension he could not sustain for long. Moreover, this whole time his penis had been aching and leaking in his pants; but if he wanted to prove he was a good lover, he needed to delay his own pleasure in deference to hers.

He sat back down, his thighs exhausted, then kissed her solar plexus, a warm gesture meant to hide the fact that he had fallen. He placed his cheek against her stomach and trailed his palms up and down her back.

He pulled his arms around to her front, tracing the tips of his fingers down her slim belly, leading to the waist and the black horizon of panties beneath. He hooked the edge and pulled them down, never breaking eye contact. *I am already the best she's ever had,* he thought. *And I haven't even pulled it out yet.*

Something brushed his chest. When he looked down and saw a penis hanging limp between Raina's legs, his first reaction was to assume it was his own that he had, somehow, seriously misplaced. In a moment the confusion was replaced by repulsion; instead of pulling himself back onto the bed, his hands, which were already around her hips, shoved outward and down, forcing her backward and buckling her knees. He stood and screamed, "What the *fuck*? What the mother*fuck*?" and ran into the bathroom, wringing his hands, pouting his lips, unsure which part to wash first.

He slammed the bathroom door so hard that the bottles on the marble counter rattled. He scrubbed his hands with soap and used his lathered knuckles to rub his lips—but it wasn't enough. He put the bar of soap in his mouth. He spit it into his hand and gagged.

His body was suddenly possessed by a spasm. His knees knocked together, and his hand clutched shut, sending the slippery bar flying off into the wall.

He meant to grab a single bottle, to properly heft it in his hand and judge its weight before taking it back to the room and hitting him with it. But as he reached for one, the side of his hand swept away the rest, causing a cascade of glass to tumble off the edge and then crash against the floor in slow motion. The one bottle he did manage to grab was a wide one from a pharmacy. He did not understand the words on the label. As if in a dream, the characters twisted and shifted—Cs and Zs and Ss forming and reforming like oil on milk. He rubbed his eyes, blind with rage or the brain-numbing stench of mixed perfumes that rose from the puddle at his feet. He wondered where he had put his glasses. He lifted the bottle and squinted at the white pills inside. He was seized with the urge to strike something. This bottle was the perfect tool.

Chapter Seven

Mr. Deer stormed back into the bedroom, ready to smash the bottle against the head of any and all who had wronged him. But when the door swung open, not even a silk curtain moved. The furniture, the cushions, and the books all stood still, as if too shocked by his violence to move. The prostitute was nowhere to be seen.

The bottle rattling in his hand, he entered the hall. The only person there was the little girl, playing Jacks with her back against the wall. One door emitted the sounds of lovemaking. Mr. Deer wondered with a sneer whether all the women here were really men. The alternative was that he, in particular, had been duped. He grew hot under the collar, thinking that the madam had pegged him for a country bumpkin and had set up this trap as a way to humiliate him.

As if the indignity wasn't enough, at that moment he stepped on a jack, the points digging through the sole of his shoe and into his toe. He nearly dropped the bottle.

"Why don't you get your *Goddamn* toys out of the hallway?" he asked the little girl as he yanked the jack from the rubber. He hurled the bit of metal at her head where it bounced off ineffectually.

Now he filled the halls with his voice. "Where are you? *Bitch*? Come out here you God*damn* Nelly!"

The sounds of lovemaking in the next room stopped. He stomped down the stairs.

"Come *out*! Come *out*!"

Now the incense choked him. He wiped his mouth. If he found him, he decided, he would kill him on the spot.

No one sat in the antechamber. He couldn't even find him in the mirror. Where *was* he? Where was he hiding?

Nor was he in the main room with the piano. He tried making lists of the things he would do, but each grew and burned up under the intense heat of the only cogent thought he could muster: *I paid for his dinner.*

Now Mr. Deer was in the kitchen, alone. He began opening cabinets frantically, finding at last a liter bottle of cognac with a cut-glass stopper. He did a calculation in his head, weighing the cost of the shrimp salad against the bottle of liquor. Plus the cost of his hurt pride. After a moment he pulled it from the shelf. He felt calmer now. He breathed easier. He left the kitchen with a bottle in each hand—one of Raina's medication, the other of liquor. The pearls of sweat on his brow were now the only indication that he had been upset at all.

He left the brothel in dead silence. He figured there were other ways to get back at the people who had tricked him. And the alcohol, at least, made up for the damages.

The rain had let up. The drain in the middle of the road stank with the water of refuse but he walked over it anyway, spitting between the grates.

He stopped in his tracks. Turning, he hurled the small bottle at the door of the brothel. It crashed against the brass pineapple plate. The pills, hundreds of them, pattered to the ground and rolled toward the gutter. And Darren Deer walked away, his hands trembling, the taste of soap still filtering through his teeth.

BOOK THREE

Chapter One

In the corner to Roy's left sat a huddled lump leaning against the bare concrete. Halfway down the bench that ran along the wall to his right sat a drunkard, silently leaning over his knees, waiting for his metabolism to catch up to the swift arm of justice. Beyond the drunkard was the wooden door that was so huge and so heavy it had made his teeth hurt when it slammed shut behind him. There was a bare and burned-out lightbulb in the holding cell. All they had was a streetlamp outside for light and a bucket for everything else.

Roy sat shivering in his corner, his eyes forced apart until tears formed. He stared without moving. He made sure not to breathe too loudly. His head rested where the walls met, the root of his loose ponytail balanced between the two planes of concrete. If he could have willed himself further backward, he would have. A drip of mucus hung under his nose. Staring at the far corner.

An outfit of tattered blacks and grays poking through the shadows of the corner, the pants torn at the knees, the excess fabric around the feet stained brown with mud. The belt cinched a fold into the waist of the pants, and the leather of the shoes had come unfixed from the soles. Knuckle-clefts traced with a wet, black dust, and fingernails waxing gibbous—the pale nails bit into by a crescent of black grime. The fingertips were dipped in a faint blue and the backs of the hands bore scratches. Above the stained collar, the throat was forested by a black beard which melded with ragged hair. Past the shape of the head hovered the corona of a hat. The face was tilted upward as if the man was blind or did not know where he should be looking. There was no stench, but Roy could tell: this man bore the mark of the dead.

Roy had been staring at the corner for nearly an hour. He was waiting for someone to come by and post bail. But Hattie's motto was always this: if you got yourself into a mess, it was your job to get yourself out. Who bailed out who was always a matter of exchange.

If Roy couldn't take his medicine, then he would have to stay awake all night until the dead man was driven away by the sun. If he looked away for even a moment, those dead fingers would clutch around his neck, and the dirt-caked face would bend forward to chew the flesh off his cheeks. So he stared.

Though frozen, Roy's body worked on. His bladder filled with the wine from dinner, and his stomach grew bored with the shrimp salad and demanded something more. Two hours earlier, as the police had approached the door of the Pineapple, he knew he had two choices. The first was to change into some boy clothes, and the second was to eat a quick plate of cornbread. The former won out over the latter by a narrow margin.

The drunkard vomited into the bucket between his knees.

As if the sound had ended the homeless man's bout of blindness, that hoary head whipped its chin down to reveal his eyes: one staring milky and unfocused from beyond the grave, while the other gaped, a bloody hole where a bullet had entered, done its gruesome business, and left. The socket streamed with blood, red rivulets thick with curded pus and vitreous humor. The teeth were black and yellow and the saliva dripped over the lips and gathered on his shirt-front. Roy let in a slow gasp and tried to regulate his heart and continued to stare at the corner. And the homeless cyclops, the victim of some wanton violence, stared back.

Roy began to cry.

The cyclops's hands, thick with cold and toil, twitched. Slowly his limb grew strong, lifting up from the elbow until, when the forearm was parallel to the floor, the hand itself raised, straightening the arrow of his index finger until it pointed straight at Roy in judgment.

He could not quiet his sobs. His chest heaved, a haywire machine.

Hungry, the cyclops stretched until it pointed with the whole arm. The tip of the finger seemed to reach halfway across the room.

The drunkard retched again while Roy was moaning. Weeping. It had never been this bad before. It had never gotten so close. When he had seen this same apparition at the steakhouse, it had kept its back to him. If he had known it would return, he would have sacrificed his eyes to any sharp object within reach—the fork for the shrimp, the tweezers in his bathroom, Mr. Deer's fingers. Roy's sight blurred, causing the image of the cyclops to balloon to twice its natural size. He screamed.

"You shut the *fuck* up."

Without thinking, Roy snapped his head to the left, where the head of the blanket-bundle was sticking out now, bringing to mind a dirty turtle. Catching his mistake, Roy immediately looked back at the corner and was surprised to see nothing. As his heart slowed down and his muscles relaxed, he flipped his head between the dreaded opposite corner and the corner to his left where, after a moment, he was able to distinguish the features of a young Black man staring at him.

After a moment of eye contact, the head turned back to the wall and Roy said, "Thank you."

The muffled bundle muttered, "Thank *you*..."

Roy sat back, relief washing over him like bathwater.

"...for shutting the *fuck* up."

Chapter Two

Roy was amazed. The shadows on the wall stayed still. He was free of the vision. He relished the smells and sounds around him. The running of drains through the walls delighted him, and even the smell of bile wafting from the drunkard's mouth made him feel thankful. The walls of the room felt softer now, warm.

Seated in the corner with his arms resting on the benches on either side of him, palms up and fingers limp, Roy was able to gaze at the bundle and thank it silently again and again. *He will never know how he helped me,* he thought. *But if he coughs I will bring him water.*

The bundle shifted. Out of the end plopped a leg, the pants riding high enough on the calf to reveal a worn shoe, an ashy ankle, and a scratched, powerful calf. It was a lump with a leg—a bean with a single brown shoot.

During the next thirty minutes, the drunkard rearranged himself so he lay flat on his back on the bench—finished, it seemed, with retching. Roy kept turning his head from the far corner to the closer one. The thought of sleeping did not cross his mind. Even if he wanted to, the snores of the drunkard made it impossible.

Suddenly, like the halves of a chestnut placed in a fire, the bundle cracked open. The nut meat inside was sleeping. He had tight black hair and smooth skin, high cheekbones, and a slender jaw. The eyebrows were thick and distinct as if they were applied with grease paint. By Roy's estimates, Raina had slept with somewhere around four hundred men. But never had he seen one so handsome. Still, he reminded himself that this was not the time for romance. The distance that opened up between them was crawling with ticks and lice and the smeared traces of previously imprisoned bodies. He was not sure if he felt this strong attraction because he was so exhausted, half in dream, or if he was just excited to see a man neither old nor ugly and who didn't expect something out of him. Either way, he couldn't shake the feeling that this man's skin was the color of sleep and his cheeks the texture of dreams.

Roy watched this man flip onto his stomach, onto his side, onto his back—all over the course of an hour. Eventually the young man, whose back was to Roy, made a subtle movement. Roy watched him like a hawk and then stood and softly stepped over to the bench. The tilting form tilted an inch backward, another tiny rotation toward an outward velocity that would send him, blanket and all, tumbling off the edge of the bench.

Roy stood beside him, rocking back and forth on his heels to stay awake. Another few minutes with no movement. Roy crouched, his elbows on his knees, his hands curled into fists and resting quietly against each other, knuckle to knuckle. His thighs began to ache.

The body shifted. Another inch and the young man would topple. Roy knew what to do. He had done it many times before with his sisters at the brothel, many of whom used sleeping pills and tended to roll out of bed and hurt themselves.

He reached out a hand and touched the tilted side with the tips of his fingers. *If I let him go*, he thought, *he will fall onto me, and I will be holding him. Whereas if I push him back, he will stay asleep and never know I helped him out.* He held the fingers there for a moment. Eventually, with the amount of force he would use to press dough into the edges of a pie pan, he pushed the sleeping form back to where it started, righting the potential disaster and restoring sleep and safety to his savior.

Vindicated, Roy stood and turned around, looking around the room. He crossed to where the drunkard lay and dropped to one knee. Started peeing in the bucket. He did not watch as his urine mixed with the vomit, the swirling chunky soup dyed red by either wine or blood.

Behind him, he heard a massive thump. Despite his attention, the boy in the bundle had rolled off the bench and landed on his back. As Roy turned to look, his stream of urine drifted from its destination, splashing over the rim of the bucket and beyond, splattering onto the floor. But the boy did not wake up. Roy stared at him sleeping on the ground before he realized he was peeing on the floor. For a moment neither young man was doing what they were supposed to be doing where they were supposed to be doing it.

Roy stemmed the flow and rushed to his side. Only now did he mumble something. His forehead wrinkled up, pulling his eyelids open. Nostrils flared, filling with the first waking breath. Now his forehead wrinkled down, and his hand came up to cover his eyes and to press his fingers on his temples. Roy watched these involuntary processes as one would the first movements of a newborn. He realized he was leaning over this stranger, and so he sat on the far bench and waited.

He wished there was something else to look at to distract him from the figure of this inmate. Was he supposed to gaze at a wall of plain concrete instead of admiring the long, powerful fingers or the luminous skin on the back of his hands as he wiped the sleep from his eyes? If the objects of interest in the room were not restricted to a sleeping inebriate and a bucketful of piss and puke—if there was something to see that didn't repulse—then perhaps his fellow inmate would not have seemed so radically beautiful, so smooth and transcendent and pure.

So when this man did turn his head toward him, Roy only had a split second to find something else to look at. He brought his hand close to his face and inspected his nails. He readied himself to be addressed.

"What time is it?" asked the once-bundled man sleepily.

"Not sure. Don't have a watch."

The young man crossed his legs and put his face in his hands. "How did I end up on the floor?"

"You rolled off." Roy was self-conscious about not looking at him for so long. Such inattention must have seemed suspect. So he turned directly toward this other man and added, "But it's probably four in the morning."

"Jesus," said the other man through his hands.

"You were only asleep for an hour or so."

Roy worried this information would betray the fact that he had been watching him. But the other man did not notice.

The drunkard, perhaps woken by their talking, sat up. He looked straight ahead of him, coughed once, and lay back down again. Both boys breathed a sigh of relief.

"Jesus, man, that bucket smells awful."

Roy nodded in agreement. Then he realized that since that other guy's face was still in his hand he would not be able to see him nod. So he said, "Yeah."

Roy worried that if they were going to get along, now would be the time to strike, but he could not think of anything else to say. As the moment of speaking passed into memory, he felt a sort of comfort. *Talking to this man, I run the risk of getting killed. Staying silent, I am fine.*

The other man stood up and walked toward the drunkard. With his back to Roy, he fished around in his pants. Roy did not realize what he was doing until he heard the urine splashing into the bucket. Now there was an element from each of the three men in there. Comingled in equal parts. Mixed.

"Haven't changed this shit in two days," mumbled the young man.

"What?" asked Roy.

"I said, they haven't emptied this bucket for two days."

"That's disgusting." But disgust did not even register on Roy's range of emotions. He felt excitement at this opening up of the conversation and the prospect of follow-up questions. Beneath that, there was a little stab of self-reprobation as he realized he had spent almost no time since his arrest feeling sad or worried about his own future. *Too much* excitement, he decided. His shirt was still damp with sweat from the vision.

The young man buttoned his fly and went back to his corner. Roy asked, "How long have you been here?"

The man, who was leaning his head back against the wall, looked up, making a calculation. "This is gonna be my third day."

"Wow!" As soon as he said it, Roy worried this exclamation sounded too juvenile. He amended, "I'm sorry." But this was worse. It was a gesture of pity that he felt was not applicable here since they were both in the same situation. Finally, with this thought, the yellow of anxiety and the blue of sadness poured into his heart, and he was able to appreciate the scale and gravity of his arrest.

To distract himself, Roy asked, "What are you charged with?"

The man's eyes were closed, his head still sloped back. He was in the posture of a very tired man, but his voice was as clear as high noon. "Not sure yet. Moving violation, technically. But they'll think of something else. They have until the end of tomorrow to tell me."

"Why did they put you here instead of your own cell?"

"They said there wasn't any room on the other floors, so they had to put me in the drunk tank. But I don't think it's true."

"What, that there's no space?"

"Yeah."

"It *is* a full moon, though."

The man's head tilted forward, forcing Roy to remember, in an image as bright and fast as a bolt of lightning, how just a couple hours earlier the face of the cyclops had turned toward him that same way. Roy could see he did not look tired at all. He looked nervous, yes, and a little bit sad, but his face was clear and smooth and, Roy thought, darling.

"What does that have to do with anything?" asked the man.

"I mean, crime rates spike whenever there's a full moon. Same for accidents."

The quizzical look the other man gave Roy was so clear and so absolute that Roy felt he could have plucked that raised eyebrow right off his face and punctuate a question with it.

"It's true. Like how the moon makes the tides. Full moons pull the water in our brains and make us go crazy."

An expression of pure disbelief.

"Is that what landed you in here?" asked the other man. "The moon?"

"To a degree, I think."

"What did they charge you with?"

"Mooning someone, obviously."

The other man smiled. Closed his eyes. Laughed. "Be serious."

"Well, I don't know yet."

"Can they arrest you for having long hair?"

"That's actually just a misdemeanor."

The other man's smile crept back on his lips. With this advantage, Roy said, "I'm Roy, by the way."

"Nice to meet you, long-haired-boy Roy." The other man wiped his nose with the back of his hand. "I'm Woodrow."

Chapter Three

"So, Woodrow." Roy was feeling more comfortable now and even kicked one leg up to cross it over the other. "Do you come here often?"

"No, most weekends I just lock myself in a cage at home."

"No need to come all the way out here for the same experience."

"Exactly."

They looked away from each other, both smiling. Woodrow asked, "Are you from around here?"

"Nebraska, actually."

Woodrow's lips turned down to show he was impressed. "How did you wind up here?"

"I broke the law, obviously."

This laugh pushed Woodrow back; he remained sitting on the edge of the bench but stuck out his legs, crossing them at the ankles, and leaned his back against the wall. He was straight as a rod. Roy guessed he was six foot two. "No, I mean, how did you end up in Chicago?"

"Oh. I took a train."

"Seriously, man. What brought you here?"

Roy didn't know what he had expected. He knew a question like this would come up sooner or later. He had very little experience talking with people who were not planning to pay him for sex. But why share? For honesty's sake? To not bear the indignity of lying to such a beautiful young man? Little reason to tell the truth, really. There was also, of course, the element of fear. People like Roy were not treated well in prison, generally, and if Woodrow decided to give him a hard time for whatever reason, there was little chance a guard would be around to protect him. Or if there was a guard around, he would likely partake in Roy's humiliation. Roy had heard stories of guys like him leaving prison with all their hair shaved off or with injuries between the legs so grievous that walking without a cane was impossible. More likely, he saw himself being dunked into the bucket in which two portions of urine diffused within puke stew. Another factor was that, if this Woodrow learned that Roy might need his antipsychotic medication soon, it might make him uncomfortable being in the same room with him. No, Roy decided, he could not afford to tell his story.

"I don't really want to get into it," Roy told his hands. Looking at Woodrow's posture of ease, he changed the subject. "Are you waiting on someone to bail you out?"

"I am, actually. My sister is getting the money together now."

"Oh, that's nice." With relief, Roy pounced on this subject. "You live with her?"

"Yeah, me and her and one of her friends."

"Are you all from here?"

Woodrow looked right into Roy's eyes. "I asked you first."

"Fine." Roy breathed in slowly. "My name is Roy, and I was created in a terrible chemical accident."

"Come on," said Woodrow, interlacing his fingers over his chest. "Spill. What else are we gonna do to pass the time?"

"I don't know," said Roy, uncrossing his legs and crossing them the other way. "I was thinking about getting started on a batch of toilet wine."

"Very funny, Samson."

Roy gestured with an outstretched hand. "Seriously. If we're gonna be stuck here for another day, we should at least get to work on some tattoos."

Woodrow stuck his tongue between his teeth and made a staccato, hissing laugh. "You are too much."

"But really," said Roy, "I think I should try to sleep some. I don't know how long I'll be in here."

"All right, all right," said Woodrow. "But if you feel someone cutting off your hair while you sleep, don't blame me."

Roy smiled. He nestled into the corner and pulled his legs up onto the bench and looked at Woodrow's relaxed face and thought of how sweet it looked. He also peered at the far corner, where the first hints of dawn filtering in through the window had abolished the most threatening shadows. He closed his eyes. He felt like he was floating on a cloud.

Something fluttered above, covering him. It took him a

moment to realize it was one of the blankets that Woodrow had been wearing. Woodrow was already back in his sleeping position when Roy looked at him, but the quiet smile on his lips betrayed his little act of benediction. Roy wrapped himself up in the blanket, pulled his legs up tighter, and closed his eyes.

Chapter Four

When Roy awoke he saw a bowl full of oatmeal and a small apple on the bench beside him. It had been twenty-four hours since he had taken his medication. He rubbed his eyes to make sure the breakfast was really there. It was real, he decided. It was just as real as the pine bench beneath it and the dull concrete wall beyond.

Roy remembered what had happened—why he was here. It felt like a brick had been dropped on his chest, and for a moment he had trouble catching his breath. The regret and the exhaustion worked in tandem to produce a dull, frayed sense of fear. He thought, *I will die in here because I did something wrong.*

"See a ghost?"

And there was Woodrow, in his corner, with a spoon in one hand and an apple in the other, eating with gusto as if this was a family reunion. Roy, whose legs resisted being stretched out straight after a night curled in like a fetus', could only manage a weak, "Something like that."

"They took the drunkard away while you slept."

And so it was. The drunkard and bucket both were missing from their usual places. Roy felt an impulse to look at the far corner. But this area, too, was empty.

"Did they charge him with anything?"

Woodrow covered up his mouth with his hand to make sure the chewed apple did not spill out with the words. "Didn't see. Probably public intoxication, if anything."

Roy started on the apple. Small and bitter. Balancing the core upright on the cleanest part of the bench, he started spooning the thin oatmeal into his mouth, sometimes looking at Woodrow, sometimes looking into the bowl itself.

From his periphery he saw Woodrow gesture to him. "Are you gonna eat that?"

Roy stopped chewing. "What?"

"The core," Woodrow said.

Moving the puréed oatmeal around in his mouth, Roy picked up the core by the stem and walked it over to Woodrow. He let it fall into his hand and, as he turned to walk back to his seat, heard his own spoon clatter to the ground. Instinctively he picked it up and nearly licked it. He stopped himself just in time and noted the mouse-dropping that had already adhered to the bottom.

The voice from behind him said, "Here." Woodrow held out his spoon, handle-first.

Roy took it gratefully.

Despite the worry and fatigue, Roy still felt a curious sense of freshness, a washed-and-dried feeling of a new day. It seemed Woodrow shared it, too. He licked the bowl with vigor and seemed much more talkative this morning. Just three minutes after his last bit of speech, he asked, "So who are you waitin' on?"

Roy set down the bowl and immediately regretted it. Now he had nothing to do with his hands. So he set them on his lap like a lady. This combined with his crossed ankles tucked under his seat at an angle would have been recognized by any cotillion professional as nothing less than perfect form. Such refinement, though, escaped Woodrow's attention. Or, at least, his commentary.

"Oh, one of the girls where I work owes me a favor," said Roy. "She should be coming by soon."

Woodrow nodded. This was a half-truth; Deirdre did owe Roy a favor, but it was unlikely she would come by here anytime soon. All of the women of the Pineapple were terrified of any haunt of the law. When past coworkers had been arrested, Roy had watched with amazement as the remaining girls gathered in the main room to point fingers and try to find out whose responsibility it was to go bail them out. Past favors, arrest histories, relative risk, beauty, and so on were all placed on the scale. Roy was sure it was Deirdre who would come bail him out after the charges, if any, were filed since he had done the same thing for her three months prior. One of her clients felt he hadn't been given his money's worth and decided to call the cops on the whole operation. Deirdre insisted it was his own insufficiencies that had left him feeling shorted. But the cops came anyway. Luckily Hattie's family had been paying off the police since before Illinois was a state. In return, on the rare occasions when someone blew the whistle on the ladies of the Pineapple, the charges filed were diluted to the point where they were little more than nuisances. Prostitution became loitering, and Deirdre—whose client was so upset, he charged her with theft—only had to pay off a parking ticket. This last case made Roy hopeful; attempted sodomy could become something as innocent as vagrancy, or, if he was lucky, a noise complaint.

Woodrow smiled at this answer. "Oh, yeah? What kinda 'favors' have you been giving these girls?"

"Very funny." He unhooked his legs from under his seat and fixed his hair, some strands of which had come loose during the night. "I like to keep my business and pleasure separate."

"All right, all right. I get that." He wiped his lips with the back of his hand. "Where do you work?"

With the oatmeal bowls empty and the apples gone, cores and all, and a long day ahead of them, Roy felt a curious sense of wonder, as if a solid brick wall he had walked by every day for years had suddenly disappeared, revealing a garden behind it. It was the sensation that anything was possible, and that even the darkest secrets could be borne. He could see only a handkerchief of sky through the window of the cell. But he felt that was enough.

"I work at a brothel," he said quickly.

Woodrow leaned back, laughing, and clapped his hands. "Oh, Lord! Now I *know* what kind of favors you've been givin' those women!"

Roy noticed Woodrow's accent shifting, and Woodrow noticed

him noticing it. As if he could erase the stain of the South, he rubbed his lips with the back of his hand, adding, "What is it, exactly, that you do there?"

The little square of barred sky seemed plush. Roy knew he would return soon to a world where he could see it better. A black dart of a bird flew across it.

"Can you keep a secret?"

Woodrow leaned forward, smiling. "What is it?"

"I need you to promise me first. Can you keep a secret?"

"Well, depends." Woodrow crossed his arms in front of his chest.

"On what?"

"Will it implicate me in some international crime ring?"

"No."

"Am I going to have nightmares about whatever you tell me?"

"You seem like a pretty heavy sleeper, so I'll say no."

"Will this secret get me killed?"

"Unlikely."

"Then," said Woodrow, shrugging, "out with it."

"All right." Roy stared into Woodrow's eyes, stating his words with gravity so as to test his mettle. "I, Roy, work as a prostitute in a brothel in the Levee District." His face flushed as he realized how loud he had said this. He hoped no one in the hall had heard him.

Woodrow's face was a stone of hidden conflict. He held the eye contact for as long as he could manage but then bit his lip and turned his head, thinking things that Roy could not gauge. Roy, too, looked away toward the corner that had commanded his attention the previous evening.

Woodrow breathed deeply and sat back, crossing his arms again. Without looking at Roy, he asked, "A prostitute for...women? Men?"

Sensing that prudence was key, Roy did not answer right away, nor did he look at Woodrow. At last he said, slowly, "I don't get to decide who...who comes to the brothel."

He heard Woodrow breathe once, hard. Roy felt like the concrete behind him had fallen away completely and that he had been frozen in the middle of his fall backwards. He suddenly felt himself in danger. Still staring at the corner, he wondered whether he could request a separate cell. He willed his shoulder to absorb the strength of the concrete behind him, in case the worst happened, and Woodrow attacked.

His cellmate kept his faraway look. Suddenly, he shook his head and then turned to Roy, who felt he probably looked like a trapped rabbit at that moment.

"You know," said Woodrow, "only God can judge, I guess. I mean, at least you have a job."

Roy was overjoyed. Usually whenever a client would open up, Roy pounced on the opportunity to make more money. Men who felt safe psychologically with their escort were more likely to tip well and splurge on better dinners and gifts. So he was used to exploiting these little wounds, tearing them open until they were gaping and bloody and could only be filled by Raina. Any mention of childhood trauma, of business strife, of marital discord rang like a cash register in Roy's ears. Now, he still heard a sound, but deeper. Like a drum of rainwater being kicked.

"Are you having trouble finding work?" It sounded more disingenuous than Roy meant, and after a moment, he doubted whether he should have started prying like this in the first place. But Woodrow, who had leaned forward to speak, now leaned back and clasped his knees.

"Oh, yeah. I have been moving around so much I can't keep a job. That is, if I can even find anywhere that hires Black men, no questions asked."

"What kind of work can you do?"

"Almost anything. I'm a metalworker. I'm good with animals and the like. I can do carpentry. And I know a thing or two about cars." Woodrow gazed up as he recounted his talents. "I'm sure I could find a nice job somewhere if I could just hunker down and *commit,* you know?"

Roy nodded. "Why do you move around so much?"

Woodrow looked at the ground for a moment and squeezed his right bicep with his left hand. "You know, it's never ideal to stay in one place for long."

"I can't say I do."

There was a pause. Finally Woodrow asked, "Have you been in Chicago long, then?"

"Almost three years."

"And before that?"

"The Midwest."

"Which state?"

"Nebraska."

"Oh," Woodrow said, "yeah. Why'd you move, again?"

The conversation had flowed so fast Roy hardly had time to think. Luckily the door of the cell clicked open at that moment. A fat guard with a face the color and consistency of raw animal fat stepped in the room, put his hands on his hips, let his belly thrust forward, eyed each prisoner, and sauntered over to Roy. He held out his hand. Then as if talking to a child, he said, "Your bowl."

Roy, eager to get on the good side of the guard, whipped around and grabbed the bowl and handed it to him. The guard swaggered to Woodrow, who held out his bowl while leaning back, his other arm still across his chest. Roy saw their hands touch on the rim of the bowl. The guard stacked one bowl in the other and walked out of the room. Roy watched as the guard clenched the hand that had just touched Woodrow, as if it had been bit by a spider.

For a minute they both stared at the door. Roy could not understand why such boiling hatred emanated from Woodrow. *Of course the guard was going to treat us as less than human,* Roy thought. *But you still have to show him respect.*

Woodrow inhaled deeply. "So, anyway," he continued. "Why did you leave home? I can think of a million reasons off the top of my head, of course. But what was the last straw for you?"

"Oh, God. The last straw? Let me think." He looked down at

his palms, which lay open on his lap. After a minute, he let out a weak, "Hm."

"Yes?"

"I don't really like to share this kind of stuff. With anyone. I'm sorry."

Woodrow shook his head. "No, I get it."

"Just better not to dwell on it."

After a minute, looking at his nails, Woodrow muttered, "Sorry."

Roy looked out the window. The rain from the night before had done nothing to clean the sky. It hung overhead like an unwashed sheet. Roy sighed and turned, lying flat on his back at full length. It was still uncomfortable for him to be wearing trousers. It made him feel anxious to feel the fabric between his legs always rubbing together. He flopped an arm over his eyes and slowed his breathing. Suddenly having Woodrow in the room was a nuisance. There was nothing Roy needed from him, and it was too dangerous to open up. So he pledged to wait until Deirdre, or whoever, came to bail him out, so he could take the customary day off after an arrest and, by this time tomorrow, be sitting in a gorgeous dress before a fancy dinner downtown, or at the opera, or the races with some piggish client named Tommy. There, he would feel better. There, in his real life.

Woodrow's voice caused Roy to jump. The tone was warmer than before. "I grew up near Mobile, Alabama."

Keeping his elbow bent over his face and his other hand resting on his stomach, Roy replied. "Furnas, Nebraska."

Chapter Five

"I was born there. In Furnas. I grew up on a small farm in the middle of nowhere with my mother and my cat, Dolly."

Woodrow asked a question.

"He died when I was very young. It was always his dream to find land out West and start a family there. His great-uncle had been a Sooner. Pa met my mom while passing through Ohio en route to Nebraska or Oklahoma. They fell in love and she decided to go with him."

Woodrow asked another question.

"He was a very skilled man, so they survived pretty well. He got the hang of farming rather quickly, and he was good with animals."

Woodrow asked a question.

"Vermont, originally. He was from a town where he was known as the 'Strongest Man Around.' During a county fair, actually, he threw a hatchet into a tree so hard that no one since has been able to dislodge it. After my father died—"

Woodrow interrupted with a question.

"I don't know how. I was too young. I never thought to ask. Anyway, after he died we had a lot of trouble keeping the farm together. I did as much work as I could, and Ma took up needlepoint to make us some money on the side. But there are things around a farm you just need a father to do. Neither of us could reach the top shelf of the cupboard, for God's sake. Still, she managed to keep us afloat and even taught me how to read. Then, of course, the dust storms started, and we had a few years where we survived on nothing but her needlepoint and the charity of our neighbors."

Woodrow asked a question.

"We didn't really see much of anybody; my aunt came from Lincoln a few times, and every once in a while we hitched a ride with our neighbor into town for church or the fair or something. But I didn't have any friends, if that's what you're asking."

Woodrow offered consolation.

"It wasn't so bad. I really just thought that's how every kid lived their life. I did like the animals. I was very close with Dolly. After Dolly died, though, when I was twelve, I started getting a little stir-crazy. I began to feel as though farm life had something wrong with it. Maybe it was because the house was so steeped in grief that I felt I couldn't really live, or maybe the fact that the earth itself seemed to be rejecting us, or maybe it was just me feeling lonely all of a sudden for people my own age. But around that time I started thinking about running away."

(He remembered how Adrian, naked, had brushed off a piece of straw clinging to the bottom of his foot.)

"But there was one event in particular that set me off."

Woodrow made a comment.

"Well, this all happened toward the end of spring when I was thirteen, a year or so after Dolly died. The house needed repairing, and to pay for it we had to slaughter some of our lambs. We had the son of one of our neighbors come do it. He was a vet and knew what he was doing." (Here the reel of the memory clicked into place and played in full color as Roy followed along with his crude, awkward words.) "He slaughtered them one morning before I woke up because Ma knew I would be upset to see it. But what she didn't know was that I was already in the barn that night, because it was hot out and Dolly liked to sleep in the loft where it was cooler. So I was sleeping up in the loft with her—"

Woodrow interrupted with a question.

"Did I say Dolly? I meant to say Maggie, the cat we got after Dolly. Anyway, I was already in the loft when Adrian, the neighbor, started killing them. So... I saw the whole thing."

Woodrow asked a question.

"No, I never had before. When Ma had to slaughter a chicken for dinner or something she always kept it out of sight. She knew how sensitive I was. I wouldn't even let her squash a fly. Anyway, the killing of the lambs upset me so much that I tried to run away from home that very night."

(What Roy neglected to mention was what exactly upset him about the killing of the lambs: it was not their terrified bleating or the rivers of blood that stained their wool, nor was it the way in which Adrian's muscles held firm as he gripped their heads to better cut their throats. Nor was it even the way in which the blood-splattered Adrian bathed himself afterward, in the same location as he had the summer before but in a manner infinitely less timid, infinitely more brusque. For Roy, who was stuck again in the same corner, the body of this man—which had, in the interceding year, grown to fill a massive part of Roy's thought— was suddenly something to be terrified of. No longer the acme of growth and beauty but a rigid instrument of destruction. Roy's attraction was suddenly linked to not only shame, but to death. But even this was not the last straw. It was not the slaughter itself or the unnavigable sexual psychosis that did it. No, what made him run away was a sound encountered the following night, a bleating that woke him up and forced him to see, standing in the far corner, the apparition of a headless lamb. Its raw stump of a neck dribbled blood in the moonlight, and the scraped bones of its spine glinted like milk glass. Roy tried to scream but couldn't. It turned toward him, its gaping throat still pulsing with the intake of air. It bleated and Roy bolted out the open window, running across the fields until he had passed through one neighbor's property and then another's, until his screaming lungs could borrow no more air from the sobs that racked his body, and he collapsed into a ditch a mile from home, still in his pajamas.)

"I only got a mile from home before I passed out in a ditch. I didn't wake up until noon the next day. And by the time I woke up, there was a black blizzard filling up the whole of the sky, coming right at me."

Woodrow asked a question about a term Roy had just used.

"It's a huge dust storm. Because the dust is so brown it's almost black. And because it blots out the sun. So I was trapped in that ditch for three hours as the dust howled overhead. Every piece of skin that wasn't covered was rubbed raw. It filled up my ears and ground in between my teeth. Though I tried to protect them, it got into my eyes too. It was the worst exposure I ever got. I was blind for three days."

Woodrow asked a question.

"Yeah, I healed up all right. It was getting home that was the hard part. Luckily my cat, Maggie, found where I was. She led me back home, meowing for me to follow her. The sheriff was already at my house when I got back. My mom had called me in as missing. But when they saw I was all right they called the doctor, and he gave me good eye drops. But I don't think this is the interesting part of the story. Please let me know if I'm boring you with all the details."

Woodrow agreed, with levity, that this part of the story was boring but encouraged Roy to continue.

"Soon as I got my sight back, I made up my mind. I was going to do odd jobs at the neighbor's farm for a little bit of money until I could buy a train ticket to Chicago. I would leave my mom a note telling her I loved her and that I would be back for her eventually. And then I would find a way to make it in the city."

Woodrow asked a question.

"You tell me. Does it look like I 'made it'?"

Woodrow laughed, and Roy did too.

"I did save up the money, though it took me a couple years. And I did run away, though I forgot to leave Ma a note. And I did get to the city, though I never really 'made it.' And there I was, almost sixteen, with no skills and no friends and no job and no place to stay, with nothing but a knapsack and a few coins in my pocket." (He declined to mention that the knapsack also contained a pencil stub, a raccoon skull, and a tiny rhinestone wrapped up in a page from a sewing book.)

Woodrow asked what happened next.

"I fell in with a weird crowd. Older men who would pay me just to eat dinner with them. It wasn't prostitution, yet. All they wanted was a little attention. A little human contact."

Woodrow made a comment.

"Yes, it was strange, but I had nowhere else to turn. Besides, it was a long time before my situation got bad enough that I had to do more than just eat dinner with them."

Woodrow claimed his ignorance.

"Of course you know what I mean. Well...maybe. Yes, a lot of them just wanted to sleep with me, but there were a few, mostly businessmen from other cities, that wanted very specific things. I had impacted wisdom teeth. Do you know what that's like? The only reason I was able to get them taken out was that, for five nights a week for three whole months, I treated a millionaire bullet manufacturer like a baby."

Woodrow expressed shock and puzzlement.

"Diaper and everything. But what men really liked, and what got me here, in a way, was to have me dress up as a girl for the night."

Woodrow demanded elaboration.

"Because, they felt that to hire a real woman would be too much. Or maybe not enough. Maybe they felt a sense of power, being able to make another man be their woman, sort of, you know? Not that I was always 'the woman,' though. Or maybe they were just interested in sleeping with other men, but had to make the relationship presentable in public. I don't know, really. I never thought to ask them."

Woodrow asked a question.

"Raina."

Woodrow asked a follow-up question.

"Honestly it doesn't matter. Around the house people call me Raina, but some clients like to call me Roy, even when I'm in a dress. It's all the same to me."

Woodrow asked a personal question.

"I'm not going to respond to that."

Woodrow apologized for his pointed tone. He posed a different question.

"It's complicated. I have never felt like a boy, really. I have no problem being seen as a boy, but I've never *felt* like one. I've never felt like a girl, though, either. I honestly don't know what either of those things *would* feel like. But I've never thought that I needed to do anything differently or change anything to be more like a girl or more like a boy, because I don't *like* either. But I know that if I ever want to live in the real world it will have to be as a boy. I do like wearing dresses and makeup, and I do like...*being* with the male clients..."

Woodrow tried to connect two definitions.

"But those things make me a girl, you know?"

Woodrow persisted.

"Well then, I guess we just have different definitions of it."

Woodrow asked him to continue.

"Yes, as I was saying, being Raina feels good sometimes, but I know it's only for now."

Woodrow asked a question.

"No, I wouldn't call it that. It's not a game or... Well, I guess I don't know what it is. Anyway. I was in Chicago, hanging out with this crowd. I would pick up clients at bars and joints as discreetly as possible, because I knew if the police discovered who I was, then I would go to jail, or worse. And I did have some pretty close calls. But one night, one of these men brought me to meet one of his other favorite Chicago girls, one named Constance who worked at a ritzy brothel. Now, this place is gorgeous, and the women all are stunning. But my client, who wanted to have me *and* this other girl stay the night with him, is told by the Madam, who was this kind woman with all these huge, shiny rings, that outside women are not permitted. I thought she was saying this just because she could tell who I was. So the man, who still wanted to sleep with Constance, tells me to sleep downstairs in the parlor, and he would collect me in the morning. I couldn't complain. That couch was as soft as a dream. But in the middle of the night I heard somebody walking around in the parlor—"

Woodrow voiced his dread at what was coming.

"No, don't worry, nothing bad happens. I hear this person walking around and they lift down this little vase off the wall and drop something into it."

Woodrow asked what it was.

"It sounded like a coin. I wasn't sure if I was dreaming or not. I woke up at first light and looked in the vase, and there was one of the Madam's rings at the bottom. Real ruby. When my client came down I told him to wait until I had talked to the Madam, in private. You see, I was worried that someone had tried to steal it. While I had no special liking for the Madam, and I had sympathy for anyone in this city who needed to steal to get by, I thought it was too strange an event not to address. So I got a private audience with her and explained what I had seen and showed her what I had found, and she was overjoyed. She said she had placed it in that vase for safekeeping when she was drunk the night before and had completely forgotten about it. She was very grateful. She said the ring used to be her mother's."

(Roy skipped over only a couple details in his retelling, the first being that the Madam that he saw during the night, while indeed drunk, was wearing a different dress than she had been wearing earlier—a winter dress instead of summer, one with red and green stripes and a snowflake pattern. The second being that

Hattie said she had misplaced the piece of jewelry not the previous night but rather on Christmas Eve three years prior.)

"After that, she started asking about who I was and where I came from, and I told her my story. She was impressed by all I had done. She asked me if I would have any interest in working for her for a while. She said she needed 'a girl of my talents.' God, you should have seen my client when I threw his money back at his face and told him that someone else could swaddle him tonight. That was when I actually began to feel like somebody."

Woodrow asked a question he did not exactly know how to phrase.

"You'd be surprised. A lot of men like what I have to offer."

Woodrow asked a follow-up question.

"No, I wouldn't call it that. 'Tricking' implies I'm lying to them. It also implies that these men don't know what I'm really like. I don't wear wigs or fake breasts or anything. I think it's pretty clear what's going on. In fact, there has only been one man who was enough of an idiot to not know what he was getting into when he rented me."

Woodrow asked a question.

"Yes, that's exactly right. That's why I'm here."

Woodrow asked a question that Roy found apt.

"Yes, all in all, I would say I've had fun. There are times when I miss Nebraska. But, up until last night, things had just been getting better and better. I want to go back my job as soon as possible."

Woodrow retrieved a detail from earlier in the story and asked about it.

"Yes, I miss her. Almost every day."

Woodrow asked a question.

"Yeah. She's out there, still."

Chapter Six

Roy sat up, feeling like he had just come out of a deep sleep. He was afraid to turn to his cellmate. If he did not approve of Roy's life choices, what then? Would they spend the rest of their time together in silence? Roy wished he had lied more. Dreading Woodrow's reaction, he turned.

He sat on the ground with his legs stretched out in front of him. He played with a piece of twine. Roy watched as he wound it around his finger and tied it into a bow. He put his arms behind him and leaned back on them.

"Well, Roy, that's a mighty fine tale you got there. That would make a great picture or something. 'The Case of the Missing Ring.' I love it."

"If you're asking for an autograph, the answer is *no*."

In the moments of silence succeeding Woodrow's laugh, Roy felt something shift. Telling his story in such great detail had forced him into a submissive position; he no longer had the upper hand in terms of mystery or intrigue. He had forfeited his power in the relationship.

Woodrow said, "I wish my story were that theatrical."

Roy smiled, happy for the hint of reciprocity. "I'm sure it can be. Anything can look theatrical if you wear as much makeup as I do."

"Yeah, well, I'm about ready to chew some of this scenery, I'm so damn hungry."

"Same. If you're a ham, you better watch out."

They smiled, the volley successful. Roy felt exhilarated, like after he had slept with a client and could sit alone and count the money. He wondered with a bit of pride whether anyone else could have matched Woodrow's quips with the same energy and accuracy as himself.

He had the impulse to tell Woodrow, "Don't feel obliged to tell me anything in return," but it was vetoed by his better judgement by dint of its passive aggression and pettiness.

They spent the next few minutes in silence. Eventually the keys clinked in the door, and a guard walked in with a new bucket. Behind him, another guard pushed a Black man into the room. He wore a maroon suit and a canary yellow cravat. He sat on the bench close to the door without looking at either of them. Roy and Woodrow looked at each other. *Well, look at that,* Roy thought. *We are in cahoots.*

"Hey," called Woodrow across the room. The man did not turn around. "What's your name?"

The man sat perfectly still, staring at the door. He looked like he was trying to will himself out of the cell. And he must have been a willful man, because at that very moment the door swung open. The same fat guard from that morning read off a clipboard, "Mr.

Thomas?"

The dapper man stood. "Yes?"

"Come with me." They exited together. The door slammed shut.

Roy and Woodrow looked at each other again. The giggles started soft but built up strength until both were hunched over. When the rhythm faltered, one of them would scoot to the edge of their seat and stare at the door like a setter dog, and send the other into peals of laughter. Woodrow's impression was so accurate that Roy felt tears leaking out of his eyes. He had only ever felt this sensation before when he and the girls of the Pineapple cooked dinner together; spices passing from hand to hand, taking shifts to stir the soup, and flour streaked on every apron and forehead. It was camaraderie and cooperation. It was the very joy of company.

The door clinked open again. A different guard, short and hirsute, carried in a tray. Lunch was creamed corn and bacon scraps. He set their plates on the benches, just out of arm's reach. He sniffled his nose as he left.

The inmates set to work immediately. Both aspects of the meal were unpleasant. The creamed corn was runny and metallic, and once Roy got the notion in his head that the cook had spat a loogie into the bowl, he could not eat another bite. He was able to eat most of the bacon, until the tough meat made his teeth ache. Once again he offered his leftovers to Woodrow, who graciously accepted.

Woodrow leaned back once he finished and closed his eyes. *A siesta may be a good idea*, thought Roy. He first wanted to fix his hair. He let it down and ran his fingers through it until it smoothed out. Then he pulled it back into the old piece of string. He secreted to the bucket and peed in it. He sat back down, looked at Woodrow, yawned, and closed his eyes.

"Do you know," started Woodrow, jarring Roy from his sleep, "what a bivouac is?"

"Yeah. Isn't it like a camp for soldiers?"

Woodrow's eyes were closed as if he was talking in his sleep. Unlike during the night, his face now seemed tired, drawn down by lead weights. "Exactly." One eye cracked open. "How'd you know that?"

"I read a lot," said Roy. Assuming this fact would pigeonhole him as an egghead, he amended, "There is not much to do during the day in a brothel."

Woodrow smiled and looked away. "Yeah, I read a good bit too." Roy realized now his statement had come across as bragging. Since he could not take it back, he decided to move on.

"Why do you ask?"

"About bivouac? There's a poem called 'The Bivouac of the Dead.' Pieces of it are inscribed in almost every Civil War cemetery in America. There was one near where I grew up. I didn't know—"

The gate rattled and the hairy guard came in. He took Roy's plate and realized his bowl was missing. When he saw it stacked near Woodrow, he turned back to Roy and asked, "Did he take your food?"

Roy, still aiming to make a good impression, shook his head, and said in his most placating voice, "Oh, no, I offered it to him because I couldn't finish it."

The guard looked at him a little longer. Roy wondered whether he would not have been better served by speaking a little more gruffly. *Feminine charm may not be a good tactic when we are all supposed to be men here.* Either way, the guard took Woodrow's bowls without looking at him and locked the door as he left.

"I'm never offering you food again," teased Roy.

"Just wait until you see dinner."

Roy had his legs crossed at the ankles, and he swung them under the bench. He waited for Woodrow to speak. He kept repeating to himself that Deirdre was coming soon. After all, it had taken them nearly seventy-two hours to bail out Theresa when that man charged her with "disturbing the peace."

Finally Woodrow spoke. "I lived near this cemetery my whole life. The owners of the land petitioned the county for a steel plaque with the poem inscribed on it, but the county kept turning them down. Eventually they just got one of us to do it. My dad was a blacksmith, so I knew a little bit about engraving. I think I can still remember it, actually:

"The muffled drum's sad roll has beat
The soldier's last tattoo;

No more on life's parade shall meet
The brave and daring few.
And Glory gua—

"Wait, shit," said Woodrow. "No. It's...

"On Fame's eternal camping-ground
Their silent tents are spread,
And Glory guards with solemn round
The bivouac of the dead."

Despite the hint of irony in Woodrow's voice, Roy found the words beautiful. Woodrow recited it with his eyes closed, as if it was coming to him in a dream. Roy wished he would say it all again.

Woodrow continued, "I was thirteen. I had no idea what 'bivouac' meant, or 'tattoo,' or even 'solemn.' But I had to carve out the letters just the same. And stick it on a pole in the cemetery behind the big house. I found out later that the reason the county refused to give them a plaque was because this family, they didn't even have any Confederate soldiers buried there. They just liked the poem and wanted it for themselves. It was an aesthetic choice." Woodrow's foot bounced up and down. "I didn't even know what half those words meant until I left Alabama. It was all just hoity-toity nonsense." He looked Roy in the eyes. Those eyebrows, dark and smooth like a rip in silk. Something was brewing under the surface.

Feeling a need to keep the embers hot, Roy asked, "Who lived in the big house?"

Woodrow took a leisurely breath. "The Dabneys. Rich, white family."

Roy nodded as if he knew them. He imagined himself prodding Woodrow with a long, sharpened stick to get him to talk. He decided he would not press him further. If he wanted to talk, he would.

So they sat in silence. The name, Dabney, hung in the air like the last word in a novel.

By chance, they looked at each other at the same moment. Roy began undoing his hair tie, watching Woodrow watch him. He had read a book about a man who could charm snakes by staring them right in the eye and playing the flute. He wasn't sure if this was the same thing, since Woodrow was, all told, more approachable than a snake. But there was, in their shared look, a mutual recognition of difference. Roy was sure that had he told Woodrow every detail of his life story, they would not be talking anymore. So while he was happy he had someone he trusted enough to confide in—prison, it seemed, made quick friends—the fact that he had to keep the details private discouraged him.

Roy broke their eye contact. He was quick to turn the blame on himself. After all, he was the one who had bragged about reading a lot, he was the one who made huge sums of money in a glamorous job while Woodrow was battered around America by unemployment and hunger. Roy had never had to worry about the color of his skin. Differences like these were insurmountable, and the divide could never be crossed—the stories never told without an asterisk at the end. And it would be better, he decided as he tied up his hair, if neither of them pretended things were otherwise.

It was then that Woodrow spoke.

Chapter Seven

"The Dabneys sat on one hundred acres just outside Mobile. They lived in a mansion at the top of a hill in the middle of the property. Theirs was the last plantation in Alabama to free its slaves. But because so many of the freemen and women had nowhere else to go, most of them stayed on the Dabney's plot and began sharecropping. Do you know about that? Sharecropping?"

Roy nodded.

"And you know it's just another form of slavery, right?"

Roy nodded, slower.

"Well, my family grew up there. Like that. In total, there were probably thirty families on the Dabney property—nearly one hundred and fifty people besides the Dabneys who numbered seven or so if you counted the live-in stepgrandma. It was its own world, there. We had our own economy, our own general store, a school, a church—even a trash service. I never even stepped outside the property limits until I was twelve. Among the Blacks was a clear hierarchy, with those who worked in the big house at the top and then the craftsmen and teachers beneath them. Then, at the bottom, the farmers."

Roy expressed his surprise.

"Yeah. We had no idea what was outside. All we knew was what was right in front of us: the work, the schooling, the Dabney boys racing through the fields on horseback, getting the first pick of the fruits, and bothering anything in a skirt. Those were the only things we knew. We were on a separate Earth."

Roy asked a question.

"For a lot of reasons. Some of them stayed because it was where their family grew up. Some, because they didn't know what the rest of the world was like. They felt like a bird in the hand was worth two in the bush. But most of them stayed because the Dabneys kept everyone in crushing debt. Since the family was in control of what they paid the workers, as well as the stores on the property and everyone's rent and all, they could keep us under their thumb. They would skew things so that everyone had to pay through the nose for just the necessities. Then they would tell us we couldn't leave our tracts of land until we had paid off the mortgage. You know where that word comes from, don't you? *Mort* is Latin for 'death.' Never in my life have I heard of someone paying off one of those things."

Roy said nothing.

"But then things started to change. People got word from their relatives up North where there were a lot more jobs and a lot less discrimination. We heard wonderful stories of people finding work in New York, in Detroit, Omaha even, and Chicago. It sounded too good to be true. My whole family, grandparents and all, would sit around the kitchen table after dinner and talk and talk and talk about how we wanted our lives to be. But our debt was all around us. It was the wallpaper and the ceiling fan, the screws keeping the boards together and even the boards themselves. It grew for every second we kept the lights on, with every schoolbook and pound of sugar we used. Everything we read and ate and slept on trapped us. We couldn't escape it. It was inside us."

Roy waited to speak.

"But one day, my thirteenth birthday actually, we noticed the Gavins were missing. They lived pretty close to the main house. The father dealt with the livestock and the wife wove rugs. They were gone, just like that. No note, no nothin'. Totally emptied out the place. The only things they left behind were a kitchen table and several hundred dollars of debt. Now, there were rumors that they had tried to escape but were caught in town; others told tales of them being eaten by Rawhead and Bloody-Bones in the forest. But even as we told these stories, we all were thinking the same thing: at the end of the day, the Gavins had acted on an amazing idea. When we traded theories about whether they got caught in the bayou or died of starvation, we would be smiling. Even if they had died, they were free of the debt, at least. We were inspired. It was as simple as that."

Roy asked Woodrow to continue.

"Well, it shouldn't come as a surprise that a few weeks after that, another family just vanished. A week after that, a family had their two sons disappear. Week after that, two families packed up and left on the same day. The mom of one of those families was the handmaid to Mrs. Dabney. You bet the family noticed then."

Roy asked a question.

"Well, all they did for the earlier families was issue a warrant for their arrests, should they ever be found up North. But they knew that no one would be able to tell one Black family from another up there, and no one would care, either. They were not getting the results they wanted."

Roy suggested his idea of what happened next.

"Well the first thing they did was hire the prettiest, most fair-skinned Black woman you've ever seen, like a pail of milk with a drop of coffee in it. They started her working in the house. It was the oddest appointment ever, I will say. Everyone else in the kitchen said she didn't know a snail fork from her own elbow. So we all began cooking up our theories."

Roy asked a question.

"I'll get to mine. But the wide assumption was that they had just panicked at the loss of their help and had hired the nearest girl with a pulse. Her prettiness, according to the popular theory, was incidental. But when the other cooks spread word that she had come all the way from New Orleans, I began to suspect something else was afoot."

Roy waited.

"Her name, by the way, was Evangeline."

Roy asked Woodrow for his personal theory.

"Well, I wondered what would make the family take on such a

pretty and incompetent girl, who would burn the greens and serve the roast half-cooked and then clog the whole kitchen with the dozen or so young men swarming after her. Then I realized: they were gonna try to marry her off to the man with the most debt, in order to make sure his family stayed."

Roy asked whether that was what happened.

"Well, not exactly. See, I had a friend named Grover. He had thought and thought about this issue. Smart guy. Teacher's assistant. And he and I got talking one day on the porch, and he asked me my theory of Evangeline. So I told him. And he nodded. But I could tell he had something else going on in his head. After a minute he asked me who would be the person with the most debt in town, since, by my logic, that was the person they were going to set Evangeline up with."

Roy interrupted with a question.

"Well, of course I don't mean literally, but they had things they could do to pretty much guarantee she married who they wanted. As her employers, they could restrict who she spent time with, and they could always threaten to fire her if she was running around with the wrong guy. Anyway, on the porch that day, I thought about who was the person in town who owed the most to the Dabneys. And I started laughing, and Grover started laughing too, because we knew that would be Sully, the hobo who had been bumbling around the Dabney property for decades. He owed so much to so many people that the general store kept a separate ledger just in his name. We laughed and laughed thinking of

Evangeline getting hitched to him. No, Grover had a different theory about her. He thought it would be better for the family in the big house if they never married her off. That way, they could keep her as a lure for as long as she was still pretty."

Roy asked a question about the girl named Evangeline.

"I don't know. I mean, I wasn't really drawn to her in the first place, so figuring this out didn't change my opinion."

Roy asked a question.

"I don't know. She was not really my type."

Roy asked a question about Grover's theory.

"Well, just wait. At the time this theory rung true for me. We thought we had cracked the code. So naturally we started telling everyone about what Grover thought, and it spread around. We noticed the Dabney sons stopped riding their horses through our fields, and the daughters stopped taking company on the porch in the evening. They closed the shutters of that big white mansion and only came out once a week to stand at the very front of the church, blocking everyone else's view of the pulpit. And of course, a few weeks later, another family up and vanished without a trace."

Roy asked a question.

"That made six, I think, not counting the few sons who headed out on they own. Their own. But anyway, here's where it gets interesting. One night we hear Mr. Dabney and his hunting pals come around the bridge, all of them hollering, with torches in they hands. Looking for Sully. He had broken into the house and ravaged Evangeline that night. Well, Sully was not a popular man by any means, but he was never known to be violent. Still, we figured we couldn't really account for a man who was as wild as him and who had probably never seen a woman so beautiful. All the while, Grover seemed to be thinkin' about something. But he wouldn't tell me what."

Roy undid his hair and put it up again.

"So we waited for news. 'Round midnight, a little boy came runnin' through and told us that they had found Sully hidin' in the springhouse. We left our dinner tables and started toward the Dabney's."

Roy held his breath.

"From five acres away we could see the fire."

Roy exhaled.

"By the time we got there, Sully was just a smoking corpse. None of us really knew what to do, since none of us really knew him to begin with, and we were all of us in agreement that such a crime deserved such a punishment. But still, we went home rattled. It didn't help much, too, that they hung up Sully's body from a tree the next day."

Roy paused and then asked a question.

"Well, The Dabneys told us that they sent her away somewhere she could be safe, a city where she could live as if nothing had happened. As I said, I wasn't close with her."

Roy made an observation.

"Yeah, well, that's because sometimes I have trouble believing it happened to me. I see it all happening. I mean, I remember it all, but whenever I get to the really dark parts, it seems like it all happened to someone else. You know?"

Roy said he did know.

"So there's that. But also, we haven't gotten to the end yet."

Roy asked what happened next.

"Well, everyone was scared stiff, of course. We didn't have any runaways for almost a year. The Dabneys got what they wanted all along."

Roy asked a question.

"Hell no. Who would the police believe? The Black people in the field or the white family in the mansion? Sully had no family and no friends. Even if we had thought that his murder had been unjustified, we wouldn't have bothered calling the police. But again, I want to stress that for most of us an affront on the honor of a woman like Evangeline was a death crime. But I think it still put this idea back in our minds that there wasn't really any escape for us. Going north was the same as hiding in the springhouse. Either way, you're gonna be found out."

Roy asked a question.

"Yes, I felt the same. The only one who really seemed disturbed was Grover. He would come over to the smithy every day, and we would talk about it. I thought he was just whistling Dixie. Until he disappeared."

Roy made a conjecture.

"That's what we thought, too. Made us even more wary of the

Dabneys. But we couldn't think of any reason why they'd want to kill him in the first place, let alone kill in secret."

Roy asked a question.

"We guessed, but we had no idea. You have to understand, there was no information coming on or off the plantation. We only knew what we saw ourselves. That or conjecture. I will say, though, that the popular opinion was moving more and more toward 'monster abduction' than anything else. So we waited and lived our lives. My father passed away, and the smithy business went to me and my sister. Two of the Dabney sons went off to college, and the mother had a tumor removed. They hired a new handmaid, an old woman named Bathsheba. Can you believe that? Bathsheba. She was from a different era. Oh, and we heard more and more stories of Black men getting lynched throughout the South."

Roy asked a question.

"Rape, mostly. Of white women."

Roy made a sound.

"I know. Seems like we Black men just can't control our wild animal impulses. Anyway! The Dabneys were still spiteful, though. The cost of milk and eggs got steeper and steeper, and they started getting stricter on mortgages. I mean, they couldn't whip you or anything. But if you came up short one month you'd find your credit gone, a cow missing for damages, and your stove repossessed straight out of the wall. Those were the hardest years of my life. I must have shoed a thousand horses to make up for Dad being gone. I even started engraving funeral plaques for people in Mobile and Montgomery. My sister eventually got a job inside the big house with the Dabneys, but that was not much better than what I was doing. She would come home with these chilblains on her hands, from scrubbing clothes with soap and lye. Don't let anyone ever tell you that having a job earns you some kind of dignity. There are jobs not fit for animals. So, long story short, it went on like this till I was sixteen or so. Around the end of that September, Grover came back. The rumor spread so fast it beat him by three days. He came to me first, knocking on my door during dinner one night. He looked the way they say men of the desert look, with roughened skin and this glint in his eyes. He told us not to tell anyone else he was here. So we hid him in the bedroom and finished our meal as if nothin' had happened."

Roy asked why.

"We figured the Dabneys were watching us. Better safe than sorry. After dinner, he and I got to talking. And he said he had found Evangeline. And asked her about everything. And she told him that what the Dabneys told us wasn't true. She told him Sully never raped her. She never even met Sully. She said she was fired for an unknown reason and had since been working in a dry goods store in Mobile. She was married already to a Black man, and they had a kid together, named Randy."

Roy asked half a question.

"To scare us! Don't you see? To show us that our lives didn't matter, that if we so much as thought of crawling out from under their thumb, they could kill us as easy as that! It had nothing to do with rape, Roy. It was a fucking *business* maneuver."

Roy began a sentence.

"Because he was the least important to the community, yes, and wouldn't pose a serious loss if he were dead. Exactly. Grover had figured all this out. He knew why they did what they did. He said he would need help getting the message out once the time was right. He said I would know when that was. Grover disappeared again, leaving us to wait. After a week I felt like I was sitting on a hot stove and just needed to jump off. Two weeks later, and I had almost forgotten about the whole affair. It wasn't until almost a month after that, in the dead of October, we started hearing shouts. We all ran out of the house and headed to the property. And sure enough, through the branches of the magnolia trees we saw a huge fire roaring right around the big house. God, I tell you, we all bolted through the woods. Me faster than anyone. I was so *angry* that I hadn't told someone sooner. It could have saved a life. Who was it gonna be? My best friend? My schoolteacher? Grover? We passed the creek and were a half mile from the house when we saw it. It wasn't someone being burned alive. It was the *house*. The house was on fire. The windows and doors shot flames ten feet out. The grass around it turned brown and crackled. The gravestones behind the house cracked with the heat. The metal placard I carved melted. And then the roof collapsed. And it wasn't until then that we noticed the doors had been barred."

After a moment, Roy asked a question.

"It had to have been him. There's no other explanation."

Roy expressed his amazement.

"Yeah. Since we were all together, I explained what Grover had told me. About Sully and Evangeline. Everyone was shocked. But after an hour or so, once they had had some time to process it, they began to spit on the rubble. The whole house, you know, was ashes. I kid you not. By morning there was nothing but half a brick chimney. We didn't find any remains ourselves. But there was an awful lot of ash to sift through, and we didn't really bother. We assumed the firemen would sort it all out. Besides, we were too busy."

Roy asked a question.

"What do you mean? Packing our fucking bags. There was not a living soul on that whole property by the time the ashes cooled. My family and I hitched a ride to Mobile. My sister sang the whole way there. There was soot on my hands still, but my heart had never felt so light."

Roy asked a question.

"Hm? Oh, we split ways in Mobile. I told them I wanted to live by myself. Besides, it was a liability to have me around. Though Grover and I look nothing alike, if anyone ever found out my family was from that plantation, and that they had a son around Grover's age, we would all be done for. So I took off on my own, getting jobs in railroads, working in some smith shops."

Roy asked a question.

"Oh, right. Traffic violation, remember? They pulled me over for having a dead taillight, and then they started grilling me. When they found I grew up on the Dabney plantation they stuck me in here. See, they can't tell one Black man from another. Once my sister comes and verifies my ID, they will let me go. But for now I just gotta wait."

Roy asked a question.

"I hate to say, but I just don't know. Maybe he died setting the fire. Maybe he stayed on the plantation after everyone else left and then got arrested or something. Odds are, he hitchhiked through Texas and out of America. I don't know for sure, though. I really just don't know."

Chapter Eight

The room had changed its substance. Roy felt as if the cell had come loose from its moorings and now drifted on the open sea. There were no ties to anything outside this room. Deirdre could dawdle all day for all he cared, and dinner didn't even cross his mind. All that mattered was already here. Looking at Woodrow and looking away when he returned the stare, and then finding something to do with his nails or his hands until he looked up and saw Woodrow still staring at him. This is how it went for twenty minutes, neither quite knowing what to do with the thrill of freedom from an old burden and the sudden imposition of a new one.

The door rattled. The fat guard entered with a clipboard. He stood in the doorway with his legs spaced out so wide he looked like he was straddling a horse. He called out Woodrow's name.

"Yes," he replied.

Roy wondered if this was how things would be. He would be glad that Woodrow was getting out before him, of course. But he would also feel cheated. He thought, *How could a Black man with no money and no job get out of jail before me?* He suddenly felt nauseous. *God, I am such a brat.*

The guard said, "Just checking you were still in here," and he left.

The men looked at each other. They waited until the footsteps died down the hall. Then they burst out laughing.

"How on earth could you have—"

"—up and disappeared—"

"—are you a ghost? Can you walk through walls?"

"What kind of vanishing-act magician do they think I am?"

The only thing that put a damper on their fun was the knowledge that Woodrow's presence in the cell was somehow of great importance. Roy suspected he would be getting out first after all.

With this lighter mood, they were able to turn the conversation outward. They talked briefly about their tastes in books and music. In this way they passed the time until dinner came. Roy had never eaten a pork chop so cold or beans so salty. Again, he gave what he couldn't eat to Woodrow.

They rested after the meal. Woodrow warned Roy that Saturday nights like tonight meant a lot more people tossed in the holding cell. For the entertainment of the coming inmates, they agreed to pretend that they were long-lost nemeses plotting for each other's blood. "I will be Baron Knifehammer," said Woodrow, "and you can be Raven, Queen of the Moon." In the dead of night, they agreed, Roy would slink toward Woodrow's sleeping form, scream, "Die!" and whack him with his shoe. Roy had to hold his sides to guarantee that no guts spilled out.

An hour after dinner, the door opened again, revealing both the hairy and the fat guard. Roy felt this was a rare syzygy. They called Roy's name and, after he stood and stated, "Yes," told him that he was charged with one count of being drunk in public, and that his friend had come to bail him out.

He remembered how he had begrudged Woodrow when he thought he was leaving before him. Now he felt the stab of guilt. He turned to his friend, Woodrow, who slipped him a wink. Though Roy had been winked at more times than he could count, though he had slept with more men than he could remember, and though he had been inured to every wile and trick in the common man's book, this one wink somehow held the pagan power to make him blush. He could manage only a smirk in return as he was led out of the cell and into the empty, still city.

BOOK FOUR

Chapter One

Every year when Hattie saw the first yellow leaf of autumn she would rush to the brothel and mark up the price of wine. She was known to run into dining room one day every fall, acorn in hand, which she would slam on the counter as if she was a legal prosecutor and the nut proof positive of some heinous crime. With the same frenzy, she would scribble out a memo to the girls to be pinned on their corkboard: "With the approaching cold weather, please do not forget that wine is never less than forty dollars a bottle, cider ten dollars, and dessert fifteen dollars." As it was Hattie, not the girls, who negotiated the prices for their services, she did not bother telling them that by the first snow their bodies would be worth nearly twice what they had been in summer. This was the seasonal economy of the Pineapple.

And the men could not complain. As the weather turned, where else were they to go? Wives seemed icier while a north wind blew, and cold streets were known to breed loneliness. Not to mention that nights were growing longer. There were simply more dark hours to fill.

The promise, of course, was of warmth. The warmth of cider, of cakes in bellies, of rooms upholstered in velvet, and finally, the precious warmth of a woman's bosom. So the ladies of the Pineapple loved the later seasons. And whether the men found the dawn streets even colder after an evening with the courtesans, the women themselves did not care. For them, the change in temperature meant only one thing: profit.

Tonight, in the middle of October—when leaves peppered the ground, the streetlamps offered light but no heat; the few dogs forgotten outside barked pitifully; and hundreds of Chicagoan mothers stood closer than they ought to their stoves—tonight, Raina prepared.

With the doors to the boudoir and the bathroom both locked, she rinsed her hair with egg; washed her face; applied cold cream; plucked a stray eyebrow; separated a cuticle from the rest of her body; applied foundation, blush, eyeshadow, eyeliner, and mascara; drew a new shape for her lips with lip-liner; and filled in this outline with scarlet. A perfect hour had passed, and there wasn't even a smudge. Her face done, she pulled on her panties, careful to arrange the contents in such a way that her penis was not obtrusive. Slipped on the dress and the gloves and the lilac perfume. Then the jewels. Tonight she opted for simple silver hoops to match her silk-thin chain, from which hung a heart-shaped locket, empty. The silver bracelets, she felt, were too heavy compared to the earrings and necklace, but she had no other choice. They were the only things she could wear without risking mixing metals. While Dot, her coworker, knocked on the door, Raina decided to ditch the bracelets altogether and go bare armed.

She stopped in front of the mirror. She looked like the other side of the moon.

At the threshold she turned on her heel and shook out a pill from the bottle. She had switched to a new prescription a month ago when her last bottle was broken; these ones were effective but left her mouth dry. She remembered her time in the cell with a mixture of pleasure and fear. Yes, she had never felt closer to death—she had nearly felt its fingers brush her neck. But there was an exhilaration to it too—the wild thrill of being stuck with nothing but yourself and then discovering that that is enough. It was a dip in her day-to-day, a hole of unaccustomed depth. Lying in bed she had imagined herself curled up there, sleeping.

But Raina rarely slept, now. As she headed down the hall, she reminded herself to be careful, to do her job and then retire to her chamber and prepare for the next day. She had put on her talismans of strength: black nail polish, silver earrings, and perfume. She was charmed and charming. Protected and ready.

Downstairs, Hattie stood up when she saw Raina. The other girls arranged silently around her. Often, Raina had men ask her what they all did behind those closed doors. She liked to ask them what *they* thought they did. The theories ranged from the fanciful to the obscene. Some men imagined that the girls were always laughing and teasing each other, doing each other's hair and trading clothes and jewelry. Other men, especially those who professed themselves well-versed in the ways of the world, said with authority that women who could not be carnally sated with just one man could not be carnally sated by men at all—meaning that their libido must necessarily spill over to the realm of other women. These men condemned what they imagined to be an orgy-house while in the same breath proposing the idea that male customers were doing the women a favor by relieving them of some of their hysterical energy. Raina had read Havelock Ellis and yawned and remarked that these same men were the ones most likely to cry when told to leave in the morning. In her years of experience, no man had ever imagined that the Pineapple operated exactly how it should for what it really was: a place of business, operated and run by businesswomen. As Connie liked to say, "The oldest profession is still a Goddamn profession."

So tonight, these professionals sat in a circle and waited for Hattie to speak.

"Hello, ladies, and good evening."

The girls responded in kind.

"Tonight is a very special night, you know."

The girls did know. They showed their excitement by inspecting their nails, blowing their noses, or closing their eyes.

Hattie continued. "Tonight, one of the biggest lobbyists in America will be dropping by our establishment."

Three women raised their eyes. These were the women who were always picked first: Deirdre, the one whose tan skin and bottle-blonde hair strove to match Hollywood glamor; Marie, who was twenty-two but looked fourteen; and Candy, who had monumentally large breasts. The rest of them slouched in their chairs, content to be the runner-up choice for one of the rich lobbyist's friends or workmates, so long as he wasn't unspeakably unhygienic and would finish his business before midnight. These second-tier women included Connie, the resident redhead; Dot, who faked a Swedish accent to accentuate her golden hair; Alexandria, the Black woman who mainly appealed to Black men or white Southern men; Sakura, the Asian-American whose birth name was Constance but who changed it at Hattie's insistence; and Raina, whose appeal, while not insubstantial, was niche. Still, rates were kept flat across the board, and in this season, there was very little risk that someone would be sleeping alone.

"So I trust you ladies to be on your best behavior, and remember: smiles are free." Turning her body toward Raina without looking at her, she added, "Lord knows we do not need any more bad press."

None of the other women smiled. It was raining, and they were tired. And lunch had not been very good today.

"Ready, all?"

"Ready," they mumbled.

At once every girl got to her feet. Sixteen heels clacked as the women stood in their assigned locations around the room. This was the performance of the open door. In that two-second window in which Hattie entered or exited the main room, the women intended to give the men a vibrant impression of movement, life, and beauty. Hattie motioned to Constance, who started playing the piano quietly. Hattie's hand was on the doorknob, and she motioned to the rest of them, who began to rush back and forth across the floor on quiet feet, twirling and dancing and showing just enough leg to inspire. They formed groups and dissolved. They fixed each other's garments that did not need fixing. They giggled loudly and whispered to each other. What they whispered didn't matter. Bits of poetry or prose. In this way, the women of the Pineapple turned their place of work into a place of consumption. Even bees do not operate with such harmony.

And it was all for this: the moment when Hattie opened the door and slipped into the anteroom. While the women were not supposed to look, it was too tempting to resist. The faces of the men on the other side registered somewhere between shocked and dazzled. To see such a trove of jewel tones and gemstones would astound any man who knew the world to be no more than the gray, garbage-lined streets outside, or the rigid, airless boardrooms downtown. There was never any lust on their faces, it seemed. The peek into the women's room elicited feelings much more elemental and much more childlike than lust. That is to say, wonder, hope, and imagination. The lust was just an afterthought.

Raina did not see into the antechamber tonight, but she knew that anyone sitting in the middle part of the couch must have seen her arm, striking, thin, and pale as bone in an extended position very much to its advantage. Connie, whose eyes were trained at the door, turned and said she saw nothing extraordinary. Some trio of businessmen, a Black guy, one old man, two mob types, and Charlie, a regular. Charlie always courted Connie. She rolled her eyes. Alexandria reassured her, "Remember, hon, fondue tonight." If they could get through this evening, at least they would have cheese. So they danced and whispered, dreaming of pieces of bread dripping with gooey gruyere, while in the next room, eight men believed they were at the gates of paradise.

Constance was playing harder now. Raina knew Constance's parents had wanted her to pursue music, but some of her peers in her conservatory, intimidated by her skill, began rumors about her status as a citizen. Raina felt for her. If she could slam the piano keyboard cover down on the fingers of those peers of hers, she would have, gladly. But all she could do now was appreciate her skill, thank her for her playing, and when Hattie wasn't listening, call her Constance.

Leaning on the doorway to the kitchen, the little girl, Pearl, stood. Though she had been less and less around the house recently, she never failed to watch the lineup from some corner of the room. It was her favorite part of living here. Her mother had worked at the Pineapple for almost twelve years before passing away from the flu. She was a ward of the house now, legally Hattie's daughter but really the cook's responsibility. Raina promised herself she would help take better care of her someday. She swore that as soon as her life stopped being so busy, she would devote some attention to this orphan. Raina wanted to be the one person at the Pineapple who always took time to do what Pearl wanted and who, without becoming her mother-figure, would at least be someone she could rely on. But for the moment, all the women of the Pineapple had a job to do. They did their dance and hoped that Pearl was hidden enough to not be seen.

There were still a good ten minutes until the doors opened. The peep followed by this long wait had a substantial effect on the men, who would pay more for these women after being baited by the single glimpse. So for these minutes, the women took turns giggling, whispering, and dancing around the room, like rolling tables on which gramophones sat, playing a record of a human voice.

What was it that reminded Raina, at that moment, of Woodrow? It had nothing to do with food, since the food here, while not always stellar, was still incomparable to prison food. Nor did it have anything to do with sleep, since her bed was so strewn with blankets and pillows that the comparison to a prison bench never entered her mind. Nor did talking to the other girls about her experience in the prison itself contribute to her recollection. No—it was Marie's red ring, the imitation ruby that reminded her of the story she had told Woodrow. *I can't believe I told him that,* Raina thought, spinning in place slowly to Constance's song.

As Alexandria approached her and took her hand to revolve around each other in a lazy *pas de deux,* Raina felt like that period of time spent in the cell was separated from her by the depths of the sea. While she, Raina, stood aboard the boat in her dress and her jewels, she could see Woodrow and herself seated on the seabed, conversing quietly, sharing the pleasure of each other's company in the deep blue swelling current, incredibly far away, incredibly out of reach. She realized that she missed him terribly.

And even though those moments in the cell were some of the brightest in her memory, she was surprised, as she studied Marie's ring, that she did not necessarily long for them. They were too far off to wish them back. To have those feelings back now would mean giving up everything she had here.

She had a sense of being stuck between two realities, like when the revolving door at the Marshall Field's department store jammed.

Raina approached Deirdre. They spoke at the same moment, Deirdre saying, "I cannot breathe in this dress," and Raina saying, "Out, out damned spot!" Both women giggled as if a joke had passed between them, and they went their separate ways.

All told, she loved her current life. She had a therapist and medication. Not to mention the pleasure of holding power over men. Every night she had someone else to think about, some new terrain on which to practice the construction of her image, the placement of compliments and neglects and insults too subtle for these men to register, but which, taken as a whole, could translate into the impression of a milquetoast maiden or a sultry, dark mistress. And she had friends here, too, people who did not care about how she dressed, people who respected her burgeoning intellect and who found her beautiful, inside and out. Compared to the spiritual and literal penury of Nebraska, in Chicago she felt like a millionaire.

She dreamed that, if she had Woodrow right here, she could

just knit him into her life without losing anything on either side. But she knew this could not be done. She knew that for every window to open, a door needed to close first. And this was the problem. She could not see the next step. She could only spin and dance with the others, only stand in front of the door and wait for it to open of its own accord.

So why did she stare at the floor while silk fringes dragged over it, feeling like screaming, screaming until her voice tore out of her throat and clattered to the ground like a shell? Why did she feel her current moment was a dream, and that only the things that were real had occurred in that hermetically sealed memory of the cell? Why did she leave all her bones in that place? She felt empty, blind, and powerless. The jewels that littered the necks of the other women were pieces she had already seen. Nothing, it seemed, could reach her.

Hattie was back. The ladies, as if driven by an electric current, arranged themselves in their order. Constance abandoned her jazz piece half-finished. Raina watched as Pearl perked up in her corner. The door opened, and the men filed in.

She recognized Charlie immediately. He came every month or so and arrived very early to wait for Connie. He wore the same brown suit every time. Though they all knew he was first, Hattie ushered a group of three men up before him, casting the Black man and the old man even further back, and beyond them, the penumbra of the men who had arrived too late. The businessmen looked like a father and sons, the patriarch with a balding head and enough fat on him to, Raina imagined, grease the wheels of the government in favor of whatever group he lobbied for. His sons were no better; both were blond and lanky. They flanked their father so that only half their bodies showed behind his bulk, as if they were not two sons but rather one very wide son. With his hands in his pockets, the lobbyist looked down the line and thanked Hattie politely for her hospitality.

Raina knew how to scare off fellas like that. All it took was a little squaring of the shoulders, a slight rotation of the arm to bring out the deltoids and triceps. And she made sure to stare him right in the eyes, to eliminate the allure that a demure girl earned by averting her gaze. Suddenly the epicene balance of her body was tipped violently toward the masculine. Behind this guise of muscle and jutting angles, she was safe.

Indeed, the lobbyist looked her up and down with a quizzical expression. He passed a comment to a son, the right-hand one, and snickered. Raina pegged them; in order, they would choose Deirdre, Marie, and Candy.

And she was almost right. Deirdre and Marie went forward in turn and introduced themselves to the father and the right-hand son, who promptly walked them to a table. But when the left-hand son looked down the line with protracted malice, Raina shivered. His brother (*Are they twins?*) looked up from his table to him, smiling in anticipation of the punchline.

To keep his hands safely in his pockets, he simply jutted his chin toward Raina.

She could feel the girls on either side of her grow tense. Even Hattie showed a crack. A single, blinding bright moment of panic. Raina watched her calculate. Was it better to risk another run-in with the law, or try to persuade the client otherwise? If it had been anyone but the son of a lobbyist, the equation would be much simpler. As it was, Raina stared and her and begged, *Do not let him near me.* And Hattie replied, *I'm sorry.*

"Oh, yes, excellent choice She's one of our favorites. Ask her about Henry James. She's—"

"Raina," she said with her outstretched hand. If they intended to find a sad Nelly, she would make sure they found instead a perfect lady. He took her hand and kissed it, hard.

"Enchanted."

Hattie kept the process moving. Next was Charlie. Raina looked down the line. Behind him stood a Black man in fine clothes who turned to her that same moment.

A mallet slammed into her heart, and her skin grew suddenly cold. Her eyes were stuck on the eyebrows of this young man, the curve of his lips, his fine ears, and his rich, brown eyes. Though she had no idea how he found her, Woodrow stood before her now, watching as she was led away from the line toward the table where three cruel, ugly men sat waiting.

Connie, stepping forward, played her part well. She giggled, took Charlie's hand and said, "Well hello, stranger."

Chapter Two

Deirdre sat next to the father, a smile nearly splitting her face in two. Marie sat next to one son. The two men introduced themselves as Jack and Mike McMartin. Only after Raina deliberately turned to her own date and asked his name aloud did he share that it was Hal.

There were already three bottles of wine on the table. The women rarely drank for safety reasons. Marie and Deirdre were already smiling and looking at the clients. Raina knew she was being rude, staring at the tablecloth as she was, but she was busy sorting through her thoughts. She felt her skin burn icy hot where she knew Woodrow was looking at her. The McMartin men stared at their menus and said nothing.

"So," said Deirdre cheerfully, "where are you all from?"

The men acted as if they hadn't heard her. After a minute, Jack said to his son Mike that he may get a Tom Collins. Mike responded to his father that that sounded good. Meanwhile, Raina's hands grew heavy and torpid in her lap.

"My," said Deirdre, reaching for the wrist of Jack with her sparrow's fingers, "what a beautiful watch you have." But Jack's wrist snapped back as if her fingers' touch had shocked him.

"Whoops," she said, "sorry, I didn't mean to...uh..."

Deirdre looked around the table, begging Marie and Raina for help. Raina did not look up, but Marie, the sweetheart, took it upon herself to knock her empty wine glass off the table. It landed on the shag with a thud, which the whole table could hear over Marie's hushed, "Oh!"

She looked around with the most genuine blush Raina had ever seen a woman of the Pineapple muster. "Oh, dear. Don't worry, I've got it." The men, meanwhile, kept their eyes on their menus.

Here, Raina watched as Marie leaned forward to push her chair back with her legs, giving the whole table a peek at her cleavage. As soon as she was standing, she turned around and bent at the waist to pick up the glass. The men at the table, like all men, were weak. For all their haughty indifference, each of the three looked up to ogle her protruding, girlish ass. Just as soon as their heads were up, Raina said a sharp, "So," forcing the men's heads to turn despite their greatest efforts. It was the best bait-and-switch they had. Some men had to have their weaknesses demonstrated, so as to remind them why they were here.

"So," she repeated, "I don't know about you all, but I'm feeling a little thirsty." It was good business to express your needs to the men around you. It made them feel good to know they were satisfying some sort of lack. It was instinctual, according to Hattie.

Looking her in the face for the first time, Hal asked, "What'd you like?"

She thought, *I'd like a smart, funny, and beautiful boy taller than you by a foot and with a wit and grace finer than your tiny, hairy head could understand.* But instead she said, "A gin and tonic." She broke eye contact with him and gently crossed her arms over her chest, as if his presence made her feel the need to be held. When she glanced back up he was smiling.

Deirdre asked the table a question and the men, robbed of their pretense of disinterest, had to respond. Raina scanned the room without turning her head or moving her eyes too much. She could not tell where he was, but she felt his eyes all over her.

Within a few minutes, the men were laughing at a joke of Marie's. Deirdre finally got a hold of Jack's watch and asked him where he got it.

"That's a funny story, actually," he said, draining the Collins and switching back to the wine.

"Dad, we have heard this story a million times," said Mike.

"Well, *they* haven't." He stared at his son for a second longer than was necessary. This, Raina decided, was the conversational equivalent to bending him over his knee and spanking him. Once the heat of indignity was cooled, Mr. McMartin folded his hands on the table, looked down at his pudgy fingers, and said, "Well, ladies, you know I travel a lot for business." Raina felt she had heard this story before. "I was up in Richmond a few years back and...hey, would any of you happen to know about the radio man?"

"The radio man?" asked Deirdre. "Who is *that*?"

"Oh, well, he was a man who lived just north of Richmond who loved working radios. And when I say he loved radios, I mean he *loved* radios. He had hundreds of them in his house and was a whiz at repairing them. They said his ear was so sharp he could tell what was wrong with someone's transistor from another room. He knew which programs came on the air when, who the news announcers were for every station, the names of the actors and writers of every serial drama and Western since the 20s. Rumor had it that he would play multiple radios at once, all throughout the night."

"Oh!" exclaimed Marie. "How strange!"

"But what about the watches?" asked Deirdre.

"Oh, he was also good with watches. Mechanically minded. Repaired them to support his radio habit."

Raina let her eyes wander. Jack's frame grew blurry while the tables behind him drew into sharper focus. Without moving her pupils, Raina tried to see the dark shape that had just seated itself at a table beside Alexandria. She could not tell if it was him.

"So the radio man lived alone for decades," continued Jack. "Women, I guess, are much more complicated machines than watches." Deirdre smiled, shut her eyes, and crinkled her nose. "One day the landlady left a note telling him that the neighbors wanted him to keep it down. And he turned the music down, and that was that."

Raina could not resist. She broke her gaze with Jack to get a better look at the table behind him. There, Woodrow leaned over his folded arms, speaking to Alexandria, looking right at Raina.

She noticed he had ordered only water for their table. She began to panic. She felt a blush was about to rise in her face, and she had no reasonable excuse for it. The clients would begin to suspect that her mind was elsewhere this evening.

If there was a goddess or patron saint for prostitutes, she smiled on Raina at that moment. As soon as she looked back at the table, Hal landed his hand on her thigh, giving her hot, red neck the perfect pretext. He must have been pleased by her flushed face, because he moved his hand an inch higher while his father rambled on.

"But of course, the music came back on the next night, and the next. This time, the landlady was forced to slip a fifteen dollar fine under his door, to be paid immediately. But," he said, shaking the last drops of wine from the bottle, "the bill wasn't paid that day, or the next day, either."

Marie asked, "Oh my God. And the music?"

"Just kept on playing. Now, I don't mean to scare you ladies," he said as he reached over to steal the last of the wine from Mike's bottle, "but I can't hide the facts of life from you, either." His eyes alternated between the three women. His sons were now looking around the room, wondering, no doubt, whether they had chosen the best women. Jack turned to Raina, and she tore her eyes from Woodrow. "The landlady had to call the cops on the radio man, seeing as his rent was due two weeks ago and his music was still playing. They used a skeleton key on the door and found hundreds of radios playing at once and a hundred more under construction, ones of all shapes and sizes—tiny military ones and huge ones meant for families, tall as grandfather clocks. Rotting food in the fridge, a pile of unopened mail on the floor..." Here he leaned in. "...and the radio man himself was nowhere to be seen."

Raina's gasp came out louder than she meant it too. From Jack's look she could tell the story was not quite over.

"Anyway, no one knew where he went. Some said he had defaulted on his rent and gone to live somewhere cheaper. Or maybe he got mugged or stabbed coming back from the grocery store. Some of his neighbors wondered whether he hadn't evaporated straight into the airwaves. But the bottom line was this: there was no trace of him anywhere. So they turned off the radios, and the apartment was quiet for the first time in, gosh, years. Decades, even." Raina looked over Jack's shoulder. Woodrow was still staring at her. With the subtlety of a double agent she motioned with her eyes toward the restrooms in the corner. Woodrow nodded slowly, his mouth moving all the while with some observation he was sharing with Alexandria.

Raina realized there were still things she had to address before she could break free. First, Hal's hand squeezing her nylon. Second, Jack's fat mouth, which would not stop talking.

"The police realized the radio man had no next-of-kin to give his stuff to. So it fell on them to clear out all the radios and watches that were gathering dust in his apartment. That's actually where I got this little number," he said as he twirled his watch around his wrist, "at a county auction up there. So one day when some workmen were clearing out his radios, they noticed something was weird. They were moving some of those old, massive Philcos—you know, the floor-standing ones that used to be in everyone's living rooms. Anyway, this one Philco was unusually heavy. So, mostly to spare their backs, they unscrewed the top to see if there was anything that could be taken out."

Woodrow excused himself from Alexandria and walked through the doors to the restrooms.

"And when they opened it up, they found the radio man's body inside."

All three women gasped. Raina stood, forcing all five sets of eyes to her. She dismissed the concern of the other girls with a subtle shake of the head. "I think I need some water," she said, rushing toward the restroom.

Jack raised his hand and called after her, "Hey, come on now! I didn't mean to scare you!"

Chapter Three

Here was a dilemma: was Woodrow waiting for her in the women's room or the men's?

She stood before the doors like Theseus at a fork in the labyrinth. She knew she had no more than three minutes before the McMartin men would get suspicious. So she tried the women's room, only to find Pearl sitting on the countertop, swinging her legs in the air. She had been twining a strand of chewing gum from her mouth around her finger and froze when she saw Raina. They stared at each other for a moment. Eventually, Raina began asking whether a Black man had come in a moment ago, but she realized that sounded ridiculous. She smiled at Pearl, wished her a good night, and went into the men's room.

Woodrow was bent over the sink, washing his hands. He smiled at Raina in the mirror as she entered.

"Excuse me, sir," she said. "Looks like one of us is in the wrong restroom."

"That would be you, Madame," replied Woodrow, bowing scandalously low before wetting her hand with a slobbery kiss.

"That's Mademoi*selle* to you." She slapped him full across the face.

Only then did they allow themselves to laugh.

"What are you doing here," she said. "Why didn't you just call me?"

"I never got your number," he said. "And 'Dirty Slut' is not in the phonebook."

She prodded his sides with rigid hands to make him leap up from the sink.

"*Jesus*, woman!" His face dripped, his eyebrows holding the moisture like moss.

"And what's with the getup?" she asked. "You were in rags last time I saw you."

"You were also wearing rags, sweet cheeks," replied Woodrow.

"The point being, you should have given me some warning. Now I have a client tonight, and I must be getting back to him." She had no desire to go back, of course, but she knew coquetry worked equally well for friends as for clients.

"Hold on there, Nancy-boy. Can't you just give him the slip?"

"No. I am assigned to him tonight." She looked at the door, realizing that some wine-bloated McMartin man might barge in any moment. "Listen, here's my card. Let's get lunch tomorrow."

"No no no, listen—" He took Raina by the shoulders. "I have to talk to you *tonight*. There's no ifs, ands, or buts about it. Please, Roy."

She looked him in the eyes. "You know that's not my name."

"Sorry," he said, letting her go. "I'm sorry. But can I see you after your evening with Mr. Cracker? It's important. I swear on a fifty dollar bottle of wine. It's important."

He looked at her so earnestly that she felt it had to be a ploy.

"Please?"

She realized she had never been in the men's room here. She filed this moment under "places I have interacted with Woodrow where I had previously never been." Alphabetically, "Men's Restroom" came before "Prison Cell." He brought novelty, if nothing else.

"Fine," she said. "Here's what to do."

Chapter Four

"Feeling better?"

The McMartin men were in better spirits. That is to say, drunk. Raina brushed away their concerns with a gesture.

Like springing a trap, Hal's hand clasped the meat of her thigh as soon as she sat down. Raina knew the way to make a man feel like the most virile piece of flesh in the world was to cross her legs so that his hand was sandwiched between her thighs. Some in this situation blushed, others did not. Hal, she saw, was of this latter type. Seducing men like him was easy. He would pretend to listen to his brother tell a story about a trip to Madrid while at the same time twitching his pinky finger so that it worked up the nylon inch by inch, until she would slink her hand onto his already-raging erection and just let it lay there. He would look at her like she was the first woman he had ever really seen and, with formal apologies, excuse them both from the table, while the other prostitutes looked at their colleague and wonder why she didn't try to extort another round of drinks from him.

Upstairs, this type of man would try to show her something she had never seen before. If she kissed him standing up he would lift her into his arms like he was carrying her across a threshold, a move that must have done a lot more to charm docile country girls than a seasoned prostitute like Raina. If she gave this man oral sex, he would pull a move just as tender as it was conceited. Namely, he would stop her in the midst of her work to bend down and kiss her on the mouth, as if to say he respected her enough to show her affection despite the rank taste of his own pre-come. If she lay down on a bed, this type of man would attempt to remove everything she wore with just his teeth. Even if he managed not to bite her, there was no man on earth who understood the system of clasps and garters that comprised a woman's undergarments. (Except, of course, for Roy.) More than once Raina had had to help a man who had unwittingly closed a clamp on his own tongue, connecting his mouth to a garter or a sock. Raina knew to avoid such pitfalls. A man like Hal had a hundred tricks like these up his sleeves, all of them sleazy and all of them awful.

Raina and Hal entered her room. It would have been a different story if he were flexible in his fantasies. Raina eyed her bookcase, wondering whether to pull out a volume and read it to him. But her experience showed her that men like Hal liked to take the book from her hands, whatever it was, and proclaim they themselves had read it, or otherwise, that is was not worth reading at all.

So, too, would it be useless for her to just have sex with him. She knew his type would be able to look past, and maybe even enjoy, her genitals. She felt at no real risk with this man, who would probably have the good humor to sleep with her no matter, even if he just wanted something to laugh about later with his brother and father. As long as she got paid she did not mind. This was a job, not a marriage.

But men like this did not just want satisfaction from a prostitute. They needed something deeper, something more sinister, even, than sex. They would not be satisfied until they were assured that they were the best lover in the world. Any night of the year, Raina would choose a pump-and-dump pig over one of these self-obsessed Casanovas. The former, at least, didn't care that Raina never orgasmed with her clients. The Casanova type would not pay her until she had melted in his hands like putty, orgasmed three times, and promised him she had never had a better lover in her life. Not only were these men no better lovers than their counterparts, but they were also annoying as all hell.

They stood in her room. Times like these she wished she had a vagina, since it was harder to fake orgasms with a penis. Hal brushed her hair behind her ear. She turned to him and giggled demurely.

"What is it?" he asked.

"Nothing."

"Come on," he insisted, wrapping his arms around her.

"Nothing. Just that... Well, most people don't bother pushing my hair behind my ear like that."

He smiled at her. "Well, I'm not like most people."

She leaned in and kissed his lips, which were the color of dead skin. She kissed twice, slowly, looking up at him afterward as if she had tasted peppermint in his mouth instead of plaque and wine.

"Excuse me while I slip into something a little more..." She looked at him over her shoulder as she glided to the bathroom. "...well, you know." She locked the door behind her.

The bathroom was still filled with the stench of perfume from when Mr. Deer had destroyed her bottles. In this way, it still felt haunted.

Raina yanked back the shower curtain.

Woodrow jumped, suppressing a cry. He stood pressed into the corner like a centipede when the lights come on. Raina motioned for him to keep quiet. She took the champagne bottle from his hand. With him watching over her shoulder, she placed it on the counter and set to work.

She emptied a few of her pills into the bottom of her drinking cup. With the base of a perfume bottle, she crushed them into powder. She opened a cabinet and pulled down two champagne flutes. In one, she dumped the powder. In both, she poured champagne.

What she didn't predict was how the powder would cause the champagne to bubble over. Woodrow, seeing an imminent spill, snatched up this glass and sipped off the foam, while Raina looked on in silent horror. He realized he was drinking out of the wrong glass, and nearly dropped it before Raina took it from his hand. Woodrow's eyes went big, but Raina rolled hers, to show him that he didn't have to worry—that he would be fine.

Once it was done bubbling over, it was impossible to tell there was anything dissolved in there at all. Raina motioned for Woodrow to return behind the shower curtain as she changed into her negligée. She took the glasses and exited the room, easing into a grin.

She guessed Hal would be in one of three postures. Either perusing the library with his tie-knot casually undone, lying in bed in his shirt-sleeves, or lying in bed fully naked. An apparent disinterest in books landed him on the bed, but she wasn't sure whether it was the coldness of the room or his modesty that kept his clothes on.

"You look stunning," he said.

She thought, *I know*, and handed him the champagne. He downed it in two gulps and leaned forward. But she would not let him touch her. She insisted on a game. She made him ask whether he could touch her toes.

"Can I touch your toes?"

She glared at him.

"Sorry," he said. "*May* I touch your toes?"

She smiled, closing her eyes, and stretched out on the bed.

"May I touch your ankle?"

She thought for a moment. Eventually she nodded. After a few minutes of this, his fingers were on her thigh. By the time he got to the edge of her panties, his fingers had grown sluggish. Presently, they stopped altogether.

"Hal?" she said.

"*Hal?*" she repeated, louder. He was fast asleep, the glass dribbling its last toxic drop onto the bedspread. She whispered, "It's that easy?"

Louder, she said, "Come out, Woodrow."

He opened the door like a child scared of his mother's anger.

"It's safe, come on out."

And out he slunk.

"Jesus. What was that stuff?"

"Sedative," she said, stepping back into the bathroom to grab the bottle. "Will you get rid of the extra champagne?"

He grabbed the bottle and took a long swig. "And why do you have sedatives just lying around?" He offered her the champagne.

She lifted her hand to decline. "They're my medication. They keep me calm." She went back to the bed where she pushed Hal onto his back. She plucked the champagne flute from his hand and walked into the bathroom.

"Jesus. And you're on that stuff all the time?" He pulled from the bottle.

"Ideally, yes." She rinsed out the glass from the tap.

"What happens if you don't take it?"

She replaced the glass in Hal's hand and took the empty champagne bottle from Woodrow, setting it up next to Hal. "What happens? I turn straight, like you. It's awful."

Woodrow picked up a letter opener from her table and brandished it at her. "Now watch out. Just because I'm not wearing enough makeup to patch up drywall, doesn't mean I'm not cute."

"You're not wearing enough makeup, period."

She lifted up the bottle once more and wiped the traces of Woodrow's lips and fingerprints from it. She pressed Hal's lips around the edge. Just in case anyone checked.

"Now," she said, "comes the hard part."

"*You* finish off a bottle of champagne in two minutes and tell me that wasn't the hard part."

"When he wakes up, he may excuse a lot in the name of drunkenness. But he will not excuse a tease of a prostitute."

"So what does a saucy 'stute like you do in these situations?"

After a moment of silence, both their eyes fell to Hal's crotch where the outline of an erection still stood.

"Oh, no," said Woodrow.

"You don't have to look."

"I will leave."

"Don't be such a girly-man."

"Coming from the boy wearing panties."

"At least I'm not afraid to suck a dick."

"This is the *good* kind of fear. This is the kind of fear that saves lives."

As they spoke, Raina had pulled Hal's member out from the fly of his trousers. She stared at it, immobile.

"What?" asked Woodrow, who, despite his protestations, stared at the dong alongside Raina. "Never seen a pecker before?"

"Yes," she said. "I mean, no. I'm just...wondering whether I need to...make it go all the way, or if I just need to...to get it..." She turned to him and squinted. "...wet."

Woodrow threw up his hands. "I am not responsible for whatever hoodwinking, fella-drugging necrophilia shit you are pulling here. I just wanted to *talk* to you."

Raina spat in her hand and brought it to Hal. "Okay then. Start talking."

Woodrow kept eye contact with her as she got started. "It's kinda hard to talk to you while that slick dick keeps clicking away under your palm."

"What, this?" asked Raina. "This is just business."

Woodrow laughed. "God have mercy. Well," he said, plopping down in the armchair in front of the library, "as you can see, I am out of jail."

"Good," said Raina.

"Yes, I'm relieved. But the reason I came here tonight, the reason I'm dressed up so well, is, well..."

"Wait," said Raina, "before you go on, can I ask you one quick question?"

"If you stop jerking off that dead fella, sure."

"First off, he's not dead. Second, I will not. Third, how did you know I was here?"

"Well, truth is I didn't. This is not the first Levee bordello I've visited."

"I thought the Columbia went out of business?"

"It's the Colombia now. With an A. They serve margaritas."

"And how do we compare?"

"Well, seeing as I paid full price for Alexandria without so much as touching her, and now I'm in here with you while you jerk off another unconscious guy, I can honestly say it's not the worst experience I've had."

"Perfect. That's our motto. 'Not as bad as you've had.'"

"Right. Anyway, I'm glad I found you tonight, because tomorrow, I gotta leave Chicago."

Raina's hand slowed. "What? Why?"

"Because I was at a diner the other day and a cop sat on one side of me and another cop sat on the other."

"What?" asked Raina, her hand speeding up suddenly. "What does that mean? And how did you get into a diner?"

"Hey," he said, "more and more diners are serving Blacks now. And it means that they are watching me. It means they don't believe I'm not Grover. And that means that I am a liability to everyone I know within this city. It means the police are gonna track my friends. It means they will be watching me with eagle eyes until I slip up and they can arrest me for something minor and make me serve a sentence for the rest of my life just because they think I'm someone I'm not, and for the love of *God*, Raina, are you trying to start a *fire*?"

Raina's hand stopped. Hal's penis was looking rather red. "So you're leaving?"

"Yes," he said, looking down. "I'm leaving."

She opened her nightstand drawer and scooped out some Vaseline. She crawled on the bed and lubricated Hal. "Where to?"

"Don't know."

"How long?"

"Forever."

"So I'm never going to see you again?"

Woodrow leaned forward on his elbows. "Well, that's what I'm here to talk to you about." Raina stared back. "I need to lay low for a while. A month, at least. Before I can get started somewhere else. I need to be in a place with no cops and no underworld and no anything. I need to disappear."

Raina could smell a proposition from a mile away. "Yes…"

"I have a car, I have enough money. I have maps and clothes and a hundred possible destinations."

"Yes…"

"But I just…" He gestured. "…I don't want to do it…" He looked at his fingers which were frozen, outstretched. "…alone." He looked up at her. "You know?"

She nodded her head. Her arm was beginning to feel sore. "I do know. So you are asking me to come with you."

"Well," he said, suddenly leaning back. "I'm not pro*posing* or anything. You're not gonna get a ring out of it. I was just thinking, if you wanted to take a break from your work here, or from Chicago as a whole, maybe you would want to come with me."

Raina looked at the wall, thinking.

"Oh," he said, "I forgot the most important part. You said, didn't you, you wanted to see your mother again?"

"I never said that." Raina suddenly felt the size of the divide between them, as if a chasm could only be properly measured when one person tried to reach across it. Her mind drifted to the fondue that was waiting for her downstairs. *Damn,* she thought. *I love fondue.* Part of her wanted Woodrow out of this room and out of her life, so she could enjoy her solitude and luxury, a life of quiet study and constant attention. She felt very impatient. She wanted Woodrow out so she could get on with her real life. And besides, her hand was cramping.

"Oh." Woodrow picked up a book from the side table. "Does that mean you don't want to see her?"

"Not necessarily. I guess I just haven't thought about it in a while."

"Well," he said, opening the book, realizing it was upside-down, and flipping it over. "You can think about it. I don't want to pressure you."

Her hand spasmed. She lifted it and flexed it, cursing aloud. Woodrow jumped up as if the curse had been for him. "Here, I got you." Raina watched with amazement. Without another word Woodrow grasped Hal's penis and began jerking it with an artful, milking movement. She looked him in the eye and said, "Is that what they teach you down in the South?"

Grinning, he tapped her on the cheek. She matched his playful slap with a real one.

"Hey! No fair! I'm not gonna hit a girl."

"I'm not a girl," she said.

"Oh, I forgot." And he punched Raina in the gut. She toppled over Hal's legs, laughing. Woodrow looked at her and laughed too.

"Here," she said, setting her hand over Woodrow's. "You don't have to be so careful about it. You're not gonna break it or anything."

"Hey," he protested, "I take pride in what I do." In a few pumps, they had set a rhythm. Raina on the base of the shaft and Woodrow working the head with his palm. A tiny moan escaped Hal's lips. They paused. They looked at each other. Then they pumped faster than they ever had before, daring each other to break eye contact.

"Don't you wanna make it so that he comes somewhere else?"

"No," replied Raina, "that doesn't matter."

"But what if his family sees the dried-up jism on his shirt? They'll mock him mercilessly."

"Let them. No, he will just close up his coat like this, see?"

"Okay. You're the professional."

Hal's breath came in shorter gasps. His member was throbbing. Woodrow and Raina looked down and instinctively pointed it so he would finish on himself. In three bursts that made his pelvis rise, Hal came on not only his shirt, but the pillow behind his head, the headboard, and his own face. Neither expected it to shoot so far. They dissolved into laughter, Raina rolling around on the bed and Woodrow rolling around on the floor.

After a few minutes, Woodrow rose and asked for a towel. Raina handed him a rag. They decided to wipe off Hal's face, at least. That would be too great an indignity. Raina watched Woodrow spot-cleaning this mean, rich boy's face, and she decided. *Yes.* She would go with him. She would lead him wherever he needed to go.

At that moment, as if he could hear her thoughts, he looked at her and tossed the come rag at her face.

Chapter Five

Objects stared at for too long turn gray. Such was the fate of the door of the Pineapple, whose corners and doorknob had been sacrificed to the intensity of Woodrow's gaze. If you had asked him offhand what he was waiting for, he would only have been able to tell you, "For the door to open." Not "for Roy" or "to leave Chicago." All of reality existed in relation to the opening of that door. That was the effect of fixation.

It had rained the night before. One of his shoes had a hole in it, and moisture seeped into his sock. He watched as a crumpled bit of newspaper swirled in the eddy of a puddle, while around it, the surface was pierced by drips from the rooftop above. He smoked a cigarette and looked back at the door, pleased to see its corners and doorknob restored. *A watched pot never boils*, he thought.

His mind was dampened and cooled by the climate. Part of him was ashamed at having to rely on Roy, or anyone, for company, or anything. Another part of him was eager to no longer have to view every person passing on the street as a potential threat, a plain-clothes crocodile. He dreamed of a corner of America too young or too old to have teeth. Another part of him stared at the blank of tomorrow with exhaustion and fear. There was no way to know what was coming. Where he was sure, he felt relief. Where he was unsure, he felt terror. But these disparate parts focused their energies toward one point: waiting for the door to open.

He looked down the alley to the street, where his car was parked. He dropped his cigarette into the puddle and watched it extinguish. He stared at the door for a moment. Immediately he lit another.

It is hard to believe when something so anticipated actually happens. So when the door swung open he could not, at first, believe it. But when he saw Raina in a skirt and a traveling blazer, the disbelief morphed into anger.

* ~ * ~ *

"Well," Woodrow said, tossing his cigarette to the ground, "I forgot it was Halloween."

"Sorry about this," she said, looking him up and down, "but the 'ugly oaf' costume was already taken."

"You got boy clothes in that bag?"

"Maybe. Why?" She took a step toward the car.

"Because if people see a white woman on the road with a Black man, they will ask questions."

Raina asked, "Like what?"

"Like, 'chloroform or laudanum'?"

"Oh, please," she said, taking another few steps to the car, "you are too cute to have kidnapped me. If you wanted to steal me away, you could have just asked. Besides," she smiled, "they'll just think you're my chauffeur."

He raced to stop in front of her. "Change."

She set her heels together. "Make me."

Slowly, Woodrow reached around her head—slipping his fingers between her neck and her hair—to the clasp of her pearl necklace. There, his fingers fumbled. The clasp held. After a moment, he let his hands fall to his sides. To their left, they heard a drop of water splash into a puddle.

"Okay, well, imagine I had figured out that clasp and had handed you your necklace all dramatic-like."

Raina laughed throatily and breezed past him.

"Seriously!" he called out as she tossed her bulging bags into the back. "It's less suspicious seeing a Black man with a white man. Please, Raina. We have to be safe about this."

She looked at him. The way his arms were stretched out straight down his sides with his head tilted a little in one direction made him look impetuous. As with a child, she knew she could not reason with him. *Besides*, she thought with bitterness, *he is probably right*.

"Fine. I will go change into boy clothes."

* ~ * ~ *

Woodrow, surprised by her change of heart, managed to call out to her, "You can keep the pearls!" The door closed behind her.

"I like the pearls."

He rocked in her wake like a leaf. To his left a droplet splashed on concrete.

Woodrow considered himself a thoughtful person. He thought of his life as a drill, one that had at various points bored through some impressive thing: dense reading material, rocky strata of poverty and toil, and muddy deposits of doubt. No matter the substance it drilled though, the course of his life had been straight. So straight, in fact, that if one placed one's eye correctly, one would be able to spot the pinprick of sunlight at the top. With a pine-board home as a starting point. *Home*, he thought. *What an ugly word.* He stepped in the edge of the puddle and watched the ripples spread outward. *Home is something unstable that is dangerous to stand on. Home is a pit of quicksand.* He knew he had to keep moving. He had to address new challenges every day just to stay alive. He did not have the luxury of having a formal education or a supportive family. Every moment alive was a concerted effort on Woodrow's part, a never-ending resistance to forces beyond his control. Every breath was an effort against history.

He turned to face the building and looked up. He wondered which window was Raina's, but then he remembered that she did not have a window in her room.

His face upturned, his eyes wide open, he was the perfect target for the fat drop of water plunging down toward him from the rooftop.

Chapter Six

Raina eased the door shut behind her and paused. There were no sounds in the Pineapple at this hour. If she had not become so used to the nightly bustle, she could have believed that this building was a carefully disguised tomb. She climbed the stairs, walking only on the near edge of each step so as to avoid any creaking boards.

Once on the landing, she made sure all the other girls' doors were closed. The names *Alexandria, Connie,* and *Dot* glimmered on the nameplates with the gray light of morning. Dust hung in the air and settled onto the thick carpet. She clicked her fingernails against each other just to make sure she could still hear.

She opened the door to her room and almost closed it immediately with an apology. It took a second for her to realize she was at the correct room after all, and it was the forms she saw within that did not belong. She was not disturbed by the body of Hal McMartin, who still snored on her bed, with tiny dried patches of semen resting on his chest, his penis nestled safely in his trousers. What disturbed her was the little girl, Pearl, who stood on the other side of the bed and turned to her with her hands behind her back. She eyed Raina with a look neither guilty nor apologetic, but blank—blank as a word in an unknown language.

Raina whispered, "Hello."

Pearl blinked.

Raina was relieved to see that the letter she wrote to Hattie still lay on her side table. So too were the books still neatly arranged on the shelf. She turned to verify that the few bottles of perfume and cream she decided not to take were still upright and accounted for in the bathroom. Not a hair was mussed on Hal's head, and the champagne bottle still rested in his hand. Everything was in its place. What, then, had Pearl disturbed?

She closed the door behind her. "What're you doing in here, Pearl?"

Pearl started walking as if her feet were bound together. As she passed the edge of the bed Raina saw why. Pearl wore an old pair of Raina's heels, which trailed behind her feet like backwards clown shoes.

Raina knew very little about kids. Still, she figured they did not like to be laughed at. She had also heard somewhere that they responded better to adults when the adult spoke to them on their level. So, shoving her skirt in between her thighs, Raina got on one knee before Pearl.

"You like those?" she asked.

Pearl nodded.

"Then they're yours. Just don't tell anyone where you got them, okay?"

Pearl bit her lower lip and nodded. Raina stood up and Pearl began to clomp out of the room. Raina turned to her and shushed her gently. Pearl bent down and removed the shoes, shuffling away in her bare feet.

Raina thought, *What I have just done was kind, but it was not enough.*

Immediately she called for Pearl to wait and, opening her nearly empty jewelry box, pulled out a string of cheap glass beads of a light blue color. The string was long, and when she laid it around Pearl's neck, it brushed the floor. Raina smiled at her and said she looked great. Pearl beamed back and darted out of the room, her footsteps so light they barely made a sound. Raina smiled down the hall at her and thought, *That is better.* She slipped into boy clothes. *But still*, thought Roy. *Probably not enough.*

Chapter Seven

Roy returned to Woodrow with his hair curled up and tucked under a hat, his earrings out, and his legs wrapped each in their separate tube of fabric. Woodrow whistled through the open window and called him, "buddy." Silently Roy sat in the passenger's seat of the too-nice black Ford and leaned over, clasping a string of pearls around Woodrow's neck. They did not sit evenly on his collar. Roy tugged them back so they would stay presentable and even.

"Am I pretty yet?" asked Woodrow.

"There aren't enough pearls in the world."

And then they headed west.

For the first few miles, they did not speak. Roy wondered whether Woodrow had packed any food. He had forgotten to eat, and now his stomach growled and churned. But they did not speak, each enjoying the sudden sense of freedom, the limitless possibilities that only presented themselves in the early morning after rainfall.

Roy picked up a map from the glove compartment and opened it up. He looked at the squiggles on the page and the words printed so small they were more like suggestions than actual names. He asked, "How far is it?"

Woodrow answered, "Seven hundred and thirty miles."

"Oh boy. How long will that take?"

"Five days."

"And how are we getting there?"

"Lincoln Highway."

Roy did not know much about the Lincoln Highway, but he felt assured by Woodrow's confident voice so folded up the map and looked out the window. Within a half hour, they were out of the city.

As the buildings grew more stunted and the grass that sprouted between the cracks of the sidewalk sprung into bushes, small trees, and even whole plots of forest, it dawned on Roy that he had no other job prospects. He had no skills; he had no friends outside Chicago, and he had very little money saved up. A newspaper clipping drifted into his mind: something about an heiress being kidnapped by a thief and slain outside New York. Roy's hand involuntarily reached for his pearls, only to discover that they were already on Woodrow's neck.

Looking at him, Roy's doubts multiplied. He had agreed to accompany Woodrow on the shallowest of pretexts. He should have known better. After all, half of his clients said they only wanted company for the evening. Still, none of his clients were funny. As if a sense of humor meant you were a good person. With his eyes locked on the road and the band of pearls around his neck, Woodrow looked like the oldest and cruelest member of some royal court who, Roy assumed, took skinny white boys like him out of the state to murder them and eat their eyes. *Oh God*, thought Roy. *He must want to eat my eyes.*

He decided to inquire.

"Woodrow?"

"Hm?"

"How did you afford this car?"

"It fell off a truck."

"A truck carrying cars?"

"Yep."

"It must have been a big truck."

"Huge."

Roy went for the more blunt approach.

"Woodrow, has someone died in this car?"

"Not yet, no."

"Did you pay for this car?"

Woodrow pouted his lips. "Not yet, no."

"Woodrow?"

"Yes?"

"Why did you steal this car?"

Woodrow's laughter was infectious. After a minute, Roy was laughing too.

Woodrow said finally, "I was only following the orders of the white man who gave it to me."

"Which were?"

"'Please, take my car...'"

Roy waited. Woodrow waited, too, until the road straightened out. Then he turned to him and said, "'...to the parking lot, young Negro, and there's a shiny new nickel in it for you.'"

Bent over laughing, Roy was able to appreciate the fine cross-stitching in the gray leather dashboard.

"I didn't know you were a valet."

"Neither did I! I was walking down the street when this old white man asked me to park his car. He must have never seen a Black man dressed so snazzy."

They turned onto the highway, the sun shining behind them. Roy worried briefly that they would have nothing else to talk about for the other seven hundred and twenty-seven miles. But he was surprised, after sitting quietly for a few minutes, how pleasant the silence was. He felt he had nothing to prove.

Chapter Eight

Just to be safe, Woodrow insisted they sit at different tables. So Roy stationed himself at a booth near the back while Woodrow sat at the counter. The diner was buzzing with a swarm of travelers and truck drivers. So no one noticed when the young Black man nearly choked on his mashed potatoes when he saw, in the mirror behind the counter, the image of the white boy with long hair, whose front teeth had each been capped with a kernel of corn. Nor did anyone notice when the Black man, a few minutes later, made eye contact with the reflection of his counterpart, only to smile and release a rivulet of chocolate milk from his lips, which dribbled down his chin and back into the glass. The diner hummed and clinked. No one noticed anything. The young Black man and the young white man paid separately and left three minutes apart. Just another set of strangers.

Not that they were the oddest pairing on the road. The dust, which had returned to ravage the West after a years-long sabbatical, forced trucks full of farmers up north. Woodrow and Roy watched as families of ten piled out of a single rusty truck, or families with broken-down cars waited by the side of the road for a miracle. These people would eye Woodrow and Roy's ride with envy. Roy preferred not to look back.

In the car on this first day, basking in the admiration of a thousand homespun car enthusiasts, Roy asked Woodrow, "Have you ever felt more proud in your entire life?"

"Only when I walk around naked."

For which Roy slapped him on the arm.

That afternoon Woodrow asked Roy what he wanted to do in terms of sleeping arrangements.

"You know my old job," said Roy. "I'll do anything for the right price."

The sun was setting into their eyes. Woodrow's face, which was already cracked with squinting, cracked further with a laugh.

"I mean, would you be willing to sleep in the car, or do you want a motel?"

"I don't mind either way."

"Then the cheapest option it is."

Here Woodrow performed a tricky maneuver, zipping past a huge truck whose bed was laden with furniture and luggage and whose cabin carried a man, a woman, and a baby. Both the man and the woman gave Woodrow the finger, and Roy would have sworn the baby did too.

That evening, in the car, Woodrow unwrapped the scraps he had nabbed from the diner and they nibbled on bits of bacon and half a greasy biscuit. Still, they agreed it was better than prison food.

When night fell they pulled off the side of the road to sleep.

They reclined as far as the seats allowed and stared up at the roof of the car. Roy passed his fingers over the material. His guess was correct: velvet.

Ten minutes later, he asked Woodrow a question. "What is your favorite book?"

Woodrow thought for a moment. "The Bible."

Roy nodded. "Good choice."

"Nah, I'm just fucking with you. It's *Bleak House*."

Roy laughed. "Mine's *Madame Bovary*."

Woodrow looked at him. "God, now I wish I hadn't brought so much arsenic."

A few minutes later, Roy asked, "Can I ask you a more serious question?"

Woodrow shrugged.

"Why do you hide your accent?"

For a moment he worried he had prodded a beast. But Woodrow eventually answered, though there was an edge to his voice. "I guess I figured no one would take me seriously if I sounded like a hick. It's the same reason I try to read so much. If I ever want to be anything serious, no one can know I was a farmer."

A few minutes later Woodrow asked him, "What is the worst experience you ever had with a client?"

"Well," said Roy, after a moment, "I can't give you any names. But I *can* tell you that some of the worst clients happen to be the richest and most powerful men in America."

"Oh my God," said Woodrow, flipping onto his side to face

Roy. "You gotta tell me who."

"My lips are sealed."

"Aw, come on, man!"

"Nuh-uh." Roy mimed zipping his lips shut.

"Well," said Woodrow, flopping back into his seat, "you gotta at least tell me what they wanted you to do."

Roy stared out the window. He had not seen stars like this in years. His stomach, unused to the coarse food, grumbled once. He moved his crossed hands higher up his abdomen to mask the sound.

"Well...there are of course some things they don't ever do," said Roy, enunciating each word. "And while I can't give you any specifics, I will tell you that the things that they *do* do are pretty disgusting."

"What? Please just give me a hint. Just a hint for your old friend, Woodrow."

"I just did."

"What?"

"Give you a hint."

"What? When?"

"Just now!"

Woodrow's eyebrows stood on separate planes on his forehead.

Roy spoke slowly, looking straight up. "Repeat what I just said."

"Okay, all right, I see, we're playing a game here. Hmm.

224

'Things they won't do...'"

"'Don't do,' I said."

"Okay, fine, ya dirty sphinx. 'Things they don't do' and...the things they...do?"

"What did I say *exactly*?"

"The things they do do?"

"Bingo."

"What?"

After a moment, Roy heard Woodrow gasp, then burst out laughing. "You have got to be *kidding* me!"

Roy smiled. After a minute, he shushed Woodrow, saying, "Come on, you and I have to scat early tomorrow."

Roy closed his eyes to Woodrow's howls of laughter. And that was how the first day ended.

Chapter Nine

The car was no longer black, but brown. Forecasts hailed the other day's rain as the last of autumn. This was the final nail in the coffin for farmers who had tried to hang on to their families' homestead. They abandoned homes in droves. Luckily this dusty eastward exodus did not interfere with the schedule of Roy and Woodrow. For hours at a time, theirs was the only car on the road headed west.

The second night, they slept in the car again. Woodrow insisted he drive. Even though Roy promised he was a quick learner, his absolute lack of experience convinced Woodrow to never let him behind the wheel. "One type of stick," he said, gesturing to the gearshift, "is *not* like another."

Woodrow had not changed out of his nice shirt, and Roy, following his lead, had also not changed. By the time they got back in the car after lunch, they both were attracting flies. They decided then and there that they deserved a real bed tonight, a closed door, and a hot shower.

They chose a budget hotel and had to ignore the cleaning woman who gawked at their car as if it was made of gold. They got the cheapest room available, one with a single queen bed, and signed under the names "J. Alfred Prufrock" and "Mr. Dalloway," and retired to their chamber.

Dingy was not a sufficient word. But despite the cockroaches that darted under the sink when they turned the light on, the threadbare sheets, and the water-stained ceiling, Roy dove into the bed as if it was the waters of the Mediterranean. He breathed in the layered stench and loved it. He had never felt happier being horizontal. By the time he looked up, Woodrow's naked butt was disappearing into the bathroom, only to be followed by the sound of the water spraying on high and the sound of his voice singing, "America the Beautiful."

Eventually the water shut off and Woodrow emerged, still steaming. Roy balanced his head on his hands and watched him approach the bed and topple, torpid, next to him.

Roy's head was level with where Woodrow's towel clung to the top of his butt. The glare from the streetlamp outside cast a buttery reflection on the curves of his skin, at one end filling in the dimples of his lower back like honey in a black walnut spoon. The light then traveled up the twin ridges of the muscles that flanked the spine until it reached the dappled terrain of his upper back, patches of shadow like a Rorschach test. The head cast a shadow over the neck, but Roy did not mourn this, as the loss of the neck gave him even more time to admire the whorl of the ear, the beautiful, dense hair, and the cheekbone peeking out over the edge. Suddenly, Woodrow dragged his arms around until they rested, folded, under his head as if he was expecting a massage. This movement came with a huge breath. Woodrow's abdomen swelled and sunk as Roy thought only sea creatures could do.

Roy knew he had to look away. He imagined this body lying with the women of however many brothels he had visited before the Pineapple. It made Roy feel sick. He got off the bed and entered the bathroom, not bothering to wipe away the condensation on the mirror. He would burn off the thoughts that clung to him like leeches. And the shower did improve his mood—at least, until the hot water ran out, forcing him to leap away with a gasp. He wound his hair and squeezed out the water and realized there were no more towels.

"Woodrow?" he called.

"Hmph?" His face was still buried in the sheets.

"I need your towel."

"You're not the first girl who's told me that."

"Woodrow, please. I am wet."

"Yeah, they usually say that, too." Roy could hear him approaching. Then a ghost poked through the crack in the door, held up by a thin, black arm. Roy pulled the towel from Woodrow's hand.

"Thanks," he said, wondering what he would see if he rushed out of the room right now. He decided to do the right thing instead and dry himself off and give Woodrow a moment to dress.

Woodrow was in his white drawers—a white so white it looked like a single, giant tooth around his hips. He was rooting around in his wallet. Roy grabbed underwear from his bag and returned to the bathroom. When he came back out, Woodrow had his money in stacks in front of him.

"I'm worth more than that," said Roy in a smoky voice.

"I couldn't buy you if I wanted to."

"Oh?"

"I don't have small enough change." He swept the dollars into a stack and stuck them back into his wallet. "How much did you bring?"

"Eighty dollars." After a moment, Roy added, "Let me pay for half the room."

"That would be great, thanks." Woodrow lay on his back in the middle of the bed while Roy sat on the edge.

"Also," continued Woodrow, "could you start chipping in on gas?"

Roy rubbed his hair with the towel. "Of course I can."

"Thanks." He turned over on his side without getting under the covers, freeing up Roy's place. After Roy had rinsed the taste of the day out of his mouth, he switched off the light and got under the covers, his back facing Woodrow's through the white sheet.

Roy waited until the shape and weight of the room began to press through the darkness. Gradually, the door to the bathroom stood out in his peripheral vision, and Roy grew increasingly aware of the weight and heat of Woodrow's body next to him. *Would it really be so bad*, he wondered, *if he woke up with my arm around him? I could always chalk it up to the involuntary movements of sleep.* But this desire was eclipsed by the even softer desire for rest. He knew if he touched Woodrow, the excitement would keep him up all night.

So he focused on the darkness. In another minute, the white sun in the prairie painting on the wall revealed itself. *How ugly,* he thought. Then he could begin to make out the hands on the clock on the nightstand. The edges of the tables and bureau traced themselves out of the gloom. The dull glow of the doorknob hung in midair like the moon.

Roy sighed and let his mind flow down the path he used whenever he felt lonely. He closed his eyes and it was summer, cicadas screaming and the mud around the barn baking to stone, the smell of grass and manure and pollen. Roy hid in the barn so he could wear a dress while milking the cows. He hummed. He did not hear footsteps approach. He did not turn around until Adrian was already in the doorway, overalls strapped over bare shoulders, sweat gathering in the crease of his chest and his back, arms bulging with the weight of two buckets of stones. He stopped in his tracks and stared. Then dropped the pails, furious but silent, grabbing Roy and tearing off his dress in a motion so savage it burst the seams. Roy stood there dreamy and naked. Until Adrian pushed him onto the hay and kicked off his boots and unbuttoned his overalls and began.

Roy could switch between any of a hundred such stories. Adrian discovering Roy's jewelry cache. Adrian discovering Roy with Adrian's old shorts. Adrian discovering Roy watching him bathe. They all began the same, and they all ended the same. The only differences were details.

Roy opened his eyes, suddenly back in autumn in a dusty motel room, conscious of Woodrow beside him.

And in the door to the bathroom stood the dark shape of a man.

Roy stared at the heart of the dark form. He tried to think back to this morning. *Yes*, he thought, *I definitely took my pill.* He closed his eyes, waiting for his heart to slow down. But when he opened them, the form was still there. Darker than before and thicker. Roy consciously kept his body still. The muscles that begged him to curl up in a ball under the sheets and scream and scream and scream were told, *No. You will die if you move.* All the while, his eyes were trained on the form, not daring to let it out of his sight.

He could read the clock in his peripheries. Ten minutes had passed.

He felt a rustling next to him, and his heart nearly stopped. Blood flowed back into his face when he realized it was only Woodrow, turning in his sleep.

The edges of the black form were beginning to set.

After another twenty minutes, Roy felt Woodrow's foot stretch until it touched his own through the blanket. At this point of contact, the anxiety was cracked and melted. It began to whirl and flowed away as if down a drain. After a moment he was empty—clean. He could move. He closed his eyes. And when he opened them, the doorway was empty. He let out a breath and closed his eyes again, for good.

Chapter Ten

It was not that neither of them wanted to speak. Actually, Roy had a hundred things to say. Every dog he saw walking along the road brought to mind some comment he wished he could share with the man in the driver's seat. But he was determined not to cave in. Something had spoiled overnight. Now neither man was sure they were doing the right thing. Both were haunted by specters: Woodrow's was a man in a suit with a badge or some important papers, while Roy's phantom hung suspended just beyond the material and harbored some darker purpose. They had no way to address their demons, so they hardened their hearts against each other instead. They were anxious and unsure and aimless. And the motel bed had cramped their necks.

In his line of work, Roy had had to present a number of different personalities—like a chameleon, but with a shorter tongue. Some nights he had to play the desperate librarian, others the bodacious vixen. Today he felt like the situation demanded his favorite persona: that of the frosty matron. He was reassured, however, by the fact that Woodrow turned to look at him more than once that morning. Though they were both clean and fresh, there was something in his eyes, some tiredness, as if one end of his nerves had been nailed down back in Chicago and every mile of road hence drew them out tighter and tighter. His foot no longer bounced, his hands no longer drummed the dashboard. His back was as stiff and still as an icicle. He was so rigid that Roy wondered how long it would take him to notice if Woodrow were to die at the wheel.

What's worse, when they stopped to eat, there was a fly in his pie. It must have been baked into the filling since its body was already trapped in the gluey, amber syrup stuck to a hunk of apple. Roy quietly laid down his utensil, put a dollar on the counter, and went to wait in the car.

He watched Woodrow through the windshield. He was still eating a cheeseburger with fries, his elbows resting on the table, gazing down at a copy of *The Island of Doctor Moreau*. Roy watched as he placed his finger on a word and looked at the counter. He twisted his head left and right—presumably to find Roy. Roy did nothing to make himself seen. He figured that if Woodrow was going to find him, he would find him regardless. The only effort he made to be spotted was to remain solid and stare at Woodrow's panicked face—the lips pursed a little, the muscles in the neck standing out, and the shoulders hunched a little beneath the white linen shirt. Finally, Woodrow headed to the back where the restroom was. He knocked on the door and must have discovered someone in there, since his countenance relaxed, and he walked to the counter where Roy had been sitting. Roy watched as Woodrow picked up the abandoned fork and took a sly bite from the side of the pie, carefully returning the utensil to its previous position so there would be no evidence. He took his own seat, smiling through the pie, thinking he had committed the perfect crime.

Roy covered both his eyes with his hands and leaned his forehead on the dashboard and laughed so hard he didn't make a sound.

When he looked back at the diner, two policemen were entering. Roy waited for Woodrow to react. But he didn't. He sat stock-still. Why worry? Woodrow seemed as calm as could be. The two overweight white men at the counter may as well have been firemen or priests. Woodrow just kept his nose in his book and read.

It was another minute until Roy realized that Woodrow had not turned a page in a while. Focusing on his face, he realized his eyes weren't moving either. He was frozen, Roy realized, with fear. Roy felt a plunging sensation in his chest, and his first impulse was to run in there and scoop up Woodrow in his arms and carry him back to the car. But the feeling passed. It seemed the ice between them had killed this warmer instinct, or at least cooled it. Instead, Roy just clutched at his collar buttons and wondered which specific word Woodrow's eyes had been stuck reading for the last four minutes.

Woodrow, for one reason or another, looked up at him right at that moment, catching his eye and expressing his confusion by bringing his two slabs of eyebrows together. He stood slowly and fixed his lapels. His first step showed the same doubt as that of a professional tightrope-walker whose hesitation at confronting death could only be noticed by someone sitting safely in the sidelines. Roy noticed. He noticed, too, how Woodrow contrived to bring up his hat at the exact moment when one of the officers turned to look at him, thereby evading the largest degree of scrutiny. Roy also noticed that the cheeseburger sat unfinished on his plate, and his copy of *Moreau* lay abandoned on the table.

Woodrow got into the car and eased them out of the parking lot without another pause. There was a fleck of ketchup on his pinky-knuckle but Roy did not want to bother him by pointing it out.

"I thought you were in the restroom." Woodrow's sober tone wiped Roy's smile off his face.

"No, I decided to just wait in the car."

"We're gonna have to start sitting together soon. We can't risk getting separated."

"All right," said Roy. "That's fine by me."

Once they were fifty miles away from the restaurant, Roy asked, "How far are we from Furnas, you think?"

Woodrow shrugged one shoulder. "Day. Maybe two."

Roy looked out the window. This tension was not entirely negative. There was something marvelous about the shape it made, its texture. Yes, the doubts presented themselves like contestants at a spelling bee: *Does Woodrow regret taking me here? Is he in more trouble than he's letting on? Did I do something to make him hate me? Is there anything I can do to get him to like me again? Is he maybe just depressed by the scenery? Could he be in physical pain from some disease he never told me about? Tuberculosis or polio? Has he figured out that I see things? Does he feel ashamed for that thing we did to Hal? Should we turn around, perhaps? Should we just part ways? Can I still get my job back? Why are we fleeing, anyway? Is he really in as bad of trouble with the police as he says? Is he steeling himself to tell me something? Could he be in love with me? Could he be so attracted to me that he is having a crisis, wondering why he suddenly feels attraction to someone other than a woman? Does he hate me? Did I do something wrong?*

It did not help, either, that the dark shape of a man had begun to creep into his line of vision, standing along the horizon on the outskirts of the fields.

But each fear, having nothing to sink its claws into, slipped off the smooth, blue sides of such an enormous silence as theirs. So long as they were in the same car headed in the same direction, Roy felt they were together, working toward the same purpose. There was no choice in the matter. At least, not until the car stopped.

So Roy did not dare disturb it. Woodrow eventually noticed the fleck of ketchup on his knuckle and licked it off. Roy stared out the window and let the flat, stunted land summon memories from his childhood. *This road will lead to somewhere eventually, no matter what happens. The only thing we know for sure is that*

Woodrow just ate a bug. So he let his head fall back on the cushion, folded his hands in his lap, and tried to ignore the pure black scarecrow that stood fixed in the distance.

Chapter Eleven

The next night was passed in the car. Roy woke up before Woodrow and spent five minutes staring at him sleeping before looking out the window. He took out his medication, the new formula in the big bottle. It had enough pills to last him a year. Today he took twice the dosage, just to be sure.

The sun rising behind the car gave every shoot of corn a long, black shadow, which lay in rows like prison bars. The stalks, whose green barely shone through the coating of dust, did not seem to know it was time to wake up, shed their dusty blankets, and rejoin the world of the living.

"Have they always been like that?"

Woodrow was staring at the fields over Roy's shoulder.

"No," said Roy, "I don't think so. But when I was growing up, things were always like this. I think they got a lot better while I was gone. The dust came back just this year."

"It's sad," said Woodrow.

"Isn't it?"

Roy realized this was one of the first serious conversations they had ever had. He was impressed by its gravity and wondered whether he had done his part correctly. Woodrow got out to pee in the field. Roy, ever-conscientious, waited for Woodrow to return before getting out to relieve himself.

They were less than twenty miles outside Furnas now. Every mile passed meant even dustier corn. Every mile, the fields became more barren. Approaching the county as the sun rose behind them, the land had the illusion of becoming more intense, more substantial in the starker light.

Roy whipped his head around, following a certain wooden post that shrunk into the background.

"What is it?" asked Woodrow.

"Nothing," said Roy.

After another minute he added, "I think we just passed the spot where I hitched a ride to the train station. For Chicago."

Woodrow looked in the rearview mirror. "That's crazy."

Roy's hands spread on his legs. Something had changed. The ground seemed tilted, or the car was too hot, or his hair too sweaty on the back of his neck. He suddenly felt like screaming. He felt he needed to be alone.

Then the car passed another wooden post by the side of the road exactly like the one before, and the tension was released. Once he saw that his experience was fungible, it was no longer such a burden. He was safe in his role as an outsider. Plus, he felt the wall between him and Woodrow was not so tall anymore. He looked over and noticed his hands were relaxed on the wheel. Roy smiled. The feeling of peace was mutual.

In this even easier silence they passed the next few miles.

Gradually, landmarks that Roy could not ignore began cropping up: the road to the doctor's house where he and his mom had hitched a ride with a neighbor when Roy got mumps, the gulch that he had only seen run with water once, and a red and gray boulder sticking five feet out of the earth, which Roy once claimed was the biggest rock in America. And on the horizon grew the little town, the closest thing to civilization that Roy saw until Chicago. It felt like his life had been opened up like a book and presented for Woodrow to read. Looking at the sunbaked and tawny fields around him, he felt ashamed of what his story had to offer.

"By the way," Roy said, twisted around to open one of his suitcases in the back. "Here's this."

Woodrow looked away from the road for only a moment to check the cash in Roy's hand. "No," he said, "don't worry about it."

Roy held the fresh fold of bills in the air over the console. "You sure?"

"Yeah," said Woodrow, waving him off. "It's no big thing."

"Okay," said Roy. He put the money back in the purse. Out of the corner of his eye he saw Woodrow sucking in his lips as if he was preparing to say something. But the only sound was the hum of the car flying over asphalt.

Ten minutes deeper into Nebraska, Woodrow asked, "Is there anywhere around here that sells food?"

Roy looked around. "Depends. Can you digest dirt?"

"I'll save that for dessert."

"There isn't really a place around here. There should be a

general store coming up, though."

Out of the ashy ground arose a square on the right of the road. In front of the building a sign read, in fading red letters, "Hardt's General Store."

Woodrow braked a little too fast and pulled into the lot. On the porch of the store sat a man in suspenders and an undershirt. Gray hair puffed out from his collar as if he was hiding a weasel under there. Only one of his eyes looked straight forward at Roy and Woodrow, while the other stayed on the road to watch for customers. Yellowed patches under each arm. He had a pipe in one hand and a coke in the other. He drifted back and forth on his rocking chair and muttered something.

"Hello," said Roy, quietly enough to show he did not want to talk. Woodrow, matching Roy's reserve, merely nodded. But before they could gain the threshold, the man spoke.

"Wait a second," he said. "Come on out here, you."

Roy could sense Woodrow's body grow rigid. They stepped back onto the porch. But the man's eye did not register Woodrow at all, staying on Roy instead.

"You the Manger kid, right?"

Roy's first thought was, *No, the Manger kid is dead.* It took him a moment to connect the name to himself.

"Yes," Roy said. "I am."

"Well damn, boy," laughed the man, "it's been so long, I thought I'd never see you again!"

Roy didn't know what else to do but smile.

The man continued, putting his pipe aside, "You let your hair grow out so long I thought you had a sister!"

"Nope," said Roy, laughing, "just me." He realized he had stepped between Woodrow and the man, who he now recognized as Mr. Hardt's brother, John.

"I haven't seen you around for years. What you here for?"

"Oh, just thought it was about time I saw my mom again." Woodrow had slunk inside already.

John's smile slipped. "You mean, you haven't heard?"

"No," he said, the color sucking out of his face. "I haven't."

"Well, she ain't doin' too well, you know."

"She's not dead, though, is she?"

"No. But, yeah...not doin' too well, you know. Everybody around here either dead or movin'. I s'pose you had the right idea, leaving when you did."

Roy did not like to look at this man. He let his eyes trace the horizon at the edge of the fields. He heard Woodrow browsing through the aisles in the dark interior of the store. He asked John who was taking care of her.

"Neighbors come around every day or so. Jameses. With food and medicine and the like."

"But she doesn't have anyone staying with her?" Roy felt like a scientist quietly recording numbers from the mouth of a machine.

"No, not that I know of."

Roy turned to John, who also was staring out at the fields. A truck filled with hay barreled past.

Slowly Roy let his soul move. Like a door it swung open, revealing a red and frothy tide behind it. It flooded every part of him, filling his nerves to bursting, pounding in his temples and swelling his heart so large it hurt.

"What do you mean," he asked John, "that no one is staying with her?"

John shrugged, still looking off.

"Look at me, John."

John turned his head.

"I asked what you meant when you said no one was with her."

John pushed on one of the arms of the rocking chair to shift his rear further back. "Well," he said, "she doesn't have no kin closer than Lincoln, and hiring a nurse is expensive. She gets along all right, I figure. She's always been a fighter."

"I don't care if she's Jack Goddamn Johnson, Mr. Hardt. Why isn't anyone doing anything?"

Roy could not be sure but it seemed John's walleye tried to straighten itself out purely out of fear.

"Well, I don't know. This is not the type of thing we really want to intrude on, you know."

Roy thought of a million things he could have said to Mr. Hardt. Instead, he turned on his heel and stormed inside the store and stood in the furthest, coolest, darkest corner, letting the air refresh his throat and calm his ire. He stared at a bag of flour until his heart slowed down, and he no longer wanted to tip John

Hardt's chair over the edge of the porch. *It's not his fault,* he told himself. After a minute, he was calm.

During this time, Woodrow did not bother him, which added enormously to his credit as a friend. When Roy finally did turn around, Woodrow approached him and asked if he was all right. Roy nodded and smiled when Woodrow laid a hand on his shoulder, not really hearing anything he said. He replied, "Thank you. I think I just need to look around the store a little."

And quite a store it was. Despite the remote locale, in its day Hardt's served as the closest general store for hundreds of families out here and therefore carried a vast amount of wares: tools, toys, food, clothes, bedding, furniture, radios, animal feed, seeds, farm equipment, and a hundred things more. Everything was a little dusty, yes, and the wares had not been refreshed in a long time. But that could not be held against the Hardt's—they would never sell anything faulty and were famous for giving kids peppermint sticks. Hardt was a beloved man who, judging by the presence of the younger, less bald man currently behind the counter, must have died within the last four years.

Roy floated through the aisles like a ghost. He touched the dresses for sale. Compared to the things he wore now, these may as well have been cut from burlap. But he still remembered looking at them with wonderment as a kid and having his mother pluck them out from his hands when she caught him. His mother. Someone who had lived, and worked, and loved him. No longer an image or a memory painted onto some wall to declutter the space of Roy's mind. As he traced her steps from years ago, her image stepped from its frame and into the third dimension, not begrudging him anything—just happy to see him again after so long.

And suddenly, there was Betty. This was an updated version, no doubt, but he could not mistake her. She was a little taller than he remembered and her hair a little more lustrous. But they had kept the eyelashes the same shade of black, and they must have used the same mold for her hands, since her fingers curved just like before. Like a family of little caterpillars. Even the dress was the same: gingham with a lace collar. Her eyes had stayed ice blue all this time.

If Roy's clothes had been looser, he could have owned her once. But the sleight of hand had not passed the scrutiny of his mother, who forced the ten-year-old to remove the doll from the small of his back and made him march up to Mr. Hardt to return it. Mr. Hardt had told him it was okay and had given him a peppermint stick anyway, an act of mercy that did not stop his mother from grabbing Roy by the hand and yanking him out of the store, red-faced. After that, he had merely stared at Betty from an aisle away, wondering which Christmas would deliver her to his house, which miracle could bring them together.

God, he loved his mother. He felt guilt set itself upon his heart. He had no one to blame but himself. As if he had torn a bite out of his own flesh.

Woodrow approached him, holding two cans of corn and a can

of pork and beans. "What're you looking at?"

"Just wondering why they wouldn't base a doll off of me. Seems they could make one much prettier than this." These words hung in the air, blasphemous. Roy wondered how much of his past he was willing to sell for Woodrow's approval. He parted from Woodrow and walked into the next aisle. Walking toward the animal feed he began to see flecks of black out of the corners of his eyes, a symptom, he hoped, of exhaustion.

He passed the next aisle and watched as Woodrow inspected the colored pencils. He picked up a pink one, checked the tip, and put it away. Roy leaned against the aisle, tired. Woodrow lifted and inspected another pencil, putting it back blessed. *Blessed, yes. Everything he touches is blessed. And I am just dirty. I leave the ones I love to die.*

In the next aisle, Woodrow asked Roy in hushed tones if he wouldn't mind buying the food now, so it didn't seem like they were traveling together. "Of course," said Roy. He bought it without incident. And he did not say good-bye to John as he left.

A few minutes later, Woodrow joined Roy in the car, put a big paper bag in Roy's hands, and started the ignition.

"What is it?"

"Open it."

Roy, whose very fingers seemed to be humming with fear and tiredness and shame, cautiously removed the object from the bag.

What he didn't know about Betty was that her eyes closed as you tilted her back. As he righted the doll, she stared at him with those huge, icy-blue eyes. Before Roy could think of something to say, he looked at the porch they were passing, John refilling his pipe while the black, humanoid figure stood behind him, like a cut-out into a different dimension. Roy thought, *I will deal with that later.* And then, looking down at the doll, *I will deal with* this *now.*

So he turned to Woodrow, weeping, and thanked him. He passed the next hour smiling, crying, and eating corn straight from the can.

Chapter Twelve

Roy could tell the passing fields apart using the same insight that a mother uses to distinguish her twin daughters. He could not point out exactly which rocks or which fences informed his memory, but he remembered without fail: the Johnsons', the McGradys', the Roberts'. They were on a road of powdery and fine dust now, and they could not see out the back window for the cloud they were kicking up. It was a trip deeper into the Midwest, and deeper into Roy's memory.

Woodrow asked, "Recognize any of these places?"

"Yes," said Roy. "All of them."

"We close?"

"Twenty miles out, I'd wager."

Woodrow whistled. "Boy, this place is big."

Roy sat Betty on his lap. "I know. I like it."

"How will we know which one's yours?"

"It will be the one with the field of dry corn in front of it."

"Roger."

They drove on. *At this rate,* thought Roy, *we will arrive at the house just before sundown.*

Suddenly Roy's organs all shifted forward at once. Betty

plunged headlong from his lap. As Roy's head hit back onto the headrest, he looked outside to see what made Woodrow to stop so abruptly. There, in the middle of the road, sat a brown turtle, hidden in its shell.

"Jesus," said Woodrow. "Sorry." He relaxed his arms. "Don't your turtles know any manners around here?"

"Usually they at least put their lights on." They sat and stared at the turtle, which Roy decided was the most misshapen animal he had ever seen. Roy picked up Betty and laid her in the footwell in the back, no longer feeling the need to hold her. In fact, he did not feel anywhere near as close a connection to the doll as he had expected.

Woodrow started craning his neck around, measuring whether he could pass the turtle on either side. When he looked back at the brown mass, Roy knew he was gauging whether he could drive over it without carnage. His hand settled on the gear shift.

"Don't you dare," said Roy.

"We have to get going," said Woodrow.

"Let's just *move* him," said Roy. "No need to be lazy about it."

As they got out of the car, Woodrow said, "That turtle needs to get his license revoked."

Roy was immediately aware of the smell of manure. *My childhood*, he thought. But as he approached the turtle, the smell grew stronger. After a moment, the irregular, brown shape revealed itself to be a dried heap of dung.

"Oh, shit," said Roy.

Woodrow cackled, bending in half. He put his head on his forearm and laid it on the hood of the car. Roy also leaned on the car and covered his eyes with his hand. He said, "We have been in the city for way too long."

Eventually Woodrow gathered his wits about him and stood upright, saying, "This reminds me..." He walked into the field to pee. Roy stole a glance over his shoulder to see the stream spring from Woodrow's body. On one hand, he admired the strength and vigor of the flow. On the other, he felt very glad he was at a safe distance from the spray.

The pee was interminable. Roy looked behind them to the cloud of dust their car had kicked up. Usually a dust cloud like that hung in the air for a few minutes before settling. But for some reason their cloud was not getting lighter at all. Another few moments and he realized it was actually getting darker.

About a mile behind them rose the darkest wall of dust that Roy had ever seen in his life, billowing and bulging like a tumorous growth.

"Woodrow," he said, "get back in the car."

The last spurts of urine were welcomed by the parched ground. "What?"

"Black roller."

"What?" he asked, zipping his fly. Seeing that Roy was not facing him, he followed his eyes.

"Holy Joseph," he said. And jogged to the driver's side.

"Pull off the road," said Roy.

"What? Why?" asked Woodrow, who was struggling with his seatbelt.

"If there's another car coming, they'll crash into us. They'll be driving blind."

Woodrow's tire found the filling of the dung heap nowhere near as dry as the exterior.

Once they were safely pulled into the field, Woodrow peered out the back window at the encroaching cloud of dust. After a minute he whispered, "Jesus. Is he your friend?"

Roy felt calm inside the car. "Who, the dust cloud? Yes, we go way back."

"How long is he staying for?"

"Depends. When I was a kid he usually visited for a few minutes at a time. Sometimes an hour."

"Okay. That's not so bad," said Woodrow as he undid his seatbelt.

"Except..." At Roy's words Woodrow's eyes rolled toward him expectantly. "Well, the only time I've ever seen one so large was three days before my twelfth birthday."

"Aw. Well at least it didn't spoil your party."

Roy remained silent.

Woodrow's arm flipped down. "It didn't spoil your party, did it?"

"We were stuck inside for four days."

"Four days?" Woodrow's mouth hung open.

Roy nodded. "But this one looks a little smaller, actually."

Woodrow looked back, astounded that anything could be bigger than the solid block of cloud rushing toward them.

"Jesus. What did you do?"

"Learned whist."

"That's pretty bad."

"Torture."

Following Woodrow's example, Roy reclined his seat too. He touched the roof of the car, just to make sure it was still velvet. He pushed the crank on the window to check that it was still tight. Just in case.

"I wanted to thank you, again," said Roy, "for the doll."

"No problem. You really seemed transfixed."

"By 'transfixed,' do you mean, 'like an emotional wreck'?"

"Something like that."

"This was something I really wanted as a kid, but we never could afford it."

"I know that feeling."

"I..." Roy was surprised to be confronted by a wall. He could not say anything else. He had thought that if you cried in front of someone, they would know everything about you, and there was no reason to be shy or reserved around them anymore. Crying was like wrenching yourself open. That was why he had avoided doing it in front of anyone since he was eleven.

Roy pushed through the resistance. "I actually tried to steal it. When I was little."

Woodrow, whose eyes were closed, raised his eyebrows. Two beautiful and smooth vole pelts. "I had no idea you were such a little delinquent."

"And I haven't even told you what I wanted to do with it."

"Oh?"

"I wanted to cut off all her hair."

"Oh, God."

"So that she would look like me."

"And then what? Glue a thumbtack between her legs?"

Roy picked up Betty by her feet. He raised her up and slammed her head into Woodrow's stomach. He curled up like a beetle and giggled in between his teeth. Three hits, and Roy returned Betty to her spot in the footwell. One of her eyes no longer swung closed.

Roy lay down. He could see a sliver of his own face in the window. The curve of a cheekbone, the bump of a brow. Shapes variously shaded and plucked for appeal. He stared at the single ghostly eye of his reflection, thinking, *This is what the kind of person who abandons his mother in hell looks like. This is the face of a bad person.* And while he did feel relieved to finally put a face to that description, he noted a sense of alarm in seeing how closely it resembled himself.

Suddenly the cloud covered them with a low howl, the larger particles deflecting off the metal with tiny pings. The car rocked, and the sun was swallowed up, and the world turned tan.

"Oh my God," said Woodrow. "I can't believe this."

"Step outside the car. Then you'll believe it."

Woodrow looked at him, concerned. "What would happen if I stepped outside?"

"The wind would rub you white."

Now it was Woodrow's turn to slap Roy's arm. He didn't know if it was Woodrow's intention to hurt him, but when he turned the other way, Roy quietly cradled his arm where it smarted.

"Seriously," Woodrow insisted.

"It wouldn't kill you. If it got in your eyes, it would blind you for a while. It would scratch up your skin. You really just have to make sure you don't breathe it in."

"What would happen if I breathed it in?"

"It would cause an infection in your lungs. It can be fatal."

Woodrow pressed the crank on the window to make sure it was tight. *Just in case*, thought Roy, and smiled.

Roy realized he had forgiven Woodrow—for pressuring him to leave his job and for telling him he could not be Raina for their travels. *He thinks I am not Raina right now just because I am wearing boy clothes. But I am still Raina. And he loves me. Which means he loves Raina, too.* He stared at Woodrow's profile, relishing the clean feeling forgiveness gave him, admiring how Woodrow's features seemed even stronger in the light, as if he were hewn from clay. Dense and wet and solid, the very flesh of the earth.

Woodrow's eyes turned to Roy. Roy said, "Actually, one of the longer storms I remember, I was milking cows during it. In the barn," he explained. "Because I couldn't get into the house, I had to shut the barn doors and wait in the loft until it passed. I fell asleep up there though, and when I woke up, it had already ended hours ago. My mom thought I was dead."

"Wow," said Woodrow. He looked out the back window. He said after a minute, "I didn't know you had a barn."

"Best barn in Nebraska," said Roy. "Built by my father. Actually, I had a secret place in our loft that my mom never knew about."

Woodrow raised his eyebrows. "Are you going to tell me about the first time you jerked off?"

Roy laughed hard at first. Then, realizing how accurate Woodrow's guess was, the laugh died in his throat. "No, I'll keep that secret for now."

"What did you do up there, then? Smoke cigs? Summon Satan?"

"All that, and more. No, I mainly just played with my cat. I would host... Well," said Roy, "It's not important what I hosted."

"Oh, God, were you about to say 'orgies'? With the other farm animals? Jesus, Roy. Why didn't you invite me?"

"No!" Roy could barely say the words, he was laughing so hard. "No, I hosted dinner parties, just the two of us, up in the loft."

"That's more embarrassing than orgies, honestly." He looked out the front window. "I can't see shit. Can you?"

"No, I can still see it."

Woodrow turned to him. "What?"

Roy pointed to the squished pile of manure behind them.

Woodrow grabbed Roy's pointing finger and set the hand in Roy's lap. "I think that's enough jokes for today."

Both settled back in their seats and looked out the window, trying to make out the closest edge of the nearest field through the dust.

"Both cats?"

"What?" asked Roy.

"Did you host dinners with both your cats?"

Roy turned to him. He knitted his brow. "What are you talking about?"

"You said you had dinner with your cat. Did you do that with both the cats you had, or just one?"

"What cats? I only had one cat."

Woodrow tilted his head. "I thought you said you had two."

"No, I..." Roy tried to remove his foot from the trap as it closed. "Oh, you mean Maggie. I got her so close to when I left home, I don't really count her as my cat. But no, I never did the dinners with her. The guest list was pretty selective."

"Ah, I see. A V.I.P. kinda deal."

"Exactly." They turned on their backs, each looking out their respective window. Roy decided to ask, "Did you have anything like that, growing up? Any special places or games you had? Besides burn-down-the-Dabney-house, I mean."

"No, none of us really knew Grover from childhood, if that's what you're asking." He took a breath. "Me and most of the other kids on the property played a lot of variations on sports."

"Variations? How?"

"You know, just with smaller teams and impromptu balls. Like, we once used an overcured ham for a football. It worked great until it hit some kid in the face and broke his glasses."

"Oh, my," said Roy, giggling. "Was he okay?"

"I mean, he was wearing glasses. He really shouldn't have been playing sports to begin with." He smiled when he heard Roy laugh. "But no, I didn't really have much time for imagination games. We had to work a lot for the Dabneys. Well, actually...I did know this one tree that had a hollow knot in the side. The opening was a slit about this big."

"Oh, my. Am I about to hear *your* first masturbation story?"

"No, you pervert. I used to hide little things in there, like scraps of paper with my name on it, or bits of candy or ribbon. One time I cut my finger on a shard of glass I forgot I'd put in there."

"Do you still have those things?"

"What? No, it's all junk. I gave it away or used it."

"Oh. So there's a lonely slit somewhere that misses you?"

"There's more than one of those around, honey." Woodrow's smile broke through.

The car rocked in the wind. Roy imagined they were going to be sanded down until their bodies were as thin as threads. He looked at Woodrow, who was turned away from him, and imagined the wind ripping the clothes off his back, revealing the smooth and warm skin of a stranger. Skin purer because it had never tried to buy him. He tore his eyes away and looked back out the window. With the smoky sand blocking his vision, he could not distinguish anything further than five feet away. Still, he could, if he squinted, make out a darker shape in the midst of the storm. His first thought was that it was someone who needed help. His hand instinctively went to the lock. Then he noticed the shape did not move. It stared at him, immobile, despite the rage of the storm. A chill traveled up his spine.

Roy chose not to look. He turned to Woodrow and said, "Do you ever miss it? Where you grew up, I mean."

"No way in hell. I hated it there. I wanted to leave every minute."

"I see. Do you miss anyone?"

"Yeah, of course. I miss my parents and my sister and friends and such. And my dog. We had to leave him behind."

"Oh, I'm so sorry."

"It's okay. He was a smart fella. He can fend for himself."

"Do you ever think about writing a letter?"

"To Rusty?"

"No," said Roy, "to your family."

"No," said Woodrow. "I wouldn't really know what to say. I also don't know their address. I think they're in Cincinnati."

"Would your sister know?"

"Sister?" Woodrow chewed on a bit of his lip. "Oh! The woman I stayed with in Chicago. The one who bailed me out. She's not a blood relative, just a friend. She's not from the Dabneys'."

Roy stepped out onto the diving board. "What kind of 'friend' is she?"

Woodrow smiled. "Platonic."

"Ugly?"

"No, lesbian."

Roy laughed. It felt like they were finally talking about the same thing. The winds rocked the car slightly. He felt as safe as a pearl.

Woodrow continued. "But as I said, I wouldn't send them anything even if I had their address. Every family from that plantation has their mail intercepted, I bet."

"Wow. Just because of Grover?"

"Yep. They've got tens of thousands of dollars out on his head."

"Jeez. He must give great head then."

Woodrow stuck his tongue between his teeth and laughed. After a minute he asked, "Do you?"

"Give great head? Yes."

"No, I mean, do you miss your home?"

"Oh. Yeah, I do, actually. I feel bad about my mom."

"Yeah, I was gonna ask you about that. What's going on?"

"I don't know. She's really sick, but no one in town is doing anything about it."

"Any idea what she has?"

"No idea. Didn't ask."

Woodrow lay back down. "I'm sorry, man. That's really rough. You said your dad's out of the picture?"

"Yep, he died when I was little."

"Of what?"

"Don't know."

"He was the hatchet guy, right?"

"Yes."

"Were you guys close?"

"I don't remember him much. But," ventured Roy, "I am, or was, pretty close with Ma. I didn't have people to play with growing up, so all my time was either spent with her, or with the animals." Roy looked upward. "I feel awful for leaving. I really should have stayed. I don't know what she did without me." When Roy looked down, a tear spilled from each eye.

Woodrow reached over and patted Roy's hand twice. Roy was happy for the contact, but he wished he could enjoy it, instead of feeling embarrassed crying in front of this man who had already seen him weep once today. He resisted the impulse to open the door and let the burning sand whisk away his tears and the skin of his face along with them.

"Hey," said Woodrow softly. "Hey, it's all right. Don't worry." Then, more cogently, he said, "I'm sure she will forgive you."

"I know, but," said Roy, "I wish I hadn't done anything that needed forgiving in the first place."

"Yeah. Well. We all do. But the past is set in stone, and save for amnesia or alcohol, nothing can get the memories out of your head. So you either have to accept them and move on or else suffer and then die."

Woodrow's hand touched Roy's again. He stared at him with intensity, as if he was offering something. When Roy was alone, his imagination preferred a gaze more penetrating than this, a gaze that commanded, a gaze that could shred through clothes and whittle something down to its barest component. Usually Roy imagined Adrian staring at him like that in some moon-drenched bedroom or before a roaring fire in an oak-paneled chalet. This image had become his diet. The two of them spread out on the rug, the fire roaring, Roy yielding to Adrian. Since there was something elemental in Adrian that demanded worship. One could see it in his gaze. For Roy, the pinnacle of eroticism was the act of being taken from. He had no experience with the brown eyes before him, which nearly melted with the offer to help. Never had Roy felt closer to Woodrow—or less attracted.

"Sorry," said Woodrow, "I'm speaking like my grandma at you. You can ignore me." He brought his hand to the steering wheel.

"No, that's really helpful, actually. Thank you," said Roy.

After a moment, Woodrow asked, "Do you think your mother will approve?" Of your lifestyle choices, I mean."

"Oh. Well, it's not really a lifestyle choice, I don't think."

"No?"

Roy wondered how far he should press this. "No. I never chose to be a prostitute. It was something I had to do in order to, you know, not starve to death."

"And I bet the grim reaper himself laced you into that corset?"

Roy stared at Woodrow with hatred. There was too much to explain here, too much nuance to convey. It was easier, he decided, to say he was a boy, who had to do certain things for certain concrete, economic reasons. This was not the whole truth, but it was the most he could explain. "I told you," he said. "I dress like a girl because I make more money that way."

Woodrow looked away. He said something under his breath.

Roy's voice was a swinging sword. "What did you just say?"

"I said," said Woodrow, "'then why did you wanna get in the car in your dress?'"

Roy sat back in his chair. "I didn't know my clothing was of special interest to you. If you want to borrow my lingerie, you shouldn't be afraid to ask." Roy stared straight at where the snakes of sand formed on the windshield and were dashed away by the wind.

"Now hold on a second," said Woodrow, holding up his hands in defense. "I am not *like* you. I don't swing for that kind of Shakespearian crossdressing Nancy-boy shit."

"What do you mean you're not '*like*' me? You dress how you want to dress, and *I* dress how *I* want to dress. That's it! End of story!"

"You just said it was a way to make money! Make up your mind!"

"Jesus fucking *Christ*," Roy yelled, whipping his head around.

"Why is it so God*damn* important that we have to be different?"

As soon as he said it, he understood why.

How else could Woodrow have resisted loving Evangeline? Why else would he live with a lesbian instead of a gal? Why else the bravado of a straight man, if he didn't have something to hide?

Woodrow's face provided proof. As he placed both hands on the steering wheel and stared out the front of the car, Roy wished he could take it all back.

They sat like this for twenty minutes. The dark form grew darker in Roy's periphery, but he refused to look. He felt like his tongue was flapping frantically over the bloody site where a strong tooth had once stood. Friendship proved fragile. Susceptible to a single shock.

Woodrow eventually spoke.

"Listen, Roy." His voice was steady. "I'll drive you the rest of the way." He continued staring out the front window. "But after that, I am headed back to Chicago." Once the words were out, his hand relaxed on the wheel, and he lay back on his seat. He covered up his eyes with his elbow and said no more.

Roy had nothing to say in return. It was humiliating. And worse than humiliating, it was fair. He looked forward. He had to close his right eye to block out the image of the dark man, who seemed to pulse with blackness. The dust was already thinning in the air. The storm would subside in the next few minutes, and they would drive the final miles. Hopefully, when Woodrow drove away, he would take the dark man with him.

Take it all, thought Roy. *At least I got a ride out of it.*

BOOK FIVE

Chapter One

As parents in Maine liked to share the stories of the children's first snow, Roy's mother liked to share the story of his first dust storm. Over dinner she would tell the pastor that she woke up one morning after a huge black roller to find Roy missing from his bed. His gloves and sweater missing, too. She eventually found him by the barn, dressed for December, not June, trying to roll up the dust into a snowman. At this point of the story she would laugh and say it was a month before they could beat all the dust from his mittens. At the table, Roy's ears would burn. None of them understood, apparently, how closely dust resembled snow. The current landscape, for example, could have passed for the Arctic. Everything was coated with soft, curving brown, from the porch steps to the old wagon. The ground's features were swallowed in a bumpy blanket of brown. A dust drift that reached Roy's height leaned against the side of the barn. Dust even clung to the treads of Woodrow's car, caking thick where the dung had stuck. The car kicked up the loose dirt, summoning a cloud that shrouded the car as it sped away, leaving Roy laden with his luggage, holding Betty by her hair, in a foreign world of beige, a snowy scene in sepia.

He turned slowly. Within the winter wonderland of dust, the

house had changed. The porch post that had threatened to break a hundred times had finally split in half, causing the roof to bend in at that spot. The windows were milky with the sand-blasted panes, but they seemed intact, at least. The lawn was in no better repair than it had been four years before. The tall and malignant weeds still clung to the foundation, as if they were the legs of a square, blind spider, which at any minute could stand and scurry away.

Off to the right stood the barn, whose color had gone from red to ochre and from ochre to brown. He could tell there were no animals in it because the door had been left open and because it was dead silent. Roy looked over his shoulder at the road. He involuntarily leaned toward it.

The wind rose, casting fine brown powder against the sides of his pants and his luggage. He looked down and shook his leg. He decided it would be best to go inside.

He expected to hear the familiar squeak, but because of some mechanical malfunction or a warping of the wood, the screen door was stuck in its wide-open position. And while he was used to dealing with the temperamental wooden door, today it offered new challenges. The knob squeaked like never before, and he had to shove a lot harder than he was used to. He felt that something was trying to keep him out.

The dust had found its way inside. It sat on the couch like a guest. It availed itself of all the pottery on the shelves. It borrowed the blankets in the corner and blocked the picture of Roy's father that stood on the mantle. It gathered in corners, on shelves. In its passing, it left streaks on the landing. It followed Roy, marking each step he took with a criminal footprint. Roy felt like *he* was the intruder and not the other way around.

Where, then, was the wife to this pervasive new stepfather? Where was the owner of the dry rasp that hung in the air like a string of rusty fishhooks? Roy set down his bags and started down the hall, calling, "Ma?"

Her room was darker than usual. Two layers of newspaper had been pasted over her windows, giving it the air of a cavern. It smelled awful, like a chamber pot left out in the sun. It took a moment for his eyes to adjust.

The lines of her face materialized. The wrinkles met at the corners of her eyes, her lips, and her forehead. The hair hung in wisps. Her eyelids were dark as if she was wearing eyeshadow and her hands—one of which lay on her lap while the other hung off the edge of the bed—were thin, spotted, and swollen at the joints. He would have guessed she was somewhere between twenty and thirty years older than she had been when he left.

He worried he would kill her just by approaching. That was how fragile she looked. Too loud a voice could have shattered her. So he whispered, the sound as unwelcome in the hot, dark room as a cymbal in a church.

"Ma?"

Her breaths came shallow and ragged. Roy thought, *If I had stayed, she would not be dying.*

"Hn?"

The sound came from a mouse.

"Ma? You awake?"

"What?" Her words did not come out with consonants.

Roy had to go forward and touch her hand. It was too delicate not to. If he didn't step forward and hold it quickly, it would fall and break.

"It's me." He pulled up a chair next to her bed and lifted up her hand, remarking how much it felt like a leaf. "I'm back, Ma."

She looked him right in the face and smiled. "You..." She let a rattle fill her chest. She exhaled. "...are late." Roy realized she was the third person he had spoken to in a week.

"Yes, Ma. I know. I'm sorry. I'm here now." The tears brimmed in his eyes.

She set her head back and closed her eyes. "Always knew you'd come back." Roy replaced the hand and watched her. She was asleep, smiling. Her breaths still came raw and ragged, and sometimes she would exhale suddenly, as if she was huffing during a tantrum, upset at how difficult breathing could be. But the pipe always opened again. Eventually, Roy recognized a rhythm.

After a few minutes, he got up. He emptied the chamber pot. He examined the dried-out plates of food. He wished the house had better ventilation or at least electricity. He organized the kitchen and drew new water for the basin. Then he did the dishes. He would stop every few minutes to make sure the breath in the next room followed its pattern. He could barely distinguish it from the sound of the wind. His blood quickened with the labor. For the first time in years, he felt he was exactly where he belonged.

This is how he spent the next few hours. He felt infinitely powerful in these halls; he had no need for anybody but himself and his own two hands. But he also felt ephemeral, like he was already a ghost, cleaning out a ghost house in a town somewhere between this world and the next. He felt he was cleansing himself. He opened the windows and shook out the blankets. He brushed off the dust that had collected on the bottom of the plates and bowls. He even cleaned the locked cabinet containing the good china. He had to catch himself every once in a while. He was breathing so hard that he worried he would inhale a fatal amount of dust.

An hour later, he came back to check on his mother. She was sitting up in bed with knitting in her lap, the thick and fluffy yarn traveling between the spindles of her fingers, looking reanimated. She looked up at him. She was not as old as she had seemed earlier, though he suspected she was just as sick. Still, he could see her past self in her face. More than that, though, he could see Raina. The nose was the same, and the eyes only differed in luster. With twenty years reversed and enough foundation, she could have even tricked Hattie. As Roy brought her a tray of peas and steamed carrots, he wondered if she noticed the same features within his own face, or whether the admixture of his father's genes had, for her, spoiled the fun of inheritance.

He laid the tray by her side. They smiled at each other.

"Hello, Ma."

"Hello, dear Roy."

"I brought you something to eat."

"Thank you."

"How are you feeling?" He pushed the tray an inch closer to her, wondering if she needed the food to be mashed.

"I'm fine. I can't complain."

"Do you..." He struggled to find a way to configure his hands on his lap that felt natural. Had the chairs always felt this uncomfortable? "Do you have anyone who comes to help you?"

"Mm-hmm. Lidia comes."

"Lidia?" He raked through his memories. "Oh, Lidia James? Mr. James's daughter?"

"Yes. But she's Lidia McDowell now." Every word she said came out half as fast as Roy's.

"I thought she liked carpentry?"

Inez looked up and to the left. "I don't remember...that."

"What does she do now?"

Inez sucked on her gums, which were mostly bare now. "Married... Lovely woman. Cooks for me and..." She paused, breathing in slowly. "...washes."

"Are you in much pain?"

She frowned. "No... Not really. You learn to live with it."

"Have you seen a doctor?" It immediately occurred to Roy that he may be taxing her with all the questions. He promised that this would be the last one.

She shook her head slowly. "Never had the time."

Roy could not look at her. He had to break away his gaze from her drooping face to remind himself that there were other things in the world besides death, aging, and poverty. He stared at the floor and waited.

"Did you have fun?"

"What?" he asked.

She coughed twice. "While you were gone."

He looked up. "While I was gone?"

She nodded.

Tears sprung into his eyes. "Yes," he said. "I had fun." He sighed and cried and looked up at the ceiling. "I made a lot of mistakes. But I had fun, too."

She smiled. "God forgives the young. You are here. That's what's important." After a moment she asked him to mash up her food. As she spooned up the mash and gummed it contemplatively, staring at Roy like a portrait, he felt that his shame was gone, and he relished the intense sense of responsibility.

A few more orders of business had to be addressed. She had him write a note to the Jameses telling them that Lidia no longer needed to come. He left it leaning on the front door so they would find it. She had him bring his old bed into her room so he could be close if she needed anything. They did not have a bell for her to ring, so Roy balanced a chunk of wood on the side table that she could push over the edge with the tip of her finger. The only thing she told him not to do was sweep out the house, seeing as the dust in the air would harm her sensitive lungs.

While Roy prepared dinner, the black ribbon he used to hold back his hair finally broke. When he brought the platter of mashed potatoes in to his mother, she insisted he use one of the bandanas she always wore around her head. She no longer needed them. Once he had it secured around his head, he sat down in the chair facing her and ate. She stared at him all through dinner.

As he put away the plates, he felt a massive, balmy peace rest over his heart. The spikes and sores of his relationship with Woodrow were forgotten. He could forgive himself every vagrancy and anxiety of the past week. He could forgive himself the idolatry and the waste. There was the magnetic pull of duty here—duty and restfulness. He was happy to fade into the same twilight that his mother occupied, where things were not nearly as rigid, and even the bleakest memories melted into shadow. Simply put, he was happy to be *here* for a while—where nothing happened, and he could be nobody.

Chapter Two

After dinner, Inez rested while Roy read by candlelight. He only brought one book with him, *And Then There Were None*, which he had borrowed from Marie. His mother's breath dragged slowly through the air, as if some of the wind blowing outside had somehow gained access into the house. She sat upright, her mouth slightly ajar, the candle's shadow digging into her wrinkles.

The book read easily. After a few pages, he had achieved the easy pace that made reading enjoyable. His eyes scanned sentences, his fingers flipped pages, and he thoroughly enjoyed the plot.

He stood, marking his page with an old envelope. He went to his room, where his clothes and bags sat, and picked up Betty from a pile of dirty laundry. He brought the doll with him to his mother's room, deciding that, when it was light, he would set her up on the far side of the couch in the main room. Until then, he set her on the floor. *It is a gift from a former almost-lover*, he thought. *A relic from a time past.* Quietly, his mother swallowed.

After a while, her breath reached an even, deep rhythm. Her arms lay palm-up, splayed on either side of her with the fingers curled. He would have to cut her nails soon. He remarked how thin and bony her chest was—how similar it seemed to a sparrow's.

What else did he have to do tomorrow? In a corner was a pile of cloth—another set of bedsheets and maybe some clothes. He would have to wash those. He noticed the glass of the hurricane lamp was chipped, but there was not much he could do about that.

He scanned the room, turning toward the far corner, where shadows gave way to an even greater darkness—gathering into the shape of a man. He stared at the center of the shadow, his gaze locked in place. The candle sputtered on the sideboard. The brown wind howled against the rough-hewn wood of the house, and Roy's hands each lay flat on a page of the open book. His muscles tensed. Fear spread through the corners of his body, like blood diffusing in water.

He tried to remember: *Have I taken my medication today? Yes*, he decided, *I took twice the dose.*

It was not the wind that was causing the candle to sputter, since there was no draft. It was not his breath, since he did not breathe. He figured there had to be some imperfection in the candle itself that made its light come out in bursts like fireworks, alternatively pulling the shapes of the room from the gloom and then setting them back down to rest there.

Without the interceding light, there would be nothing to stop the shadow-man from reaching out to grab him, to overpower and kill him. He knew it was a predator. Not only would it be able to reach him unhindered, but it would surround him. It did not have teeth, since teeth were too simple an evil. What lay in its form was worse than even that. There would not be enough time to grab another candle, there would not be enough time to save his mother, and there would not be enough time to run. So he held his breath, frozen in place, and prepared himself for death.

He heard a cough. On its heels followed another cough, dragging up more ragged coughs, like beads on a string. He heard the clay mug being lifted from the nightstand, and his fear-frozen heart beat faster. There was someone else here, he remembered. Once his mother took a sip of water, she coughed once more, and set the mug back down.

Roy called to his mother without opening his lips. The sound vibrated in his throat. An "hmph."

When she did not react, he made a more urgent entreaty. "*Hmph.*"

She sniffled her nose. In his periphery he saw her roll her head to the other side. Finally, he opened his mouth.

"Ma," he whispered.

Her lips moved with waking. "Mm?" she asked.

"Ma," he said.

"Wha?"

Roy thought, *She must have lost her T's while I was gone.* Her fingers curled into her palms. Her head lifted from the pillow, and she scrunched up her eyes. "What's it, Roy?"

He did not know what to say. He just stared at the corner and waited.

After a minute, she opened her eyes and followed his gaze. She looked from the corner and back to him, then at the corner again.

"What are you looking at?"

Your number is up, he thought to the dark form.

"Roy?" She waited. Sniffled her nose again. "Roy? Do you...see something?"

A tiny, frantic series of head nods affirmed her guess.

"What is it?"

He could not respond. He could not move a muscle. He felt the signals traveling through his nerves, but the muscles they reached were dumb. He could not even close his eyes.

"Honey, look at me." She held an arm up in the air and waved it. He could see the movement, and he could see her hand fall back onto the quilt. "Honey, look over here. It's not real, h—" She was possessed by a coughing fit, the contractions more powerful than herself. When she lay back she was wheezing, panting. The words came out like sandpaper. "Honey—Roy —here."

The candle sputtered and relit. Roy tried to scream, but it stuck in his throat.

Suddenly, he heard a crash, and his head whipped around to see his mother's hand hanging off the edge of the bed a foot above where her mug had smashed into the ground. The water coated the dust with black and slipped between the floorboards, dripping onto the even drier dust beneath the house.

Breath flooded into his lungs. When he looked back at the corner, it was empty.

His mother stared at him incredulously. It was not unkind, but it was also not soft. It was the same look she had given him when he had lied about being sick to get out of chores for a day. Disbelief.

He panted. "Thank you," he said and swallowed.

"We need a new candle," she croaked. She was right. The one on the dresser was about to go out.

Chapter Three

With a new candle installed, the shards of the last mug swept away, and a new mug set in its place plus an extra mug for Roy, he sat and looked at his mother, her hands stacked in her lap.

"First," she said, "tell me if you're okay."

Roy took off his bandana and set it on his shoulders. "Yes, I am okay."

"Are you scared?"

"No. Not anymore."

She nodded her head. He laid his hair on the bandana and tied it at the top.

She asked, "Can you tell me what you saw?"

He tried to draw a breath but it bounced around his chest. He exhaled and tried again, drawing his lungs full of air. Once he was breathing regularly, he said, "Yes. I mean, I can try. It was a black man."

His mother's eyebrows met above her nose. "A Black man?"

"No, no, no, not a *Black* man. I mean, a man made of shadows. Real blackness. Black."

"Shadows," she said, "shaped like a man?"

Roy nodded. She licked her gums. She looked off behind him.

"And how long have you been seeing him?"

"Him?" he asked. Once he had the number in mind, he wondered whether he should lie and tell her it was less than it really was. He saw this house as an island, the only light in a sea of darkness. He was alone here with her, and he decided there was nothing to hide. "Five days."

"And what does he usually do?" She coughed.

"Stands there. Staring at me."

"He have eyes?"

"No," he said, surprised. "I guess—well, I guess I don't know whether he's staring at me or not."

She nodded slowly.

He continued. "But...it feels like he is."

She sucked in her cheeks and looked to the side. "Is he the first one?"

"The first one?" He licked his lips.

"The first thing you've seen."

"No. It's not the first."

"How long?"

"Since I was twelve."

"Seven years?"

"Seven."

She laid her head back on the pillow. After a minute her eyes moved from the ceiling to Roy's face. "Move the candle over here," she said. He set it on the nightstand, and she stared at him. She took a deep breath and let her lungs rattle. She tightened one of her hands into a fist and let it go. Then she looked up.

"When I met your father in Ohio, I fell in love at once, you know. My father sold him a mess kit." She turned her head to Roy. "He was traveling west at the time. Brought a tent and a canteen and the clothes on his back. And Pa told him where he could get a good meal in town and a clean bed, and your father said he didn't want to bother with an inn or anything like that. Said he hunted his own meat. Pa said, well, here's where you can buy some nice firewood, and your father said he cut his own kindling. Pa said, let's at least get you some nice pajamas, but your father said it wasn't worth it. He said, and I still remember this, 'It's cheaper being naked.'" She smiled to the ceiling. "Of course, this was just a joke between men, but I overheard it. For a girl of sixteen like me, working the counter at my dad's shop, why, I could not stop blushing. I blushed from that very moment until I went to bed that night."

She moved her mouth around. She took a slow sip of water and started again.

"He came back the next day, saying the mess kit was good, but what he really needed was some matches. He and Pa jawed it up a bit, and then he left again. I blushed again, but not for as long. Third day, he bought some kindling, said the wood around here wasn't as dry as he liked. He and Pa talked of fishing and hunting, both of which he did well. They made fast friends. I tell you, Roy, that man was as handsome as handsome could be. You've seen the pictures."

Roy raised an eyebrow. In fact, Roy had only ever seen one picture of him—the one on the mantle—which he was glad had gotten obscured by the dust. The image had always scared him. The eyebrows were too bushy, his jaw too sharp, his stubble too unkind. Those eyes, dark like Roy's, seemed—to a young boy who could barely reach the mantle—unforgiving.

"Well, Pa went to tend to another customer and your father started talking to me at the counter. I asked where he was going and he said, 'West.' He asked if I had a fella. I said no. Then I heard Pa's footsteps coming toward the counter. But they shook hands and hugged, as chummy as can be. And Roy, your father, he looks at my pa and says, 'Sir, I was just about to ask your daughter to get a coke with me across the street.' Now Pa must have seen the joy on my face because he said, 'Yes, go ahead and take her.'"

Inez smiled. Her eyes were closed.

"We went to the drug store and each bought a root beer float. I learned he was eighteen and from Vermont. And he learned I could eat more ice cream than any person—man or woman—on that side of the Ohio River."

Roy laughed and asked a question.

"Yes, a little. I did worry that my appetite might scare him off, but I also figured that if a man doesn't like a woman who eats, then what in the hell *does* he want her to do? So yes, I was testing him. But mainly I just loved ice cream. Anyway, we talked and talked and talked until I asked him why he was dawdling in town so long if he was so antsy to get west. He said he was staying because he wanted to talk to me. Well, I must have blushed to my shoes. But what you gotta realize is that girls back then weren't daisies. We all had good heads on our shoulders. I wanted to take on Pa's business with my sister after he died. We considered moving it to a bigger city, something up north maybe. And I wasn't looking to settle down yet."

Roy drank some water. Inez drank water as well.

"So we walked back to the store, and he asked me if he could see me again. And I told him no. And he looked as hurt as a kicked puppy, let me tell you. And he asked why. And I said because he was a liar. And he swore he never lied to me." Inez smiled. "And I said, 'You told my dad you preferred to be naked, but here you are in front of me, covered like a nun.' Then it was his turn to blush. He apologized for the lie and told me he would miss me. And then he went away."

Roy asked a question.

"Of course. I didn't tell my dad what had happened, but of course I did feel a little bad. No matter how smart you are, you're still given to the same wants and needs as any other person. Part of me wished I hadn't given him the boot. The store seemed mighty cold that afternoon."

She finished her water. Roy stood to refill it.

"No, dear, don't worry, I'm almost done. So next morning I'm cleaning the shop and a group of old church biddies comes stomping past the store, talking to each other in the sharpest words you can imagine an old church lady saying. I had no idea what was wrong. So I stepped outside and saw your dad walking up the street as naked as the day he was born."

Her laugh turned into a cough.

"People stared, husbands covered their wives' eyes, and a baby stared crying somewhere. I didn't know why everyone was so upset, though. I thought he looked pretty good."

Roy protested.

"All right, all right. I'll spare the details." Her toothless smile was contagious. "So right there in front of the whole town without a stitch of clothing on him, blushing to his roots, he asked me if I would go out with him now. And I said yes."

Roy had finished his water, too, and insisted he fill them up. He also suggested that she save the rest of the story until tomorrow when she would have more energy.

"No," she said, "I'll finish it tonight. There's not that much left."

Chapter Four

"My father of course didn't want me to be seen with Roy after his little stunt. So I snuck out that night, and we met at the park. We talked for a while, and I commended him on his courage. He thanked me, but asked that I never make him do it again. We walked around the town for a while, and I asked him to show me where he was staying. He brought me to this abandoned lot where bums slept and showed me his tent. He asked whether I liked it, and I told him it was a fixer-upper. He thought that was funny. 'A fixer-upper.' He told me about his hometown and the hatchet-throwing competition he won, and I told him about my family. I asked him why he wanted to go west, and he said because he wanted to be as far away from Vermont as he could. He said there were things there that he wanted to forget. That night, we made our way back to the fountain, and I kissed him. He asked for me to come with him, west, and I said no. He asked why, and I told him. I didn't want to be nailed down to anyone."

Roy asked a question.

"So he left, for good. And I went back home. My sister Terry had stayed up waiting for me, and I told her everything. I made her promise not to tell Pa."

Roy asked another question.

"He did. Of course he did. Someone must have seen us walking together by the fountain, because in the morning Pa was barking mad, asking me all sorts of rude questions about what we did that night. My sister and I told him the truth, but he wouldn't believe me. He said I had disgraced him."

Roy asked a question.

"Yes, well, you know how things are in towns like that. Even a family's most private shame is bound to turn into a rumor before long. It only took two days."

She took a sip of water.

"So he and Ma agreed to send me to a missionary school to teach Indians."

Roy asked a question.

"Yes, all in two days. You couldn't mess around with a woman's honor, back then. It was the only thing she had really. So anyway, they packed up my bags and told me I had a train in the morning to St. Augustine in Nebraska. It was the worst news I ever heard. And on top of that, Terry had disappeared."

Roy asked another question.

"I couldn't find her anywhere. I needed my sister, but she was nowhere to be found."

She looked a long way off.

"That night though, I heard a tapping at my window. I thought it would be you-know-who, but it was only Terry. She was there on the ground, throwing pebbles at the window. I helped her climb up the fire escape. I kept asking her where she had been, why she hadn't been there to defend me, and so on. But she didn't say anything, just handed me a card written in big, dumb, capital letters. I read the signature first, if you could call that thing a signature. It started with an 'R.' Yes, she had gone over to the bum camp to see if Roy was still there, and by some miracle, he was. So she told him what happened, and she told him about St. Augustine, and he wrote me this note and sent it home with her."

Roy asked a question.

"That was the risk. I think it would have killed Pa if someone had seen *her* near the bum camp, too. But I don't think anyone did. Anyway, the note said that, if I wanted him to, Roy would stow away on the train I was taking in the morning, and we could meet up at the destination. I figured, hey, why not. I wrote a letter back, and Terry climbed right back out the window to bring it to him. God. I could never ask for a better sister."

She took a sip of water.

"I got onto the train at seven in the morning, knowing that Roy was stowed away in the caboose. I knew I was never coming back, so I stole Pa's gold watch before I left. The ride took two full days. I thought the land was mocking me. Every passing hour it got flatter and bleaker, as if I was headed right toward the end of the earth. It was hard to believe that anything good was ever going to happen to me ever again. But I got off at Sioux City and there he was, standing on the platform with his bags, his arms open, smiling. We got married that afternoon at the county clerk's office, and the next day, Roy came into our hotel room with a big bouquet of flowers and a newspaper advertising cheap land near the Kansas border."

Roy asked a question.

"This was...1919. Before the ground began to dry and the winds picked up. We got a car on credit and arrived at the flat plot of land and looked at it. He asked what I thought, and I said, 'It's a fixer-upper.' He liked that."

She took a breath, adding, "About that time, we got Dolly from a neighbor whose cat had a whole litter.

"Your father, he built this home with his own two hands. Whatever anyone says about him, Roy, you know that he built our house himself. He was an amazing man. Remember that. We lived here for a year, just the two of us, with Dolly underfoot. He picked up farming well. We got to know the neighbors, and we did favors for them in exchange for seeds and eggs. It was very good for a long while. And then you came along. Not that you were a bad kid or anything... In fact, you were very good kid. Very sweet. You slept like a rock every night. But there are things that all parents have to face, whether their kid is good or bad."

Roy told her it was getting late. He suggested she hold the story here.

"No, Roy, I already told you. There's not much left. Where was I? Yes, kids bring strife. Suddenly our ends no longer met, and we had to stretch things further and further to get by. I taught you as much as I could in my free time, and your father did every odd job he could on the side."

Roy asked a question.

"I'm just thinking, dear. Give me a second."

Roy waited.

"And then something changed in your father. I guess it started when I asked to see the newspaper clipping he kept about his hatchet-throwing competition. He said he had lost it. The clipping. But I found it tucked away in his wallet one day."

Roy asked a question.

"No, it's all true. He did, in fact, throw a hatchet so hard that no one was able to get it out, perhaps even to this day. It nearly split the tree in half, too. The only thing that surprised me was that he had been disqualified from the competition before he got a chance to throw."

Roy asked a question. His mother took a deep breath.

"Because they said he was yelling. Acting rowdy. And then he went and threw the hatchet into the wrong tree. No one was hurt, but they didn't count his win. Even though he hit his mark from fifty paces. I asked him about this, and he explained that he hadn't slept well the night before, and got heatstroke during the competition. And the sun was in his eyes. It put me ill at ease. The things he wanted to run away from... Well, I guess they caught up with him."

Roy asked a question.

"Well, all kinds of things. I would catch him standing frozen in the barn with the saw still in his hand, staring at the house like he'd seen a ghost. Or he would wake up in the night sweating from some nightmare. He got less and less sleep, those days. And I was no better. Having to take care of you on top of everything else wore me down to the bone. When I wasn't feeling very good about your father, and I would catch him in those frozen moods, sometimes I would leave him like that for a half hour just so I wouldn't have him bothering me."

Roy asked a question.

"He wouldn't tell me. But I had my suspicions. He had a dog that died when he was little, and sometimes I would find scraps of meat or bone on the ground out back. I didn't connect the two things until he was already passed. And... Well, his dad was a cruel man. I think that had something to do with it."

Roy asked another question.

"I stopped letting him hold you, for one thing. And I didn't trust him with a lot of his tools. He was still a very strong man, remember. And once... Well, he could get angry sometimes, if I didn't snap him out of his little episodes fast enough. That's why we only have three plates of china."

Roy asked another question.

"He was a sick man, dear. As you reached five, I don't think he could tell anymore what was real or not. Yes, it may have happened a few times, but I don't begrudge him it. When he snapped out of it and saw what he had done, you couldn't get a word in for all his apologizing."

Roy asked a question.

"He knew the doctor would be too expensive. So I went behind his back and made a whole set of new dresses for the doctor's daughters. In exchange, he gave Roy a 'free' consultation. But even then, the medication they prescribed was too expensive. Your father took less and less of the dose until he ran out, and never got a new bottle."

Roy asked a question.

"Since he was a kid, I figure. Again, he never really told me."

Roy waited a while, then asked a question.

"I have no idea. His own father died when he was young, too. I never heard about him."

Roy asked a question.

"Same as your father."

Roy asked a question.

"Suicide."

Roy asked a question.

"Let's not be morbid. Let it stand at 'suicide.'"

Roy asked a question.

"The church wouldn't take him. So I buried him myself, behind the barn. Near where we put Dolly. You were too little to remember."

Roy asked a question.

"Why? Because I loved him. I still love him, Roy. I want you to understand that. He was sick, yes, and by the end, he didn't belong on this earth any more. But he was not a bad man. No. Even at the end, he was never a bad man."

Roy asked a question.

"It seems so. I worried about that. The doctor said it could be passed on. But I never noticed anything in you that would make me suspect it. You had your nightmares, yes, but hell, so did I. Well, I did see that you kept putting out a saucer of milk for Dolly after she died."

Roy asked a question.

"Yes, honey. I emptied them before you woke up. I didn't want it to spoil."

Roy asked a question.

"Well, I didn't want to spoil that, either. If you wanted to have an imaginary friend, that was fine by me. I wasn't gonna tell you that you were crazy. It made you happy. And it didn't cost me anything. Just a saucer full of milk every day."

Roy waited.

"I'm sorry to lay all this on you. You come from good stock, Roy. I see your father in you, and I see myself, too. Don't think you're some kind of mistake, or that there's something wrong with you. Be proud of who you are. Trust me when I say that every bad thing we gave you is balanced out by a hundred good things. Your father loved you and wanted you to be happy. You're an amazing young man, Roy. And I am proud to be your mother."

Roy started crying.

"I think we've had enough, don't you think? Don't worry about the water, I'm fine until morning. Sweet dreams, my Roy."

As he left she added, "And please, blow out the candle, will you?"

Chapter Five

In the morning Roy's spit came out tinted with dust. He stared at the spot on the back porch where his saliva lay smeared, wondering whether it had landed on a particularly dusty part of the porch and had therefore gained its brown color after it had left his body, not before. But when he dragged it with the sole of his shoe he realized that the color was inherent in the spit itself. His body, therefore, was corruptible, and the dust had found its way inside him.

This was only one of many setbacks that morning. He realized that the prepared food that their neighbors had filled the icebox with was dwindling already; though his mother ate next to nothing and he himself had only a moderate appetite, he did not figure the stock would last for long. And he did not know how to make biscuits. Staring into the stinking pit of the icebox, he thought he should ask his mother for the recipe.

She still seemed tired from the night before. She slept through the morning and only roused at noon. Her breathing seemed to require even more work than before. She was fading. He knew that she was fading. Still, she smiled and thanked him for the plate of mashed potatoes with bits of bacon mixed in, though by the time she was awake to eat it, it had already grown cold.

Gathering water from the pump, he took time to look around the property. He felt like he was seeing each thing for the first time. Every object stood out with the intensity of a photograph, and the sun carved crisp lines between the timbers of the house. Returning, he passed through the barn. It was strange not having the animals around anymore. The trough offered only dust, and the leftover cow patties were petrified. Spiders had made webs between each rafter and then decided the real estate was awful and had abandoned their properties. The only current inhabitants were a family of mud dauber wasps whose impatient buzzing filled his ears. The ladder to the loft was rickety. Even if he had trusted it, he was not prepared to see how the loft itself had changed.

He wondered, as he brought the water inside, whether things had been easier for his mother in the interceding years. The dust had not been as bad during that time, they said. And besides, he had never really contributed much to the farm work himself. His absence must not have been very sorely felt. Through this line of thinking, he absolved himself of his guilt.

He heard a thump down the hall. He rushed over to his mom's room and saw the block of wood on the ground.

"Ma? Are you all right?"

"Yes, dear." Her voice was like a thread of silk. "I just need some help using the pot."

He helped her with the task, noticing as he lifted her how light she was and then how disconcerted her lightness made him feel.

If she gets much lighter, he thought, *my arms will slip right through her.*

Once that was done, he offered Inez her needlepoint but she said she wanted to rest. He offered to read to her but she said she was tired. He got her some fresh water and replaced the wood on the nightstand and brushed off some of the hair that clung to her face. He did not feel like he had been here only a day. He felt like he had been here for a century.

As he opened the front door, he was shocked to see a woman and a man, both of them dressed very smartly, standing at the door. Her fist was raised as if she was about to knock. In her other hand was the letter that Roy had left out on the porch yesterday. They stared at each other for a moment, dumbfounded.

Her face broke out in a smile. "Well hell-o! You must be Roy!" She swept him up in a hug, her perfume choking him. Behind her stood the man, clean-shaven, portly, and nondescript; he wore a black suit with white pinstripes and a wide, red tie. The woman pulled out of the hug and held Roy at arm's length, staring into his face with an incredible amount of interest. Suddenly, all her features fell at once, her lips and eyes crashing back into the flawless default of Titian. There was nothing to read on her face. Looking at her was an aesthetic, instead of a literary, experience.

"Why," she said, "you don't remember me, do you?"

Roy tried to speak.

"Well," she said, stepping back and holding out her hand, "I am Lidia McDowell, *née* James." She smiled at the recognition in

Roy's face. "It's a pleasure to see you again!"

"It is a pleasure to see *you* again," he said lamely.

"And this is my husband," she said, turning. "Socrates McDowell. Don't let the name fool you; he's no philosopher!" She laughed and touched Roy's arm. "Now," she said as she stepped into the room, "we just read your note right here, and we are sur*prised* beyond all belief! I have been making my hubby here come help me with your dear, sweet mother for months now, and suddenly you want to take her *away* from us? Why, that won't do. We brought over more food than you could handle today, and we insist—" She yanked a huge burlap bag from her husband's hands. "Simply *insist* that you let us cook it up for you. What do you say to roast chicken with gravy? Fingerling potatoes? Wine? Well," she said as she blew past him into the kitchen, "we've got it all here, don't you worry, just sit tight, and we will have it ready in a jiffy."

Roy rocked in her wake and tried to remember what he had intended to do outside in the first place. Her husband took a step closer to him, also looking in the direction of the kitchen, from which sounds of slamming and metal dragging against metal were already emanating.

"You better not interrupt her in the kitchen," said Socrates. "You stand to lose a finger."

Lidia rushed out of the room. "Where are my manners?" She was headed to Inez's room when Roy grabbed her by the arm.

"Wait," he said. "She's resting."

Her mouth made a perfect little circle, and she said, "Oooh, so sorry, so sorry. I guess I'll just wait in here." She returned to the kitchen.

Socrates looked around the room without moving his lower half. Another man would have felt self-conscious at the house that, despite his best efforts, had clung to dust as if to dear life. But instead, Roy experienced an intense sense of protectiveness. A dirty sort of pride. The only thing wrong with this house was *them*.

Finding Socrates insipid, Roy turned and went into the kitchen, feeling the urge to stomp on something. Lidia bent over the cutting board and cleaved a roast chicken in half with a bang that traveled through the floorboards. Roy had to yell her name to get her attention.

She turned. "What?"

"I said, she's not hungry now. She just ate."

"Oh," she said, taking a step from the table. "Well," she said as she returned toward it, "the three of us still have stomachs, don't we?" She took up the cleaver.

The ball of Roy's foot pressed down in his shoe. "Actually, I'm not very hungry, either."

She turned to him with abject shock in her face. "Oh," she said. "I see." She set down the knife and stared at if for a moment as if it were the casket at her newborn's funeral. Instantly, she perked up again. "Well, I really should be spending my time catching up with you, anyway! Why, I haven't seen you in years! How old *were* you?" She passed her husband and stopped in front of the couch, not prepared to sit in the dust but also not wanting to offend. Roy realized he had forgotten to set up Betty on the couch as he had intended.

Roy wanted to force Lidia to stand, but there was something so frantic about her that he felt that, if he pushed her too hard in one direction, her body would fall to a hundred pieces on the ground. So he instead handed her a clean blanket. "Here," he said. "The couch is too dirty for your clothes."

She gladly spread it on the couch and sat, crossing her legs and pulling on her top knee with her crossed fingers. For all her grating enthusiasm Roy could not help but admire the fashionable cut of her skirt. He decided Mr. McDowell must be rich.

"So," she said as Roy sat down, "where have you *been*? I haven't seen hide nor hair of you since 1935!"

He would have relished the opportunity to correct her estimation of the year, but he had to accept that her figure was right. "Yes," he said, "precisely."

"And what have you been up to this whole time?"

"I went to Chicago, actually."

"Chicago!" She turned to her husband. "It's a shame your *uncle* is dead!" Turning back to Roy, she added, "Socrates's uncle used to own the most *amazing* restaurant in the north side. But it's all gone to seed recently. Lost all its spirit. What were you doing in Chicago?"

The question was leveled so suddenly that Roy had no recourse. He now understood why compulsive hoarders tended to rig their houses with booby traps.

"Oh, well," started Roy, aware that Mr. McDowell sat motionless with his eyes stuck on him. The air seemed very hot and very thick. "I mainly waited tables. I had some friends who were actors. I also was a store clerk."

None of his three attempts seemed to land on particularly receptive ears. Lidia looked at him with an empty, smiling face which bobbed slightly. After a moment she said. "Wow! Actors!" She turned to her husband. "Socrates and I just saw *Macbeth* in Lincoln—" She stopped and gasped. "Oh gosh, am I not supposed to say that here?"

"What?"

"You know... 'The Scottish Play.'"

"Oh...no," said Roy, laughing, "I think it's okay to say here."

"Okay, good. Well, anyway, Socrates and I saw it, and we thought it was just a*maz*ing. All the things with the prophecies and whatnot...it's really extraordinary. That man knew how to write a play!" She turned back to Roy and crossed her legs the other way. The crossing of her legs, he noticed, had a repulsive effect on him. Seeing her thigh hitched up and draped over her other thigh made him never want to cross his legs again—and in fact made him unconsciously spread his legs a little further apart. "Well we are just so *glad* you're back, we just missed you awful. Why'd you come back?"

"I heard Mom was ill. By the way," he said, addressing both husband and wife, "I wanted to thank you for all you've done. You really did us a huge service. If there's any way I can repay you..."

"Oh, no, *no*, our families have known each other for *ages*; we don't expect anything in return." She reached out and laid her hand on her husband's. "Your mother is such a pleasure to be around, *we* should be thanking *you*, honestly." She smiled at him. Now he became aware that the negativity he felt toward her was not only undeserved but also nonsensical. Why did he feel such cruelty? She had given so much to his mother. She had succeeded where he had failed. And she was asking nothing in return. The imp that sat on his heart was humiliated for its bitterness. Still, it refused to move.

Roy asked, "What have you been up to? How's the family?"

"We're all just great, thank you for asking! Oh..." she said, turning again to her husband. "I guess I should tell you that...my mother actually...passed away. A few years ago."

Roy remembered from his youth that there had been something wrong with Mrs. James, but he did not remember what. She had been dying then, and he could not help but assume that she had been dying ever since.

Still he said, "I'm so sorry to hear that. Are you doing okay?"

She nodded. "It was hard on all of us. But she suffered for a long time. We know she's in a better place now."

He let a second stand in her memory. Then ventured, "Yeah, disease can be rough."

She nodded and asked, tentatively, "Now your father...was he taken by disease?"

Roy decided, as punishment for her insensitive question, he would pummel her with a brusque response.

"No. He killed himself." And then he added a word that, while maybe inaccurate, at least carried the harsh clout of too much information. "Schizophrenia." Then he asked, "And your father?"

She breathed deeply, then said, "I'm so sorry to hear that, Roy. Dad's doing well. Jacob helps him with his jobs now. Jacob is becoming quite the incredible mechanic. He has his little gal, Peggy, and they are just the cutest thing."

Roy swallowed as his memory split the James's sons into two. The name came to him only after a moment. "And Adrian?"

"Oh, he's great—funny you should bring him up actually, because he is coming to town next month for my birthday!"

Roy's eyebrows rose. "Your birthday? Congratulations!"

"Thank you! He's over in Des Moines now practicing veterinary medicine."

"Is he married?"

"Not yet!" she said with trumped-up disapproval. "I have tried setting him up with some of my friends in Iowa, but he says they're all too *silly* for him. Oh, but he has plenty of time. We're not worried for him. I just lucked out finding such an amazing man so young!" She turned to the blank face of Mr. McDowell, and Roy thought, *Well, he's probably very nice to her.* She continued, "But yes, he will be here soon, and I'm sure he would love to see you!"

Roy wondered how to respond to this. He had spent so many hours of his life imagining that it was Adrian, instead of some anonymous businessman, who clambered on top of him at night. He had spent so many hours returning to that moment in the loft that it was hard to believe it had actually happened.

"Yes," Roy said, suddenly very nervous, "I would love to see him, too!"

What would he think of me now? Roy wondered.

No one had spoken for a long moment. Lidia looked at her husband again. A quiet cough drifted from the other room.

"Well," Lidia said briskly, "great! He will be coming down here by the twentieth. We'll stop by sometime with a nice cake for you two." She stood. "Well, I guess we better be moving on. You sure you don't need any help around here?" Before Roy could speak, she added, "Well, of course we will be coming by with food every once in a while. Lord knows I cook so much we don't know what to do with half of it!" She hugged Roy at the door. "We are so happy to see you again. Tell your mother we said hi. Don't be a stranger now!"

They left as suddenly as they had arrived. Their car sped away, leaving a dust trail in its wake. Inside, the slabs of poultry lay on the counter, with bowls of corn, beans, and potato on the side. The clock struck four. As Roy went to check on his mother, he realized he never asked Lidia about herself. He thought, *Didn't she used to be a carpenter?*

Chapter Six

His mother coughed weakly when he entered. As he sat himself on the chair next to her bed, she raised her eyebrows and then opened her eyes.

"Is she gone?"

Roy smiled. "Yes, she is."

She raised her head. "It's about time."

"Ma!"

"What?" she challenged. "She wears me out."

The little imp hopped off his heart and vanished. He no longer felt ashamed about his brazenness toward Lidia, now that he knew his mom felt the same. He savored this feeling and said, "What is *up* with her husband?"

She shrugged. "I thought he was deaf and dumb the first time I met him. But he just loves to hear her speak. Well, that makes one of us. But I think he earned a fortune making rubber in Missoula."

She looked at him. She squinted and then rubbed her eyes.

"What is it?" he asked. "Can you see me okay?"

She paused. "Yes," she said finally.

"You were saying about Socrates?"

Her sigh came out softer than a flower petal. She leaned her head back. "Yes, he made it rich over there and met her at some church function in Lincoln. Fell in love immediately."

"Didn't she used to be a carpenter?"

"Maybe... I don't remember. But Socrates is a man of traditional values. Did you notice her makeup?"

"Yes, I did." In fact, Roy had recognized the exact shade of Max Factor lipstick she used.

"All his idea. Remember when she got that nail stuck through her hand when she helped me take down the springhouse? Oh, well, I guess you weren't there for that. But since she got married, I haven't seen her without her nails manicured like she could slice an apple with them."

Roy did not respond. She was not usually this talkative, even before she was sick. "Ma" he said, "are you feeling all right?"

"Right as rain, dear, right as rain. Now what kind of woman marries some man from Missoula and lets him force her into stockings and skirts and fancy hats? Why, when she was sixteen, she could build a shed in an afternoon. And I don't think anything is worth giving that up. Not love or money or fame. Why, she—"

Her eyes froze on a point over Roy's shoulder. He followed her eyes to the corner where the pile of cloth sat. "Ma?" he asked. "Are you okay?"

Her mouth opened. Her eyes opened. Her hands curled up into balls. The only sound was of her nails scratching the quilted fabric. After a moment, she whispered, "The Bible."

"The Bible? You want me to get the Bible?" Roy stood in the line of her gaze. "The Bible, Ma?"

She did not move or reply. He looked around the room and saw nothing.

"The Bible," he said and ran out.

There was only one shelf in the main room, and it held, beside the Bible, a row of mail-order primers that contained the confused and often manic handwriting of Roy's youth. The Bible itself was bound in leather that broke off in flakes. At the bottom left corner, the binding had separated from the text block, revealing the glue-stained mesh underneath. It was the first Bible he had touched in years. As he passed the kitchen, Roy realized he needed to cover the chicken before it got dusty. He pushed the thought away. *Not now, not now.*

Her gaze was still fixed on the corner, paler than he had ever seen her before, eyes wide as turnips. The light in the room was muted. He felt they were in a cave lit by a candle. Roy did not know whether to stand or to sit. He decided to kneel by the bed and open the Bible on the quilt beside her.

"Ma? What part?" She did not respond. "Do you care what part?" He flipped through the pages. The book fell open halfway. There, lodged between the pages, stuck out a thrice-folded slip of cream-colored paper, clean and rectangular and smooth. He looked at his mom and plucked out the paper. "This?" he asked. He peeled it open. The creases were stained with age, but did not tear. The page had a few lines written in all caps in a scrabbled hand with no regard for the neatness of rule or the maintenance of margins. The letterhead read: "Tanya Hotel, Sioux City, Iowa," and the date read 1919. It was not until he read the signature did he understand.

Read it.

"'Dear Inez,'" he started, peeking up at his mother and her fixed rapture. "'Dear Inez. You know I have never done this before, but I wanted to let you know somehow, in writing, that you mean the world to me, and I am so happy to have you as my own. You are as pretty as the day is long, and you're smart as a fox and strong as an ox, and I love you.'" Roy looked over his shoulder. The corner was still empty. He looked back at the paper and snapped his head back to the corner immediately. Didn't it look darker over there, all of a sudden? He turned back to read, sensing his mother compelling him to continue. "'There's a lot we don't have, but we do have a lot still. You can do anything, and I can do anything. I even liked it when you embarrassed me in front of the whole town, and I would do it all again. For you.'" His mother let out a long breath. Roy's voice caught in his throat. The room was colder, and his mother's hands clung to the sheets with an iron grip. "'I promise to provide for you for now and forever. I hope you like the flowers. I love you. I love you. I love you, and I love you again. Sincerely, and with love, Roy.'"

He could not drop the paper. He could barely look up. His eye was stuck in the hole of the "o" in "Roy." He shivered and knew what he would see when he looked up. He knew what he would see if he looked backward. He was between Scylla and Charybdis. As long as he kept his eye on the "o," nothing could happen. His mother would still be alive and the dark man would keep his distance. He wanted to keep his head down until the day he died.

But he had no choice. The scales tipped, and his head rose. His mother's head had fallen backward, and her eyes were clouded over. Silence banged in his ears, and the flutter of the paper as it landed on the ground was loud enough to topple the walls of a cathedral. He could not decide if he needed to inhale or exhale. So for a long while, he did neither.

And suddenly he was alone in the room.

Chapter Seven

Soon the clock struck the half hour. He lifted his face, marveling at the crescents of moisture that sunk into the sheets and showed where his eyes had been, where his mouth was. He paid his final respects to his mother and closed her eyes. He closed the door behind him.

The dishes were dirty. He should change his shirt. He would have to get a shovel. His bandana was too tight. *I wonder where that raccoon skull went.*

Like solar flares, his thoughts leaped outward, consuming some unlucky planet before being forced by the sheer magnitude of gravity back toward the heart of the sun. She was dead. The monolith, the point around which all others must rotate. A horrible hub. An awful axis. He smiled.

Not heeding the dust, Roy landed on the couch. *I forgot to place Betty here.* But to go back into the room now would mean... His breath caught in his chest.

This was the time of day when the house was coolest—the interior shaded during the time that the sun was at its zenith.

Do souls travel fast, he wondered, *or slow? Do they rush, or float?*

He felt like there was nothing above him anymore. He floated into the air of the main room. His head landed on the ceiling. It curled his shoulders and back as he rose.

She is dead.

The clock struck noon. No, the clock struck midnight. And the wet pantomime of his crying face was printed on the fabric of the couch.

Remember when she. No. I shouldn't.

Create a space where she is not. A new planet. In this other Earth, the only difference will be that she is no longer alive. And then put yourself in it.

The clock struck four a.m.

I am moving too fast, he decided. *Slow the orbit. Take deep breaths, and let it all out.*

"All right! Enough!" he shouted when the clock struck six.

She was far away, in the next room. *She is too close.*

The golden watch of her father. It is mine now.

He wept until his throat throbbed—until he retched. He rolled around on the floor and slammed his feet on the ground. Four whole years. And the clock struck seven.

In his room, he marveled at how thick the light came in, as if it were slanted honey or a huge, yellow book leaning on the wall. Or a massive slice of yellow cake. The luggage in his room, then, could be giant squares from a chocolate bar, and the blanket set out in the corner could be a tea napkin. It was not a healthy snack, but he was feeling peckish.

I am so glad I did not wear mascara today.

Cold water felt good on his wrists and face. The other thing that felt good was to cut slowly through the chicken that that girl brought over earlier. Yesterday, he realized. Had he remembered to season the meat? Or was that just dust?

He ate some potato. The first mouthful fell to the floor, and he had to pick it up and fling it out the window.

He did not reach the couch.

He toppled forward on the ground in the main room and cried. It did not feel as bad when he brought his knees to his chest. He looked around the room. He was alone. The clock struck noon.

The books on the shelf looked better arranged by height. Then they looked even better arranged alphabetically. Then by color. Finally he tried to replace them in their original order but could not decide if this was better than the alphabetical arrangement or the color-coded one. He determined that he was currently unfit to make such a serious decision.

It was nicer on the porch. He drank some water. He was not in Nebraska, nor was he in Chicago or New York or even Paris. He was lying at the bottom of the ocean under an arctic glacier, staring up through a mile of ice at the pinprick of the sun overhead.

He stood in the hall looking at the door at the end of it. The clock struck four. The clock struck five.

Cool water refreshed his feet and his face. She was still dead, though.

The thought was like an indestructible bee trapped in a metal ball suspended over an open fire. She was dead; and then, she was dead.

Next he cleaned the dust from the chicken and cooked some for himself. He ate it with cold potatoes. He washed his dish and put it back in the cupboard delicately.

The clock struck seven. Something had to be done with the body. The moon must have come and gone during the day because it was not behind the barn nor was it behind the house, and it was not cloudy either. *The moon is just like me,* he thought. *Neither of us are behind the barn—nor are we behind the house.*

He could not retrieve his bed because it was still in her room. He brushed most of the dust off the couch and spread out the blanket and stretched out on that. He awoke to the clock striking ten a.m. He had slept for fifteen hours.

Like how the sun is never "out" but just "out from hiding." The thought came back before his eyes were even open. But his head felt better now. He felt he could handle it. He breathed and tried to think it through. He was no longer crying. *My name is Roy Manger. I am nineteen years old. My mother Inez just passed away. I am going to bury her today.*

He changed clothes first. And drank some water.

Her body was light, wrapped up in the sheet. If he imagined she was sleeping he wouldn't cry. He laid it on the couch.

The day was already warm, said the clock as it struck twelve and then one. He cleaned the house and waited. He turned every page of *And Then There Were None* without reading a word.

Now, said the clock. Seven. The planets were aligned

Though he didn't know where his father had been buried, he did know that behind the barn the ground had always seemed uneven. So that's where he buried her, hopefully close to Dolly, too. He prayed over her and left a tear in the soil as well as the liquid of a blister that the spade created and then popped.

He washed his whole body after he finished. He dragged his bed back into his childhood room. He lay in it and waited for night to come. Shadows crept in through the window and spread from under his bedframe. These shadows met on the floor as the clock struck ten. He could open or close his eyes as he pleased now. The darkness no longer held any terror.

Lying in the dark he felt like he was lying on time itself. It was possible, he felt, to return to a moment where she was still living, if he could only fall backward through the bed, through the floorboards, and into the earth. But the hours pushed up underneath him. They would not yield. He cried quietly, wishing he were six feet deeper, wishing he were forty hours earlier. But the material beneath him was harder than rock, and there was no going back. He cried harder as he realized that, despite his greatest efforts, he was rising still, imperceptibly, like how a mountain range rises, or a plant dissolves. There was nothing he could do. He rolled over on his side and pulled his knees up to his chest. The clock struck midnight, but he was asleep.

Chapter Eight

Several days passed with Roy living this new and smooth life. There were no longer any other people to worry about. His mother's grave was shaded by the barn every hour of the day, and the memory of Woodrow grew dim and pacific. He tasted things for the first time. Each bean provided a new dimension of flavor— a new context for what he thought of as "bean." He read *And Then There Were None* two times in a row and even went back to read the Bible passages he remembered. There was little to do in the fields; even if the corn had survived, it was still too dusty to work for more than a few hours at a time. He remembered enough about needlepoint to practice it before the sun set. He even finished the knitting project his mother had started. He no longer had any need for candles. He rose when the sun rose and he lay to rest when it set. For nearly two weeks he was the only person on earth.

In this time he began watching insects in their various enterprises. The spider in the closet sat patiently and inspired Roy to sit patiently too. The fly did not mind buzzing around the same window all day, and so Roy did not grow restless completing his tasks around the house. The beetle went for days without eating and, in the process, molted its old exterior. So too did Roy begin to ration the leftover food, feeling the spiritual expansion that came hand-in-hand with the mortification of the flesh. It was a rigid discipline. When he lay in his bed at night, he imagined being at the center of a web. He was peaceful.

The "I" became all-encompassing. No longer did he worry about what to wear. He wore skirts because they breathed easier and men's shirts because they were less tight. Washing his face one morning, he forgot what his own name was.

When darkness came, he cried. And in the morning he bathed in cold water. He stretched his muscles until they were long and supple. He would lie in bed after lunch and wonder where the Earth was in relation to the moon. He grew smooth like a river-stone. His movements were graceful and, without a mirror in the house, he felt for the first time like he was actually alive. He drank water by the gallon.

He woke up one day to find the spider in the closet had deserted his web. That same afternoon, there was a knock at the door. He hid in his room. He could see the car was that of the McDowells. He was glad he had remembered to lock the door. *They do not know*, he realized. *They are still living in the world where my mother is alive.* They left a basket of food on the porch wrapped in old newspapers and drove away.

They had even made a cake. Roy brought it to bed with him, where he ate half of it with his bare hands. He licked his fingers and lay on his back and realized the universe would always bring him exactly what he needed.

The red bandana served as a mouth-guard for when he rid the house of dust. Every room yielded soft handfuls of rust-colored powder, in which the occasional piece of straw or beetle would hide. These piles met each other in the main room and were ungraciously ejected from the house with a few shoves of the broom. Roy laughed while he did this. Then the rugs needed beating. Then all the upholstery. No nook was left uninspected, no closet shelf unpunished.

He decided all the furniture needed to be aired out. He dragged chairs and stools onto the front yard, where they convened with each other in groups they were unused to. He ate lunch at a table from the main room, with his legs up on a stool from the kitchen, sitting on a chair that he was certain had never left the foyer. *What an unusual wedding*, he thought. When he brought the furniture back inside, the wood was warm. They were revitalized.

He resealed the windows with newspaper and found an old can of paint in the shed. He found a length of rope and bound the porch post that had slipped so it stood upright once more, and whitewashed the whole front of the house. After another week he noticed he no longer cried before he slept. He was dreaming from the moment he laid down his head until the moment the sun rose—sometimes about Woodrow, but mostly about rivers.

He prayed in his mother's room and took walks around the property by moonlight. Not even Dolly bothered him. He drank hot tea in the morning and taught himself to whittle. There was only ever one thing in his head at a time.

The huge dust snake approached him on the road one day while he was polishing the doorknobs. He put the rags away and changed into pants. Whether Lidia or Adrian, he was ready.

The car was a familiar one. It was the same model that Woodrow owned. It even had the same license plates. His mind had to jump from one track to another as he recognized the man who stepped out of the car as not white, but Black; not stocky, but slim; not Adrian, but Woodrow. Woodrow stared at Roy and took off his hat, his face blank. Skin like ceramic with its lacquer of sweat. They stared at each other, Roy feeling secure and lofty leaning against the porch pillar, chewing on a piece of straw.

"Well, look what the cat dragged in," said Roy. They were the first words he had spoken in weeks.

Chapter Nine

Woodrow, unlike Lidia, was a welcome guest in Roy's new home. He said absolutely nothing as he entered the house, except to accept some water. The way he sat on the edge of the couch reminded Roy of the married men who were visiting the Pineapple for the first time, scared that someone would recognize them as their neighbor, their mailman, or their pastry chef. Roy handed him his water. Woodrow thanked him and turned to look at Betty, who occupied the far corner of the couch.

"That's Betty," said Roy. "I believe you've been acquainted."

Woodrow reached out and grabbed Betty's hand, his thumb filling out her tiny palm. "*Enchanté*," he said.

Roy was not afraid to laugh. Nor was he afraid to stand up and offer Woodrow a piece of cake. "It's vanilla," Roy said. "Your favorite." Woodrow declined but Roy brought two slices anyway, the marks of his fingers still clearly visible along one side.

Woodrow ate the cake, and Roy smiled, drawing his legs up into the armchair with him. Woodrow looked down the hall, then at Roy.

"Is she..."

Roy had forgotten how beautiful his voice was. Or maybe it

was just the beauty of any other human voice. He nodded in response.

"I'm so sorry." He set down his plate.

"Thank you, Woodrow."

Woodrow sat upright, his butt occupying no more than three inches of the cushion. "I wanted to apologize."

Roy felt like gold coins were raining on him.

Woodrow continued. "I'm sorry if what I said or how I acted made you feel bad."

The coins suddenly became little flecks of manure. Roy smiled like a lioness and waited a moment. He weighed his options, wondering what he stood to lose. But suddenly the furniture itself, empowered by their stint in the sun, seemed to compel him to push onward with the moral impulse. After a moment he said, "That's not how you apologize, Woodrow."

His eyes leveled at Roy's.

"What do you mean, that's not how you apologize?"

"If you want to apologize," said Roy in what he hoped was an instructive tone, "you don't say you're sorry for the way it made the other person feel." Woodrow leaned forward, bracing his elbows on his knees. "Saying it like that leaves all the blame on the other person. Instead, try apologizing for what you *did*. Say, 'I'm sorry for what I did, *and* the way it made you feel.'"

Roy could read Woodrow's face like a book. His expression was that of prose right before major action, when the sentences grow thin and pale. Suddenly he shook his head and looked down, dragging his hands from his knees to his thighs, preparing, apparently, to stand. But he froze while looking downward. He breathed in.

The words came out of him slowly. "I am sorry for what I did."

Roy gave him a smile of encouragement. He told himself, *If he leaves, I will still be content.* He asked, "Why?"

Woodrow looked at him. "Because," he said softly, as if someone might overhear. "Because I mocked you. And I left you here alone."

"I accept your apology." Now he let a wider smile reach his lips. "I'm glad you're here now." The mug clunked as he set it on the table and stood. Woodrow also got to his feet. Whether because Woodrow had grown in the three weeks since he last saw him, or because being alone gave Roy the sensation of being bigger, he was surprised and disappointed to find that his eyes only reached Woodrow's chin. "Thank you," he said, "and I am sorry, too. For the things I said. I had no right to call you out like that."

"It's all good. Apology accepted."

Roy gathered the dishes and brought them to the kitchen. Woodrow followed.

"So," said Roy, drying the plates, "what brings you back here?"

Woodrow leaned over the counter. Roy was a little concerned with the fact that he did not look at Roy when he spoke.

"Well," he said, "I got as far as Las Vegas, if you can believe it."

Roy's eyes widened in surprise. "Las Vegas! Wow. I thought

you were headed back to Chicago?"

"Realized it was too risky there. Decided to try the other direction."

"Why didn't you stay in Vegas?"

Woodrow shrugged. "It wasn't really what I wanted. It was too...bright."

"Well, you're pretty bright, too." Roy knew this comment made no sense. He was painfully aware that something strange was happening—that the plug was trying to fit into the wrong outlet. Was it possible, he wondered, to fit Woodrow into this new life of his? He hated to think that monuments of his solitude had to topple just for the sake of an old friendship. But, at the same time, to push him away may have proved too painful to bear. So Roy just put the dishes in the cabinet and pressed on. "What brought you back here?"

"Well, same reasons as before. Pretty secluded space. Plus, you're here, which makes it easier to hide out." He traced his finger in a mound of spilled salt.

"Woodrow," said Roy, putting on his best disapproving-parent voice, "are you in some kinda trouble with the law?"

Woodrow straightened out. "No, ma'am, I've never broken a law in my whole life."

Roy threw the dish rag over his shoulder. "Well, that's just because they haven't outlawed ugly yet."

"Ha!" Woodrow barked. "Since when did you get so uppity?"

Roy shrugged. "Since God decided to grace me with wit as well as beauty." After a minute he asked Woodrow what he needed here.

"Well, I don't think I can be out and about for a while," he said. "I had a scare down in Vegas. And I would be willing to help around the house. I can cook and clean and all. I would earn my keep."

"You are welcome here for as long as you need," said Roy, thinking, *I am so magnanimous.* Instead of being trapped in Woodrow's car with him behind the wheel, now Roy had all the power. It was a responsibility of alarming intensity. Suddenly he wished it were not up to him. The house groaned outward all of a sudden, and certain prospects made themselves evident. He would have to pay taxes. He would have to learn how to farm. He would have to learn how to survive or else die.

Woodrow thanked him.

And now, Roy thought, *I have this other person here, someone with even less experience than me, someone only familiar with southern soil, who doesn't even know where to find the hardware store.* Roy felt the concrete set around his feet—and he teetered on the bridge over the river.

They passed the rest of the day in calm silence. Whenever Woodrow entered the same room as Roy, Roy found a quiet excuse to leave it. As Roy passed the pile of Woodrow's luggage that stood by the front door, he wished he could shove them all in a closet, somewhere out of sight. Even the crumbs that Woodrow left from eating his slice of cake had a massive impact on Roy's inner peace.

Not until the crumbs were carefully plucked from the floorboards was Woodrow allowed to even sit on the couch again. Roy hated that he was occupying this position but balked at change. *What does Woodrow expect?* he asked himself. *I will not go back to being my old self just because he is here.*

The silver lining was that Woodrow had brought a veritable library with him, and Roy dug into books he had never even heard of before. They sat in the living room together, both rigid and silent as watchtowers. When it grew too dark to read, he sent Woodrow to sleep in his old bed, while he slept on his mother's bare mattress. The world was no longer in balance. The night was too chilly, and Roy began to begrudge Woodrow. *Why should I have to pay for his mistakes? Haven't I suffered enough already?* Not to mention the fact that Woodrow really wasn't as charming as Roy once thought, nor was he especially funny. And the fact that he returned only out of necessity insulted Roy, who once considered their friendship an end unto itself. *Even if I can stand being around Woodrow all the time, there is still the issue of money. Namely, how to get enough so that we won't die.* There was nothing left to sell here, and the property was worth only the dirt that infected it. They could not rely on Lidia's charity forever. The twelve knolls of the clock seemed to spell out death for the young housemates.

The world which was once a vast and placid sea on which a few boats floated now became crowded. Sailboats scraped each other's sides, barges crushed dinghies underfoot, the water grew rancid and gray. Suddenly Roy looked over a limitless, shifting field of riggings and sails, twisted up in each other and groaning with the million points of tension and abrasion. *This is no way to live*, he decided.

Roy lay on his back, listening to a dust storm move in and swallow the house. He thought, *I do not have the space to be myself while Woodrow is here. One of us is bound to be crowded out until he starves. One of us must be the runt. We cannot both make it a habit to take what we want.* He heard Woodrow walking around in the other room. It felt like someone with dirty shoes had decided to step into his open wound. His skin suddenly felt very itchy.

Right before he was about to fall asleep to the sound of the sand buffeting the windows, he remembered that his mother had died in this bed. He wondered what that must have been like. Then, seemingly in response to his own question, he fell asleep.

BOOK SIX

Chapter One

Roy relished the moment of peace just after waking before the worries from the previous day settled on him. Once more he heard wood groaning against wood, and a terrible metal weight settled on his chest. He heard Woodrow in the kitchen. If he never arose from bed, then he would never have to deal with him. But there was a chilly draft in his mother's room, and hunger began to nip at his innards.

He nearly stepped into the tray of breakfast set outside the door. A pancake, some bacon, and a scrambled egg. Roy lifted the tray and brought it into the kitchen.

Woodrow was bent over the stove. He turned around. He wore Inez's apron and had a wooden spatula in his hand. This was the pantomime that the intruder performed to compensate for his intrusion.

"Hey, Ma," said Roy.

"Good morning, son."

"I think I'm too sick to go to school today."

"That's very grim news, son. Looks to me like you've come down with a bad case of ugly."

Roy threw a napkin at the back of Woodrow's head. Woodrow

laughed and arranged his own plate. They ate on either side of the kitchen table, passing the salt back and forth to cover up the taste of the eggs, which had started to turn.

"So, Ma," said Roy, "what do you have planned for today?"

"You know, the usual things. Galas to attend, world leaders to meet. I may buy some fresh eggs. Oh, and dinner at the Ritz."

Roy mustered a weak smile. He understood, now, what it was that disturbed him so much about Woodrow's gaze. While he rested his elbows on the table and held his interlaced hands over his mouth, his eyes betrayed—not judgment exactly—but a sense of distance, like there was a glass pane between himself and Roy. *This is an interrogation,* he thought. *He is trying to read me.*

"Woodrow?" he said.

"Yes?"

"I want you to know that I am really happy you're here." This was one of the first times Roy had ever said something where he himself did not know whether it was true or false. "I mean it," he continued. "I loved getting to know you. It really hurt when you left." That part was true, at least. Woodrow swallowed. "But I had a lot of time to think about it while I was here."

"And?" asked Woodrow, after a pause.

"And, well, having Mom pass away... Well, it changed how I thought about things." He was surprised at this new flavor of words. It was an unexpected feeling, having his thinking slowed down to the rate of speaking. He was creating and revealing in the same moment. He continued, "Looking at the things that mattered to her, ultimately...they weren't the things she owned, or her body, or her pride." Roy looked down at the plates: Woodrow's licked clean and his own still littered with scraps. He pushed it toward Woodrow, who immediately ate up the bits until the plate was as clean as his own. "She really just wanted to remember her relationships. That's all she wanted, at the end." Something blue and huge quivered in Roy's chest. "There was no blame there. There was no room for anything but...the good stuff." He was crying now. He could not look Woodrow in the eye.

One of his hands lay on the table like that of a mannequin while the other covered up his eyes. What had he been trying to tell Woodrow a moment before? It was easier to cry than he expected. He appreciated Woodrow's silence. This way, he could tell he was listening. Still, despite the emotion, he felt an edge of self-reprobation. *Why am I trying to sell my grief to this stranger? Am I still trying to prove something?*

He felt something in his hand. He had to wipe his tears and look at it to understand what was happening. The incomparable smoothness, the warmth, the shapeliness, and solidity of Woodrow's hand could only be confirmed by sight. His fingers brushed against the back of Roy's hand as if they, together, over this table, had invented the sense of touch.

Roy pulled his hand out from under Woodrow's. Woodrow's own flopped palm up. Roy slipped his hand into this warm couch, and working separately but under the same impulse, they both curled their fingers so they would interlock, turning the gesture of condolence into one of alliance.

Finally Roy felt ready to look into Woodrow's face. The eyes and the smile were open, accepting. It made Roy's face break into its own smile and, through some golden alchemy, turned his tears of grief into tears of gratitude. Roy thought, *This must mean that I no longer love myself as much, since I am taking such joy from the approval and touch of another person. This must mean I hate myself again.* But, he reasoned, the bay, in which boats were crushing and groaning against each other, did not need to be so small in the first place. He didn't need to remove boats in order to clear up space. *Erase the land on the horizon and scoop out another depth of sea. Let the boats spread out. Let there be room for both him as well as me.*

"So what I'm trying to say," Roy continued, "is that you are welcome to stay here for as long as you want." He wiped the last tears from his eyes and stared into Woodrow's. Their other hands met on the tabletop and completed the circuit. Roy's smile lit up.

"Thanks," said Woodrow. "I missed you, too. But I don't think I can take you seriously."

"Why?"

"Because you have...the most enormous glob of snot hanging out of your nose right now." Roy broke their hands' connections and covered his face. He screamed and Woodrow laughed. He rushed for a dishtowel to blow his nose while Woodrow curled up over the tabletop, laughing until a vein stood out in his forehead. Roy, cleaned up, beat Woodrow with the dishtowel and called him a brute. He relished the sound that the fabric made against his body. Roy had to stop after a minute so that his lungs could catch up to his laughing.

Chapter Two

The next day, Roy slept in. When he finally arose there were bags of groceries in the kitchen. Not just bacon, flour, sugar, and eggs, but luxury goods as well: whipping cream, coffee, tea, pickles, almonds, and sour cream.

"Woodrow," he asked the man sitting on the couch reading, "was this you?"

Woodrow frowned, shrugged, and shook his head. "Must have been the grocery fairy."

"A fairy indeed." They ate breakfast in the living room.

Their hours were spent in a variety of physical and intellectual labors. They made repairs around the house, organizing the tools in the shed and re-seasoning the cast iron pans. They had something to improve everywhere except the barn, which they left untouched, condemned. Woodrow undertook a secret metalworking project out back and would brandish a needle-pointed awl at Roy whenever he tried to approach. "After 'awl' I do for you," complained Roy.

Far from impeding on Roy's private time, Roy found the presence of another person gave even the most mundane activities a function. Reading on the couch while Woodrow read in the armchair, or napping in the same bed—both laid flat in Roy's old room, where the sun did not enter during the afternoon—the activities developed their own shape and began to *do* something neither could name, isolate, or control. Free from external pressures, their relationship grew its own limbs. The trails they had blazed in the prison and on the road felt the tread of new explorers, and they found rest within each other.

It was a matter of course that Woodrow's arm would eventually find itself draped over Roy during a nap. Quiet arms found their way around waists as the men hovered over the stove, stirring. The sleeping situation, too, changed. The naps began later and lasted longer until they were sleeping in the same bed all night, drowsy and languid and as pure as dew. They cooked for each other and talked during the day, finding, within a short time, the fine-tuned and restful rhythm experienced by forests centuries old.

To Roy, every development in their relationship seemed to be the further blooming of a flower already bloomed. Each new step of intimacy and affection was welcomed but not anticipated. Woodrow, for his part, seemed to view their interaction in a similar fashion. When Roy attempted to speak to him about his thoughts on the matter, Woodrow nudged him quietly away. He did not want to talk about whether he had had male lovers before, and he did not want to talk about the first moment he considered Roy more than a friend. Roy promised himself to do all he could to not scare off the wild animal, which was, despite its strength, still timid. So he put away the traps and the bait and lay on the forest floor and waited for the birds to alight on his shoulders.

On the eleventh morning of their new domestic arrangement, Woodrow entered the room where Roy was slowly waking. Woodrow had just come from the washbasin and was wrapped in a towel, beads of water clinging to his back where he could not reach to dry. He crept into the room, dropping the towel and looking through the drawers for his clothes.

He did not jump when he heard Roy stirring. Calmly, as if testifying, Woodrow turned to the bed and Roy's eyes. Roy looked him up and down, wondering whether this image was just the residue of some dream. Eventually Roy sat up and pulled his nightgown over his shoulders as a snake would its skin. They stared at each other like this.

After a moment Roy stood—a foot away from Woodrow— sharing the square of intense, yellow sunlight glaring through the window. The air cooled their skin. Woodrow's breath had never sounded louder or more regal.

Something bubbled up in Roy. It was not the hot impulse of his fantasies with Adrian, nor was it the sleepy, greedy languor he was used to feeling when looking at a naked client. It was rosy and thrumming. Their eyes held each other's and the walls of the room moved slowly outward.

They stood facing each other, still as reflections. The figure in front of him could have been carved from wood. The ridges of the collar bones, the slim undulations of the abdomen, the strokes of the thigh muscles in the sunlight... He felt he was no longer looking at Woodrow, but instead at a model of some ideal—some figure in the background of a painting, looking at something beyond the frame. Roy swayed on his feet in the presence of this silence, wondering what Woodrow wanted him to do. Roy went down the list: Woodrow, standing there like an obelisk, did not look like he wanted to be slapped, or held, or kneeled before. There was nothing in his eyes that showed he was waiting for anything. *Where is the conceit?* Roy wondered. *Where is the guile?*

The bubbling sensation fizzled out. For the first time in his life, Roy did not know what a naked man wanted from him. He suddenly felt painfully exact, like a mirror set in front of a statue.

A bird called outside. *If he will not show me what he wants,* thought Roy, *then I will make the first move and figure it out from there.* He needed to discover whether Woodrow was made of flesh after all. So he built up the courage to raise his hand, to set it on the figure in front of him, to discern, by the temperature and the consistency, whether he should thank God for this beauty, or a sculptor. He quickly lifted his hand.

The sound was of one salmon flapping into another. Their hands, which had deflected off of each other in the process of being raised, fell back to their sides. It took them a moment to understand what had happened. Then the faces of the statues cracked, and Woodrow and Roy began to laugh. Their feet broke out of the plaster and they breathed freely, crumpling like leaves. Woodrow mimed the incident, clapping his hands in front of him, limp-wristed like a seal. Roy laughed so hard he fell to the ground. Woodrow, bent over double, leaned his side against the dresser. Roy stood and approached Woodrow and, without thinking, put his arms around his shoulders the same moment that Woodrow wrapped his around Roy's waist. They were still laughing when they kissed.

The kiss was too short. As soon as they parted, Roy wanted more. The second was as warm and as electric as the first and two times as long. After the second kiss, their foreheads met to deliberate: was this second kiss long enough? No, they decided in unison. So the third kiss lasted longer. Slowly Woodrow's hands moved up Roy's back like the shadows of clouds over plains. Roy felt his body turn into a prism, warmed by the ember before him. Birds sung in his chest, and the pressure building around his groin sent sparks up his spine. And the fourth kiss was even longer than the last.

They pulled away and set their foreheads together. When they kissed again, it was different. Roy felt like he was being crushed by Woodrow. Not to be outdone, he squeezed back with all his might.

Roy turned Woodrow around and tossed him onto the bed. Both smiled. Roy jumped onto him, setting his mouth on his, his hips slowly describing a tight, smooth oval in the air. Woodrow groaned. He felt he could almost taste the sound.

Woodrow pushed back, twisting their center of gravity to the tipping point, toppling Roy and setting his weight on top of him. Woodrow's hips pushed against Roy's—slower and stronger—and

Roy groaned, turning his head away. Woodrow set his teeth to the exposed neck, still shoving with his hips, while Roy ran his hands up and down Woodrow's back, legs wrapping around his torso. The bubbles were back. After a moment, Roy began to laugh, and Woodrow, pushing his arms under Roy's torso, began to laugh with him.

Like this they turned on their sides, setting their hands on each other's fronts, the tips of their tongues touching. Roy's heart beat so strong it hurt. As Woodrow's hand swept between Roy's legs, his thighs clenched around it and he pulled Woodrow closer, pleased to feel that, under the drum of Woodrow's chest, a heart just as red and just as electric was beating the same rhythm as his own. They put their heads together and breathed. Walls crumbled. Ponds ran over their dams and swelled into rivers. And, somewhere else, the sun was rising.

For the next hour they rolled and unrolled, clenched, arched, smiled, grew tired; turned, kneeled, and held each other. The details stuck out like pearls sifted from sand: the way the small of Woodrow's back would sweat as Roy twisted under him; the way Woodrow's hand trembled on the back of Roy's head; the way he could feel the ridges of Woodrow's fingerprint against his tongue. Even the taste of Woodrow's ear seemed like the most precious piece of information Roy had ever learned. He opened up his chest and set these jewels inside. They belonged to him now and were to be kept for posterity. For the first time in his life, Roy found himself free of the worry to please the other, as he was used to feeling with his clients, and free too from the shameful pleasure that he derived from his fantasies with Adrian.

As they climaxed, somewhere one of Roy's nerves short-circuited, causing his left eye to produce a tear. A moment later Woodrow collapsed into his arms, totally spent, his heart beating blood that struggled to remember its old purpose. The only thing left was to breathe and to smile. The scales clinked faintly as they found their level. And, wrapped up like that, they slept.

Chapter Three

Roy did not ask where the money was coming from. He looked over the groceries piled on the kitchen table every Sunday like the Feast of Stephen, and he pored over the new books stacked by the front door. He knew these were likely ill-gotten goods. But Woodrow was impenetrable, never so much as hinting as to how he obtained such treasures. One day Roy took advantage of Woodrow's absence and inspected his wallet, finding inside a five dollar bill, ten pennies, and a dime. Some days he would stare at Woodrow while they read, Betty sitting placidly at the end of the couch, Roy's legs stretched out over his lap, watching Woodrow's blameless, brown eyes drift through a line and snap back into place like a typewriter. Woodrow would turn to look at him, and Roy would return to his own book, sometimes kissing Woodrow's hand in an effort to dissimulate. Roy decided that if he was to be an accomplice, he would at least be a silent one.

They spent whole days in bed together. What surprised Roy about his emotions was this: the fulfillment of all his old fantasies did not yield the effect he had expected. Despite Woodrow's eagerness to please, Roy did not feel the total bliss he had expected, nor the fulfillment he had imagined a million times.

Reexamining his childhood fantasies, he called up the images of himself wrapped in Adrian's arms and recognized them for what they were: not examples of total satisfaction, but rather vignettes of death. They were images only. There was no thought, no desire in them, and Roy's perception of himself was that of a lifeless mannequin, a limp doll of a boy. The sensation was not of love but of oblivion. He wanted to be held by arms so strong and a chest so large that he would cease to exist. But he never reached that point of pure blankness—he was never lost to the higher power. Roy would stroke Woodrow's head, thinking about these developments, and feel confident that he preferred the current situation to those he used to dream about. *The oblivion will come eventually anyway*, he thought, twisting a tiny curl of Woodrow's hair in his finger. *I may lean against Woodrow and he may lean against me, but please, God, don't let me fall at his feet.*

So they debated, and they talked, and they read, and they quarreled and cooked and made love. They worked around the property and grew stronger and happier in their isolation. Roy would lie next to Woodrow at night, enjoying how the moonlight brought out the blue undertones in his skin and bemoaning the fact that to kiss that beautiful face all over would also mean rousing him from his slumber. He imagined in his lover's body the stresses of the day being mended by rest, and the million tiny shocks his body had suffered being replenished by the wholesome food. It was strange how little he had appreciated his own body until he saw it mirrored in Woodrow's. With his arm draped over

Woodrow, he was aware, finally, that his body was a miracle. At this point, he usually fell asleep.

They knew they could not live like this forever. They were one of the last families in the neighborhood. The words "desertion" and "abandoned" fluttered through the breeze like shreds of newspaper. No one knew when the dust would settle or whether they would ever be able to plant here again. Over the dining room table by candlelight, they planned. Cities were out of the question so long as Woodrow was on the lam, and most rural areas were either being consumed by dust, being sold out to big corporations, or suffering the old ache of segregation. On top of the domestic woes, the newspapers that Woodrow brought home every week revealed that the situation was growing worse in Europe. It did not seem like things could continue for much longer. Something had to change.

But they could not budge. They flowed down the deepest ravines like water, incapable of making a decision any more than a stream could scale its banks. They lay like lizards on the bed and practiced matching their rates of breath. Woodrow secreted to his metalworking projects, and Roy discovered, through trial and error, how to make biscuits. Though they lived each moment to its surplus, they knew something would have to change soon. They ate dinner at six and spent the evenings on the porch. They wrapped quilts around their legs and kept an eye on the horizon.

Chapter Four

Woodrow called from the kitchen. "Who the *hell* is that?"

Roy sat up from bed and watched the dust cloud approach their house, the tiny point in the front forming into a black car.

"Lit," Roy said, "it's Shidia." He dashed to his dresser and began rummaging around.

"What?" asked Woodrow, poking his head around the corner.

"Lidia. It's shit. No. Shit, it's Lidia."

Woodrow stared at him in confusion. Roy told him to help zip up his dress.

"Is she...one of your clients?"

"No, no," said Roy, scrambling to find the right foundation. "She's just an old family friend who I do not really want to talk to." After a second, he understood Woodrow's confusion. "Oh, and I'm dressing up so that she thinks Roy isn't home."

Woodrow nodded. "How can I help?"

"Just bring me my lipstick. And keep her occupied for as long as you can. Profess ignorance to everything. The only thing you can tell her is that it's only you and Raina here."

"Roger that," said Woodrow, starting down the hall. "Wait, who am I?"

"You can be my porter."

"Porter? Okay. What's my name?"

"Uh... Porter."

"Porter the porter. Got it."

The door opened before Raina could get her mascara on. She heard a man's voice, too low and businesslike to distinguish. She did not detect Lidia's strident words. Why would Socrates come without his wife?

She heard them sit. She telepathically urged Woodrow to offer the guest a drink. He did not.

When Raina had finished her makeup, she shoved her feet into some heels and walked down the hall.

The difference was obvious. It could not be Socrates because Lidia was not with him—and this new man did not show any of the dreary complacency unique to rich men with beautiful wives. The eyes that turned to Raina were icy, the jaw strong, the step jaunty and confident as he approached Raina with his arm outstretched. When he took off his hat, the image fell into place: Adrian James introduced himself and said it was a pleasure to meet her.

Surprise drew out the "A" as Raina greeted him. "Aadrian! Wow!" she exclaimed, turning to Woodrow and back to Adrian. "I'm Raina. I'm a relative of the Mangers. It is a pleasure to meet you! I've heard so much."

"Hopefully only good things," he said, laughing. It sounded like how Raina imagined a shark would laugh. Once the thought was in her mind, Adrian's features drew themselves out into a starker shark shape. *The jaw is a little savage, isn't it? And the high points of the forehead look more cartilaginous than bony.* She could not tell whether his tooth was really chipped or if his general carnivorous impression made her imagine he had fangs. Only his blue eyes disrupted the comparison.

"Only the best!" she said. "Can I get you milk, tea, water, anything?"

"Oh, water'll be fine."

"Sure thing!" As Raina passed Woodrow, his eyes implored her, *Who is he?*

She kept talking from the kitchen. "What a surprise! How long have you been back?"

"Only a few days," he responded. "There's not very much for me to see out here anymore. Now, I assume you are Roy's...?"

"Cousin!" She handed him a mug. "On his mother's side."

"I should hope so!" He laughed.

Raina smiled. Was she missing something? "Please, let's sit. And this," she said, gesturing to Woodrow, "Is Porter, my chauffer."

Adrian nodded. "We've been introduced." Raina noticed his hands were smooth still, spared from farm labor. How old was he now? Twenty-three? Twenty-four? His shoulders were still broad underneath his suit. He asked, "Roy's cousin, wow. Great to meet you. Are you here with your husband?"

Raina was about to say she was married to Woodrow, but she caught herself in time. She did not want Woodrow to get attacked by anybody, but she especially did not want Woodrow to get attacked by Adrian. "No," she said, "I'm trying to finish school in Illinois before I settle down."

"Very noble of you."

"And yourself?" she asked.

"I'm not married. I'm just out of veterinary school, and I'm too busy to bother with women for now."

"Oh, well, you would find that having a woman around makes many things much easier."

"Yes, but they also make many things more complicated," he said with a thin smile.

After a moment, Raina said, "Well! You must be very fond of animals, if you're a vet. Do you keep any at home?" Raina was disturbed to realize how much she sounded like Lidia.

"I'm actually not very fond of pets. Miss...?"

"Moore. Then why did you get involved in veterinary medicine?"

"Well, at one point I thought I would make a much better butcher than a vet, actually."

"A butcher!" Raina said in her best parlor-room voice. "How's that?"

"Well, we don't have to get into specifics. Talk of work is boring."

"No," she insisted, mistaking refusal for shyness, "please explain. I never thought those professions could intersect."

Adrian rubbed his hands together. "Well, my interests don't

lie so much in the lives of the animals themselves, but in the species in its entirety."

She nodded. "Well, that's very..." Her hand described an arc in the air while her mind raced for a word. "Holistic, of you. Very Darwinian."

Adrian smiled. The tooth was chipped after all. "Precisely, Miss Moore. You're familiar with Darwin?"

"Oh, I just dabble." It was Woodrow, actually, who had lent her *On the Origin of Species* and implored her to read it. On her left, he kept his silence.

"So you see what I mean. Not to delve into anything too scientific, but often the individual animal is only worth what it can contribute to the species as a whole. So I feel like I'm wasting my time saving the lives of these sick, decrepit, old pets that have nothing to contribute to the gene pool." This was something rehearsed, she realized. Words did not usually flow like that in the languor of noon in Nebraska.

"Wow," she said. "That's such an enlightened idea. Why, Porter and I were just in France, and many people there are espousing a similar view." She turned to Woodrow, who seemingly surmounted his bitterness at being edged out of the conversation and nodded twice in accord.

Adrian smiled at this kindred spirit. "See, my colleagues don't believe me. Even those who do believe me only think it's viable for fish or insects, small animals with short lives. But I personally think that they just haven't seen how bad it can get—how much of a threat certain organisms pose to the species as a whole."

Her mind raced. Should she mention music or something? She realized she had more to lose trying to change the subject. So, to keep the bird in her hand, she decided to keep the subject going as it was. "We agree completely," said Raina. "And everyone I spoke to in France agrees as well."

Adrian smiled. "Well, I won't bore you with business. You said you're from Lincoln?"

"Originally, yes."

"Are you all visiting?"

Woodrow and Raina looked at each other. "Yes! Well, really," Raina amended, "it's not anything as light as any old visit. Roy called me and told me my auntie had just passed away, and that he needed help with the funeral arrangements. I had Porter load up my bags and I headed right over." Woodrow looked at her with loathing.

"I'm sorry to hear that. So your aunt is now passed?"

Raina nodded solemnly. She wanted to keep her eye on Adrian. Every time she looked away, something about him seemed to change. The same tooth that was chipped a moment earlier now seemed straight as a razor.

"She was a very kind woman," he said. "Why, I remember... Well, you probably don't want to hear me spin my old yarns at a time like this. Please, let us know if we can do anything."

"Thank you, Mr. James, that's very kind of you. Lidia has been an amazing help this whole time." This was the first thing out of her mouth that wasn't a lie. But the deceit was too fun, and quickly she changed gears again. "Roy, you know, has always been rather sensitive." She crossed her legs. "The very day we had her body taken away by the county, he decided it was too painful here for him, and he skedaddled off."

Adrian scratched his cheek. "That's too bad. Where to?"

His nervous energy convinced Raina to back away from the conversation, and the sudden intensity of his gaze convinced her to set up traps as she went. "I'm not sure, really. He lived in New Orleans for a while, but I don't know if he liked it there. He was always like that, you know. Never really sure what he wanted."

Woodrow looked at Raina.

Adrian nodded slowly. "So you would say that Roy has some...issues processing grief?"

"It seems like it. I mean, you've known him almost as long as I have, Mr. James. You know he was always a little different."

Adrian looked at the doll sitting at the end of the couch. "Yes, I remember. I actually wanted to ask you a question. There's something I could use your help with." He pulled a notepad and pen from his inner pocket.

"Anything, Adrian."

Adrian looked at Woodrow and then back at Raina.

"Oh!" she said. "Of course! Porter, why don't you draw us some more water from the pump?"

Raina's eyes begged Woodrow to go along with it. He stood and closed the door behind him. Only someone who had lived with him as long as Raina could have detected the tiny excess of force he used to close it.

Adrian began. "Now, please stop me if I go too far, but my sister told me that Roy's father suffered from some sort of..." He checked his notes. "Schizophrenia. Do you know anything about this?"

Raina was glad she had put on so much foundation. Now it would be impossible to notice the color drain from her face. "No, I never heard about anything like that."

"You never heard about the father being mentally ill?"

"No," said Raina, "never." This was not a total lie, since it had been true a month ago. "I knew he passed away a long time ago, but that's about all."

Pen poised, Adrian stared. "You didn't have much contact with them?"

"Unfortunately not," she said.

Adrian looked at where the wall and the ceiling met. "That is...so..." He squinted. "*Frustrating*." A shark biting into a decoy.

After a moment she said, "Well, I'm sorry I couldn't be of much help."

In the silence that followed, Raina looked outside, wishing more than anything that she were not still trapped in this room with this awful man. She resisted the impulse to leap out the window.

"Madness is never easy to talk about, especially when it's in one's own family." He looked at her. "Which side of the family did you say you are on again?"

"The Moore side," she said. "Aunt Inez's side."

Adrian nodded. He wrote something down. "You and I, I think, are both ahead of the curve, Raina. Politically speaking. Europe is starting to recognize the threats that liberalism can wreak on the human species. In Germany they have already begun implementing programs to weed out the most dangerous individuals who run the risk of mongrelizing the human race. And what happens? They manage to pull themselves out of the worst economic slump in their history. But America, it seems, is determined to stay behind the times."

Her skin tightened on her forearms and neck. She caught herself wondering, *Where is the closest knife? Where is the fire poker?*

"But," Adrian continued, "we have made some progress. We recognize that individuals suffering from mental disease, at least, have no place within a healthy population. But there are degrees of danger, you see? My father, for example, was a synesthete. Do you know what that is?"

She knew what a synesthete was. Liszt, who was Constance's favorite composer, had been one. "No," she said, tilting her head a little.

"It's a mental disorder in which one's sensory neurons are crossed. It jumbles the stimulus and the autonomic sense. My father, for example, saw smells as colors."

"Wow. Could he taste defeat, too?"

Adrian smiled but did not laugh. "I never asked him. But it was not heritable, see? And it doesn't prevent the afflicted from leading a normal life. Schizophrenia, on the other hand, being a dangerous and heritable disease, is toxic to have in a population." Raina watched his pen trace zigzags on his notepad. "Anyone with schizotypal parentage legally belongs in jail."

Raina felt the only way to survive this encounter was to match Adrian. "But Mr. James, why jail? Couldn't the diseased individuals escape and then breed?"

Adrian shrugged, staring at his notes. "Well, we would have precautions for things like that. For dangerous schizophrenics, we would implement a regimen of medication that yields the diseased infertile."

Raina nodded. "Good," she said slowly.

"Listen, Raina," he said suddenly, setting his pen down on the pad. "I think your cousin needs to see a doctor. It's dangerous to have him out in the world. You are obviously a very smart woman, and I know you can see where I'm coming from." He took a breath. "I just need one perfect example..." He trailed off. He looked at her and smiled. "I'm so sorry, I hope I haven't worried you. I just thought you, as his cousin, have a right to know."

Raina nodded. "Yes, I completely understand. If I ever find out where Roy is living, I will let you know first thing."

Adrian smiled. She wondered what had chipped his tooth. Some awl or adze in his sister's workshop? A monkey wrench or a piston hitting him while working with Jacob? Suddenly, Woodrow opened the back door with a bucket of water in his hand.

"Porter," she said musically, "can you give us a moment?"

"Oh, no," said Adrian, "I was just leaving. Lidia will see red if I'm not home in time for dinner. I'm sorry to have kept you so long." He stood and kissed her hand. "I'm so sorry to hear about your aunt. Has there been a service?"

"Yes," Raina lied.

"Where?"

"Barnville."

"Barnville?"

"Barnville, Ohio. Where she was born."

"Oh. Well, I'm sure it was lovely. It was nice to meet you, Porter." He waved. Raina thought she detected the faintest hint of body odor as he passed. She watched his walk: he kept his arms pinned to his side, as if he was wooden from the waist up. Once he had walked down the porch steps, he turned around and said, "Thank you for having me. I'm sure Inez would have appreciated the help."

"It was the least we could do," said Raina, fighting against the wind to keep her skirt down. "Come on down anytime."

Adrian did not reply. He stared at her legs. When he looked up at her, he was pale. No one spoke for a moment.

"Mr. James?"

"Good-bye," he said, turning and stepping into his car with a far-off look. He drove off at a breakneck speed and disappeared into the dust.

The weight lifted off Raina's shoulders. She went inside and buried her face in Woodrow's chest.

"I am so Goddamn sorry," she said. "I should not have treated you like that."

"It's okay," he said. "I'm just sorry he said all those things to you."

She pulled back. "You heard?"

"Yes," he said. "I listened from the back window." Wrapping his arms around her, he asked, "So if he ever finds Roy, he's gonna arrest him?"

"Or take him to some lab and fill him with needles and tubes. I don't know." Talking about Roy as if he was not there made it easier for Raina.

"Do you think he...?"

"Suspected?" She turned the thought around in her head. "You know, I really don't think he did. He seemed pretty wrapped up in his own theory."

They hugged again. The house's stunned walls gradually worked their way back toward the center, providing structure, comfort, and safety. Though the sun had only just touched the horizon, a wind had swept in to rob the earth of its warmth. Woodrow and Raina agreed they were ready for bed.

She asked Woodrow to undo her zipper, adding, "Now don't think I'm trying to seduce you." He let the dress fall slowly to the ground, and he insisted she lie back while he removed her shoes. "If I had known you treated women so kindly," she said, "I would never have taken off my makeup." She made him lie back too and began to rub his feet. Woodrow reached over and grabbed hers, running his hands over her hairy calf.

"I must say, ma'am, you have some of the worst feminine hygiene of anyone I've ever met." He plucked a hair from her leg. She kicked him until he laughed. "God, you come out into the main room with your leg hair poking out from under your dress, and I ask myself, 'What kind of lady is she trying to be?'"

Raina laughed and covered her face with her hands.

Suddenly her abdomen grew cold and constricted. She sat up straight like Dracula rising from the crypt.

She pulled her leg back and set one hand on her calf, the other over her heart. "Woodrow," she said. "Did you see Adrian staring at my legs? On the porch, I mean. When the wind was blowing up my skirts."

Woodrow shook his head. "I'm not sure," he said.

Raina's thoughts swirled around her, freezing, developing razor-sharp and icy spikes, and threatening to kill her.

"He knows I'm Roy."

Woodrow's expression dropped. He sat up on his elbows.

"Woodrow," she said, "we need to get out of here."

The gravity of the moment settled on them. They were frozen together. If they never moved, they reasoned, the terror would never develop into action. They could go back to the previous moment, and their world would never have to change.

"*Now!*" she shouted.

Chapter Five

Roy and Woodrow moved around the house with the silent efficiency of bees, both operating out of same mind, two agents acting for the same end. They darted from one room to the next, shoving clothes into bags, wrapping up food, selecting one or two books apiece. Roy picked up the photograph of his father but immediately set it back down. Woodrow began a pile of the flour sacks and paper bags that acted as their luggage. As Roy passed through the main room to get to the kitchen, he noticed Betty sat perched atop the pile.

"Woodrow?" he called into the next room.

"What?"

"The doll?"

"We may need it."

Roy did not have time to worry about that. He redid the bandana on his head and got back to work.

When they had all the bags set near the door they began loading up the car. The back seat was entirely filled, so Betty would have to sit in the front with them. The setting sun made the white sacks orange and gave Roy the impression that the fields were somehow pulling away from them, retreating into cold space, leaving them stranded on the surface of Mars.

Woodrow sat in the driver's seat, and Roy told him to wait. He ran inside and pulled his grandfather's gold watch from a tiny box in the back of one of her drawers. He looked over her clothes. There was nothing here for him. He shoved the watch in his pocket and headed outside.

The car sputtered and wheezed. Roy watched as Woodrow cranked the key in the ignition; he heard the engine start and die, start and die again. He watched on, unbelieving, wondering how to wake up.

After another few minutes of trial, Woodrow looked under the hood. Roy did not bother leaving the car, nor did he ask what the problem was. In his mind's eye he saw Adrian speeding toward them in a paddy wagon. *No,* he thought, *I bet he's already in a white asylum van. No. He is coming here in a hearse.* Roy stepped out of the car and kicked its tire to force it into action.

Woodrow poked around under the hood. Roy asked him what was the matter.

"Dust," he said. "Clogging the engine."

Every inch of land between them and safety seemed to stretch out beyond the red horizon. For the first time he understood the anxiety with which sailors whispered the word, "landlocked."

Both he and Woodrow turned to look at the road at the same time. Roy's first thought was that it was a small dust storm. He had seen them that small before. But dust storms never came with a tiny, beige police car at their front.

"What the *fuck*!" said Woodrow as they raced back inside.

"We gotta hide, Woodrow."

"Where?"

That was a good question. The house had no attic or cellar and the shed was not big enough for two. None of the rooms' doors locked. Roy whipped his head around. The corners of the house had never felt so rigid. His impulse was to wrap himself and Woodrow up in a blanket and to lie on the floor. He wondered whether they could both fit in the chimney.

The idea burst in his mind like a bubble. Woodrow turned to him, sensing the thought.

"The loft."

Chapter Six

The huge sliding barn doors had been left open, and they screamed as Roy and Woodrow drew them closer together. Besides the dust and cobwebs that weighed down every corner and the nests of the wasps on the wall, the barn had also been invaded by a family of rats whose scurrying in the dark made Roy lift his feet impulsively. Cans of old tractor gasoline were stacked in a corner. The cows, who had been his childhood friends, were absent. He tried to imagine that they had not died, but had instead moved east, like him. Woodrow entered the shadowy barn beside him, holding his nose against a stench that both of them had grown unused to.

The ladder to the loft was in poor repair, so Roy, the lighter of the two, offered to go up first. It held. He helped Woodrow up. The loft itself was largely unchanged. There was less hay than before, and the floor was coated with drifts of dust, the floorboards sanded to a skin-like softness. Roy turned to the corner where his hiding place had been. The piece of glass that had once hung there had come unloose and shattered against the floor. His old high chair still stood in the corner, but one of its legs bore the gnaw marks of rats. The book about sewing had been sacrificed to the elements, and the strips that had been torn from the pages hinted at the meddling of tiny paws. The only shocking change was the scale. Had he really been so small that he could curl himself up in that corner? Had he ever been able to stand upright in that alcove?

Together he and Woodrow lifted up the ladder and drew it up to them. They kneeled outside the frame of the window and peeked outside.

The sheriff's car pulled up to the dirt driveway, and Adrian jumped out. The sheriff himself was rather large, with white sideburns and pants that came up to his ribs. Roy and Woodrow watched as they knocked on the door of the main house as if they had been invited for supper.

Roy's hand found Woodrow's as the two men let themselves into the house. It was not a large house by any means, and the men scoured its confines in minutes. They regrouped on the porch, gesturing to Woodrow's car. How could they have escaped without their car? Adrian then pointed to the barn. They started toward it.

Woodrow and Roy pulled their faces from the window and leaned on either side of it, their hands meeting under the frame. If Roy pretended this was happening to someone else, then he could be calm. If he imagined himself remembering this moment from a far-off date, then it would not be so terrifying. *Wasn't that scary?* he imagined himself saying. *That one time we were almost castrated in a barn?*

"Roy?"

His breath stopped at the mention of his name. The men

entered the barn.

"Roy Manger? Are you in here? I'm Eric Greer, the sheriff of Furnas County, and I'm here with a warrant for your arrest."

Adrian's stressed whisper followed. "Don't *warn* him, sheriff. You'll scare him into Kansas!"

The sheriff spoke again. It was easy to follow his words and imagine they were playacting, that the sheriff was not actually a cruel man and Adrian was not really a monster, but rather two paid actors, totally innocuous family men who would remove their costumes once this scene had ended and return home to their wives to eat tomato soup and listen to the radio. Roy wondered whether the sheriff's gun was filled with real bullets or stage blanks. In the shadow of the window, Woodrow squeezed his hand as if they were watching a tense part of a movie.

After a few minutes of searching the barn, the sheriff and Adrian returned to the car. Roy's mind slipped from the plane of panic to the lower plane of deliberation. Even if Woodrow and Roy ordered the spare parts at Hardt's tomorrow, it may take up to a week to get the car in working order again. That was not an impossible amount of time, truth to be told. It was tolerable. The paths of the future opened up like a stream cleared of debris. As the sheriff climbed into his car, Roy breathed a sigh of relief. They were in the clear.

"Wait a second," said Woodrow.

"What?" Roy stared at his face, which was bisected by the shadow from the edge of the window, glowing with twilight orange

369

and purple.

"He's not getting in the car."

Roy's guts clenched as the sheriff drove away, leaving Adrian standing alone on the front porch. He held a rifle in one hand and a carton of ammunition in the other. Handcuffs dangled from his belt. Adrian watched the police car speed down the road, kicking up dust behind it. After a moment, Adrian, the doll-sized figure moving around in the dark, turned and went to inspect the shed.

"It's okay," said Woodrow, sensing Roy's terror. "We just have to lie low here until he leaves." Roy did not move. "He probably is having the sheriff come pick him up in the morning. He won't be here forever. Hell, we only had a day's worth of food in there anyway. Even if he sets up camp, he won't last for long."

It felt like Roy's intestines were tumbling around inside him. The man had invaded their home. Like animals, they were confined to the barn. He realized now that he had been foolish to start loving Woodrow. They had built a castle on a foundation of sand, and now the surf would rise and reclaim the stones. And by morning they would be dead.

"Hey," said Woodrow, "don't worry." Roy turned to him. Woodrow smiled. "If we can survive the Lincoln Highway, we can survive this."

Roy smiled weakly and rested his head on the windowsill. "I'm just sorry. You don't deserve this."

Woodrow lay down and put his head in Roy's lap. "I would rather starve to death in this barn than eat at the Ritz without you."

Roy smiled. After a moment he said, "Try telling me that in a week, after I've gnawed through your leg in my sleep."

Woodrow laughed. Roy scooted until he was lying flat with Woodrow's head on his stomach. They looked up at the ceiling where cobwebs clung and where tiny pipes of clay stood.

"Why?" asked Roy.

"Why what?"

"Why do you want to stay here with me?"

Woodrow was silent. "Because I have a death wish."

Roy slapped his arm. "Seriously."

"Because I'm trying to disgrace my family."

"You are awful."

"Because I love you."

Roy took the words as coolly as he could have hoped. At the Pineapple, such professions of love were met with a quip such as "that will cost you extra" or "save that for your wife." But here, the words unveiled a whole landscape. They summoned a calm, flat river in which Roy lay surrounded by shallow, greenish water, with wide, sun-warmed slabs of slate beneath. Those words formed the water and the stones and the trees and the mountains beyond—pulled them out of the very air and set them into the earth as a jeweler would set an emerald into silver. At that moment, he felt like neither Roy nor Raina. He was not a former prostitute or a possibly paranoid schizophrenic or an aesthete or even an American. He felt naked, blind as a seed buried deep in the warm earth, pushing, he hoped, toward the surface.

"I love you, too, Woodrow." After a minute, he added, "But that doesn't explain why you would stay."

"Well," Woodrow said, breathing deeply, "how about this?" He rubbed his face with his hands. "After I had left you here, a few days into my journey west, I started getting these cramps in my gut." He gestured to his abdomen. "And it got worse and worse each day. I knew I couldn't go to a doctor, and painkillers didn't help. One day when I was walking to the store, a cramp hit me and I almost keeled over. Some man rocking on the porch asked me what was wrong and I told him. He scratched his beard," Woodrow said, scratching his chin, "and spat in the spittoon and asked whether I had parted ways with someone recently. I said yes. He asked if this person had made me laugh. I said yes. He said that was the problem. I had become so used to laughing that, when I left you, my gut muscles didn't know what to do." Woodrow's head turned to look at Roy's face, but Roy did not look down. Woodrow continued, "It was then I knew I had to come back." Roy bit his lip and smiled. "You see?"

"Bullshit," said Roy. "You tell tall tales, Woodrow."

"No," he said, cracking up. "It's all true."

"Okay, I'll bite. So you're saying you came back...because you don't have health insurance?"

Woodrow laughed. He held Roy's hand and said no more.

Eventually Roy said, "I missed you too."

Woodrow nodded. "And I'm sorry I left you alone for your

mom thing."

"It's all right. I think it was something I needed to do alone."

"How are you feeling?"

Roy shrugged. "She hadn't really factored into my life for the past few years. So her being gone, it kinda feels like how it felt before I came back." He added, "It just makes being home feel weird."

"I bet," said Woodrow. "Well once Adrian leaves, we can get the heck out of here. I don't think you could sell this place for anything but pocket change, but it would be nice to have it off your hands."

"I know. It's strange to think they'll eventually tear down all these structures."

"Like?"

"The house, I mean. The big companies are gonna tear everything down. The barn, too."

"I had no idea."

"Yeah." Roy's right leg twitched. He had an image of himself grown old and insane on this property, the dust digging its way under his skin until his heart beat only sand. He did not want to be trapped here. He would rather die. "Yeah, that will be strange."

"Where do you want to live?"

Roy stared at the dark ceiling. He could see a single star through a hole in the roof. "No idea. You?"

Woodrow shrugged against Roy's side. "Maybe southern Nebraska. Just buy a huge, barren property there and spend all my time naked in bed."

Roy slapped his shoulder. "You goon." Part of him demanded answers from Woodrow: *Why do you love me? Have you loved anyone before? What do you really think about me? Why are you Woodrow? What are the elements that comprise you? What do you dream about? What do you fear?*

But he let his tongue lie limp. These were not the questions to ask now, or ever. There was better enterprise, he reasoned, in just lying still, holding his hand, and loving him with his whole being.

With Woodrow beside him, Roy's stress diminished. He was no longer on the scaffold for his own execution. Instead, they were on a cloud, watching the bitter and dark farmhouse below slowly grow sallow. They rested on the leftover hay, peeking at the perfect square of sky visible through the window and the scattered salt of stars that poked through the holes in the roof. Eventually, sleep crept over his eyelids, and he rested.

Chapter Seven

Woodrow woke Roy with a shake. His eyes held something urgent. He motioned for him to go to the window. He pointed at a spot on the lawn twenty feet from Woodrow's broken-down car. The finger was an accusation, and the guilty party was Adrian, in his shirtsleeves. The couch had been pulled onto the lawn and blankets were stacked on top of it. Roy watched as Adrian stepped back into the house, the rifle slung over his shoulder.

"What is he doing?" whispered Roy.

"Watch."

Adrian sauntered out of the house with what looked like a can of gasoline.

"Shit!" Roy whispered, turning to Woodrow. They watched as he soaked the cushions with the fluid. "What is he doing that for?" Roy suspected Woodrow saw the endgame. He stared at Adrian like a chess player would at an adversary.

The couch burst into flames. Adrian stepped back and crossed his arms, freshly coated in yellow and red light.

"Well," said Roy. "I never really liked that couch anyway."

Woodrow shook his head. They watched as Adrian reached into Woodrow's car and pulled out a flour sack full of clothes. He tossed it onto the fire.

"*Shit!*" Roy whispered.

Adrian turned to the barn. Roy and Woodrow ducked below the window ledge.

"He knows we're here," said Roy.

Woodrow nodded.

"And he's trying to draw us out."

Woodrow nodded.

"So he can shoot us."

"So he can shoot *you*," Woodrow amended.

Roy felt like the fire was right in front of him. His skin grew warm, and his muscles came alive in the heat. He kept thinking, *This cannot be real. This cannot be real. The curtain will fall soon, and we will stand and buy popcorn and go home. We are safe. This is only theater.*

After a while his wits returned to him. He said, "Well, anything he can destroy, we can always buy again. It's just stuff, after all."

At these words Woodrow sat bolt-upright and stared out the window. Roy followed his gaze.

Adrian was lining up their luggage. He was seemingly creating a hierarchy, saving the most expensive items—the cosmetic bags and jewelry box—for last. Roy watched as a flour sack was tossed onto the flames. After a minute the sack burst open, and one of his silk dresses crumbled into ash. Charred pages of *Anna Karenina* were sucked into the blackness of the night sky. Woodrow's body tensed beside him as Adrian brought Betty out of the car. He judged her to be of some importance and placed her near the middle of the long, snaky line of luggage.

Sweat stood out on Woodrow's brow. Roy asked, "What's wrong?"

"Listen," he said. "We need to do whatever it takes to stop him."

"Woodrow," said Roy, touching his back. He was rigid as cement. "Those are just things. They're not important. He can't reach us up here. We're safe as long as we stay put."

"You don't understand, Roy. There's something in that doll..." His hands clenched on the sill. "There's something in that doll that we cannot afford to have burned."

The flames found their tinier, icier duplicates in Woodrow's pupils.

Roy asked, "What's in there?"

Woodrow laughed once. "Nearly $7,000."

"From Las Vegas," Roy said, after a moment. "From somewhere you robbed while in Las Vegas."

Woodrow nodded. Roy repressed the urge to reprimand him like a mother, to slap him across the knuckles for having broken the law. But because Roy had shared in the loot, he felt complicit. And because he had felt such pleasure eating the food and reading the books that the stolen money had bought, he started to reason that maybe the crime wasn't so bad after all.

Roy idly looked around the room. *If we threw my old high chair at Adrian*, he thought, *then maybe it would knock him out.*

If we threw the rotting sewing book at him, maybe he would be distracted. Disappointed in his own schemes, he turned to Woodrow. He could almost hear the gears and cogs whirring and clicking into place in his skull.

He waited until Woodrow's expression relaxed. He asked, "Do you have a plan?"

Woodrow told Roy his plan and Roy added his own ideas. Adrian threw one bag, then another, atop the fire. When the time came, Roy held Woodrow's face in between his hands and kissed him, once, wishing him good luck. Roy was ready to separate from his other half for the time being. But he knew that any injury visited on Woodrow would harm his body as well. And if Woodrow died during the execution of this plan, Roy could only see for his own future a vast, black wasteland. But they did not have time. They pulled apart and began.

Chapter Eight

Silently, Roy let the ladder out the back window while Woodrow stood guard. Then they descended. Roy watched Woodrow steal across the lawn into the main house, one shadow in a vast sea of shadows. Roy entered the barn through the back door and watched Adrian through a crack in the wall. Adrian lifted a bag that tore in his hands, slipping dresses to his feet. He leaned down and began to gather them in his arms, black and red tulle covering his face. Roy took advantage of the distraction and headed to the back of the barn. He unscrewed the caps to the gallon drums of tractor fuel.

Once the gasoline had been splashed around the barn and had soaked into the wooden walls, Roy grabbed two sacks of old chicken feed. He stacked these in the far corner so they looked like a person in hiding, then threw a blanket over them. He slipped out the back doors, padlocking them shut behind him. He felt a sense of accomplishment, one he usually felt after finishing reading a novel. He smiled in the dark, imagining a clean black line being drawn through this part of the plan.

He ascended the ladder and accessed the loft through the window. He left the ladder leaning there. He crept up to the front window and watched Adrian toss another piece of luggage onto the fire. The wood in the couch gave way under the weight of the blaze, sending sparks up into the night sky. The doll was next. There was no time to lose.

All Roy had to do was look out the window long enough for Adrian to notice him. As he lifted his head upward, he marked each star that slid into view, wondering whether the last thing he ever saw would be that star, or that one, or that. His knees ached against the pressure from the old boards and his stomach clenched. He felt like he was vibrating. He rose like a corpse from the crypt.

The firelight did not catch on anything as small as the dry corn stalks on the field, so the only objects within its orange aura were Adrian, the car, and the snaking line of baggage. The only three features in an expanse of black. *I wonder*, thought Roy, *whether these murdered bags had posed a unique threat to the species of bags as a whole?* The whole scene was vibrant and satanic—Roy felt vicariously drunk with the power of the destructor. He was shocked at himself when he realized that, given the opportunity, he would gladly have changed places with Adrian.

When Adrian's gaze moved toward the loft window, Roy ducked his head just in time. A part of the ceiling exploded above him, raining down flecks of wood and dust and opening another tiny frame for a star to poke out of. *It's not so hard to get shot,* he thought. *It's so simple. Anyone could do it*. Through a slit in the wallboards, he watched the next step unfold. Adrian, excited, approached the barn with his gun raised, the blaze forgotten behind him. But there was something wrong. Adrian was clutching his face. When he reached down for a handkerchief Roy saw that his nose was streaming blood. Roy smiled. Recoil. But despite his marred face and the accompanying shame, Adrian still stalked toward the barn, the gun raised like a long, single eye, staring at where Roy was a moment ago. Heart racing, palms slick, legs forgotten beneath him, Roy stared at the house and waited for the signal.

Chapter Nine

Woodrow crept onto the back porch and entered the house, keeping Adrian in his line of sight through the open windows. He heard Roy lifting the cans of gasoline in the barn and wished he would stay quiet. But he had to concede a degree of control in this situation. Falling in love always meant giving something up. In Woodrow's case, he gave up the exhilaration of committing a crime alone. And while every forfeit for love was matched a hundred times over by the boons of affection and joy, Woodrow could not help but reprimand himself for falling in love, when falling in love necessarily meant partnering up with someone who was by no means a natural-born criminal.

He jumped off this train of thought and let it chug away. He could not afford distraction at this moment. He could not even allow himself to eat a grape from the bowl on the table. He had to keep his eyes on Adrian, and keep his footsteps silent. He kneeled in front of the windows in the main room and waited until Roy returned to the loft. Adrian tossed another bag onto the fire. Only one more before the doll. His fingertips pressed on the sill and his breath grew shallow. He had to be patient. There was no room for mistakes.

Woodrow was still in the bad habit of narrating his action. Living on the Dabney plantation for so long, he had become accustomed to sharing stories of his life. For years he had transformed his daily action into tales worthy of telling and then shared them with his friends while they fished or weeded. His tools were primarily these: embellishment and omission. He wondered how he would spin the story of his current situation. He did not have to embellish much, since this was one of the bravest plans he had ever undertaken. But would his audience still be impressed if they knew that he was only risking his life in order to save some sissy boy? In his youth, any boy caught doing anything for a girl was automatically deemed a pussy. Woodrow suspected the verdict would be even harsher if the girl was not Black, but white, and not even a girl at all.

Woodrow watched the loft with the intensity that the sun stares at the earth. *Soon*, he told himself, *Roy's face will emerge. It has to.*

Adrift on this cushion of time, Woodrow wondered why he still cared so much about this old practice of storytelling. He no longer needed to filter his lived experience through a narrative he would present to others. He no longer needed the approval of the friends who would lean on the pebbly banks of the creek and laugh at any anecdote in which some Nancy-boy got his comeuppance. These friends were gone, and the house around which they had revolved was cinders, the rare and violent blood of the family within it boiled and then reduced to ash. Why, then, among the ruins of fire and of memory, did he still feel the need to impress?

Woodrow turned his eyes to the bonfire just as the couch collapsed, forcing one of its legs to topple out from under it so its wooden part stuck out while the upholstery remained in the blaze. The grin on his face was irrepressible.

Who was it in the barn, exactly? Whose face did he wait patiently for while kneeling on the floor of this dusty home in the middle of this Godforsaken state? Was it a shy and smart young Black woman like the ones his grandmother would set him on dates with? Was it a white girl from one of those magazines his neighbor had lent him when he was too young to understand? Was it his own father? Perhaps Evangeline? Or was it one of the Dabney daughters, Emma or Olivia, those alabaster harpies whose smooth skin and raven hair inspired nothing in the men of the Dabney plantation but hatred and fear? Who was he waiting for? He could not seem to remember how the story went.

Woodrow had to change his position, since one of his legs had fallen asleep. He stared at the window of the loft, feeling an impatience that verged on violence. *Where the fuck is he?*

Halting the progress of these cruel thoughts, Woodrow drew a bundle of sensations from the reservoir of memory. The feel of Roy's skin. The sensation of laughing. The taste of Roy's mouth after he had eaten fruit. The sense of safety and of purpose. The quiet peace of reading in the same room. These were the offerings, the things he needed to curb his impatience. These were the golden apples he threw to distract whatever was pursuing him.

Who was in the barn? The question looped back like a needle and thread. Automatically he waded through the faces from his past and slipped them, one by one, into the window of the barn. Perhaps he was waiting on one of the prostitutes he had visited before finding Raina, one of those kind women who did not care that Woodrow just wanted to lie down and talk to them for a while. Women who hugged him for two hours and just let him go, no questions asked. Their faces rotated past the window like the frames in a film reel. He knew what he would have told his friends if he ever saw them again. He would say that once those bedroom doors closed, he did his business as any man would. And he would not stop there. His fellow fishermen would not bite unless the tale brimmed with bravado. He would lie and say he had lain with those women five or six times over the course of the night and left them walking awkwardly the next day. That was the only way to get the men's interest, to prove that one was among them.

Or would it be his father's face in that window, the mustache touched with gray and the skull cursed with baldness? Would the figure point to Woodrow as he had years ago to tell him in no uncertain terms exactly what was acceptable for good Christians to do with other men and what wasn't? For a boy of fourteen begging his father for forgiveness, Woodrow had had little room for hatred at the time. But today, as he watched Adrian toss another bag onto the fire, he let the rage fill his chest. Like an orgasm, it peaked and dissipated. His family was dead, for all he cared. He felt a sort of freedom. He had the impulse to hum.

This part of the story, he realized, would never sell. "I waited and waited in the farmhouse for my sissy accomplice to give me the signal." No, that would never make it into the final story. The boys who lay on the bank would fall asleep.

He stationed another figure at the window of the loft. A Black man, his own age, with small ears and a big gap between his front teeth. His mind's eye did not supply the lower half of this young man, which relieved Woodrow. If the window were any lower, Woodrow knew he would see the ragged line of innards spilling out, where this boy, the original Woodrow, had been thrown across the train tracks by a group of white teenagers the same month they had arrived in Charlotte. Together the first Woodrow and the soon-to-be Woodrow had exchanged theories about Evangeline and Sully on the porch after work. They had sipped lemonade and imagined life beyond Dabney. They, too, had traded stories.

Woodrow flexed his thigh to ward off a cramp. He shook his head and returned his gaze to Adrian, who, in turn, was looking into the depths of the fire. *No*, Woodrow thought. *I am not waiting for Woodrow. He is dead. I am Woodrow now.*

Just then, like a ghost, the face he was waiting for rose in the loft window. The features were blurred by the light of the fire, and Woodrow could barely tell if it was really Roy or someone else. But he knew it was Roy, or at least, his heart knew it was Roy. He had seen plants parched for weeks at a time suddenly perk up once watered. This is what it felt like to see that face at the window. As soon as it was visible, though, Adrian raised his rifle. Woodrow gritted his teeth as Roy's face disappeared and Adrian's hastily-raised gun jumped backwards in his hands, ramming its butt into his face. Woodrow hid his giggle in the palm of his hand and crawled to the door, where he watched Adrian approach the barn, nursing a broken nose.

He realized he could never tell a story about this night. Not just because of the lawlessness, or the violence, or because he was risking his life for something as banal as love. He opened the front door and peered around the corner, waiting for Adrian to disappear into the barn. In fact, the fisher-boys would love this story. More likely than not, they would laugh at the funny parts and hold their breath in suspense as any seasoned audience member would. Adrian disappeared into the barn, and Woodrow's body tensed, ready to dash off the porch, thinking his fisher-friends would never hear the tale of tonight, because this night would never become a story. Woodrow would never shove this experience into the mold of a narrative, because he had nothing left to prove. The sentence ended at the front door. Past the row of thorny weeds, there was nothing left to tell. So he leaped off the porch, let the cover of the book fall shut, and hit the ground running.

Chapter Ten

Roy had never been to a beach, but this was what he imagined it felt like to be treading in the deepest part of the ocean. He was out of his element, that was certain, and beneath him, a beaked beast with tentacles writhed in hungry contemplation, wondering whether it should spare him or drag him down into the crushing deep.

He watched Woodrow bolt out of the house and rush toward the bonfire. He ran by it so fast that Roy could not tell if it was really him or just a shadow. But he made sure: *Yes, the doll is gone.* Out of the aura of the fire, he strained to see where Woodrow was. The night had swallowed him whole.

Slowly he remembered why he was up here. Crouched in the corner, he watched Adrian through the cracks in the floorboards as he stalked down the row of stalls, occasionally shoving the doors open with a kick. His nose had stopped bleeding, but it left a red stain down the front of his white shirt, which now clung to his skin all the way to his belt. Roy watched with glee as Adrian froze in place. He had noticed the sacks in the corner. Roy looked out the window, and there was Woodrow springing out of the gloom toward them, holding a stick of furniture whose end still held fast to a blazing scrap of upholstery.

Slowly Adrian leveled his gun at the decoy. A shot rang out, and the bundle tore open where its head would have been. At the same moment, something landed in the middle of barn. It was the burning couch leg, come from nowhere, a gift from no one. Then, the sound of the barn's front doors slamming shut. From the outside, the padlock made a merry click.

Adrian shouted, "*Fuck!*"

Roy looked out the window. Woodrow looked up and gave him the thumbs-up. He ran back toward the house just as part of the door blew away. Adrian was trying to shoot off the lock.

Smoke began to creep up into the loft. Roy cast a glance at the few relics that would be sacrificed: the high chair, the book, the pieces of glass. But these were not his—they were toys some other kid once played with. The only thing on his mind right now was the execution of the plan, the crossing off of the last item on the list. So he covered his mouth with the bandana and crept to the back window, glad he had remembered to leave the ladder leaning there. But halfway across the loft, a floorboard exploded a foot away from him.

He froze. He realized that Adrian must have been able to see him through the cracks in the floorboards. Roy turned to where Woodrow had vanished into the shadows, thinking, *At least he is safe. If I die, at least he will live.* He felt that, despite the air in the loft that was quickly becoming hot and smoky, he could feel the night air brushing past his head. He was with Woodrow, running through the night.

He looked down. For a moment his and Adrian's eyes met through the gaps. Roy remembered those eyes, that jaw, that shocking shark-image that even the floor of a boat couldn't protect him from. His heart was steeped in ice.

Something else stirred within him. Cruel vines crawled up the walls of the barn and slipped through the cracks, eager to wrap around his wrists and hold him in place there, staring. Why not stay here and let Adrian kill him? It was Adrian, after all, who caused Roy these years of anguish, who had given him the whip with which he had flogged himself every day for seven years. *Why does Adrian stand there, staring, as if the world revolves around him? Because,* thought Roy, *it does. Everything revolves around you, Adrian. I have wasted my life trying to find you, and I have let the better part of myself be consumed by your image. So kill me already. You have killed me once. It's easier a second time.*

But Adrian's aim was off. The bullet burst through the floor to Roy's right and whizzed through a hole in the shingles. Roy fell backwards, snapping out of his trance. *The smoke,* he thought. *It's muddling my thoughts.* Alarms began to blare in his head, and the wood of the floorboards began to feel hot. Adrian, for all his rage, was largely silent and seemed to be trying to extinguish the flames with kicked dust. Roy began to crawl toward the back window. He heard something break behind him, and he turned to look over his shoulder.

In the far corner stood a man far blacker than black, a black that did not look like color at all but a puncture in space itself, an edge where light and texture could no longer find purchase. Dense and massive, it made Roy twist around so he was pushing himself backward, away from it, the smoke drifting into his nose and the dust clinging to his palms.

The fire grew underneath him. But the corner was safe. Between the floorboards, the light of the blaze shot upward like a spotlight through prison bars, casting shadows on the ceiling. Roy pulled his knees to his chest and stared at the corner, trembling.

The figure pulsed with a darkness so vile that Roy wished the roof would cave in already so that some merciful rafter could crush his skull and the shifting, violent shadows within it. But no. His muscles ached with their own numbness, and his brain short-circuited. He could no more move a mountain than a finger. And the dark figure held his gaze and grew even larger. Darker.

Roy's mouth held an O-shape under the bandana, the O of complete despair, dribbling saliva from its bottom curve. His eyes would not close, and the smoke drew out streams of tears. If his heart was beating, then it was too fast to measure. If any breath entered his lungs, his chest did not move. Around him, the fire began to roar.

The figure pulsed and then began to resolve itself inward. The darkness passed through black and became pale. The color of cream emerged from this gorge, but certain spots retained their dark: the curve of the groin, the lower legs, the forearms, and the head. Through the smoke and in the dancing shadows of the blaze beneath them, Roy watched as it materialized, giving itself a form, pulling itself, with the sheer force of will, into an image.

Roy stared, his fingernails tearing through the cloth at his knees. Sobs racked his whole body. With the attention of the starving, he stared.

And in the far corner of the loft, with his hatchet in hand, Roy Manger Sr. stared back.

The sound of Adrian smashing his shoulder against the back doors rose to Roy. The fire made the dry wood pop. Roy could not make sense of it now, but he heard something falling. The flames had climbed the walls and now ran up the ceiling, raining smoldering bits of wood and shingle onto the patches of hay in the loft. Soon the room was illuminated with savage, orange fire, and Roy felt his frozen skin tighten with the heat.

Meanwhile the naked father hefted the hatchet in his hand, his eyes as dark as Roy's, but even darker for the purple rings beneath them. The body was cruel and huge, and Roy imagined himself being crushed by its toe, being mangled by its strong fingers, being torn to shreds by the gleaming teeth set deep in the stubbled jaw. His father's body would have been cruel even if it hadn't been holding the hatchet. Roy Sr. raised the hatchet and aimed it at Roy, hefting the weapon in the air, twisting that terrible body into a form of torture, ready to spring. His face contorted in a silent cry.

At that moment, the tiniest bit of bile rose in Roy's mouth and dribbled from his lip into the cloth of the bandana.

Then Roy saw something in his periphery. Some shadow dancing on the window, some illusion cast by flame. A small, black form sat on the windowsill and stared at Roy with yellow eyes. *Dolly*, he thought. His eyes, still trained on Roy Sr., noticed that this colossus had frozen in his tracks.

The car horn blared outside. Adrian gave another shove at the barn door, which held fast against his efforts. Built sturdy by Roy's father. The fire was deafening.

Trembling with the effort, Roy pried his eyes off his father and turned them to Dolly, who jumped to the floor and wove a figure-eight around Roy Sr.'s legs. Roy's breath unhitched itself, letting in a mouthful that was half air and half smoke. The statue of his father stood frozen in its mad rage, the muscles bulging, the veins in his forehead twisting in the red glare.

Roy got onto his hands and knees, keeping his eyes stuck on Dolly, not letting his gaze be sucked back toward his father, knowing that this discretion meant the difference between life and death. *Just get to the ladder,* he thought. *Just get to the ladder and you will be safe*. Roy backed up, breathing heavily, trying to compensate for the thick smoke by inhaling deeper. He pushed himself up onto the ledge of the back window and looked down out of the barn.

The ladder lay flat on the earth. It stretched from the base of the barn to a point on the ground twenty feet away. Somewhere else, the car horn finally died down, having run out of air. The sounds of someone trying to kick through wood reverberated within the barn. The barn itself groaned, sucking in wind for the sake of the fire. Roy, too, struggled to get his breath into his lungs, the lines of the ladder swimming and buckling. Like this, the barn, the horn, and Roy all fought for their air.

I will soon be dead, he thought. *Adrian is just a man and cannot kill me. All he could ever do was hand me the whip. But he could not kill me. It is the job of the whip to do the killing and not the man who gave it. The man who tried to kill me will die, too. But I will die despite my efforts. I will burn to death or I will be shot or I will break my neck on the ground below. None of my dresses, none of my wit, none of my reading or love can save me. I did not stop whipping myself when I could have. And that,* he thought, *is why I'm here now.*

Not knowing where else to go, he turned back to the loft.

His father stood at rest before the far window, alone. The glow of the fire curved around his massive chest and clung to the curves of his body, catching in his iliac crest and the angles of his shoulders. *This world was made for you, Pa.* As Roy thought this, the far side of the loft floor caved in, opening up a huge pit which screamed with flame and smoke, spitting up sparks from the black expanse over which Roy Sr. hovered like a phantom, the only fixed point in a space rippling with heat. Like a film reel, his father took the same exact step forward as last time, and raised his arm in the exact same manner; the same sequence of muscles and tendons tensed to lift the hatchet above his head, the same mask of rage overlaid itself on his already barbaric features. And Roy, meanwhile, could not even scream.

Roy became aware of a sound. For a moment he thought his mother was calling his name. But it was a man's voice that screamed his name again and again, a man's voice that grew hoarse and broke with the effort. Woodrow. At that moment, something connected in the circuit of his mind, and his brain flooded with electricity. He sat on the ledge and thought, *I want to live. I want to live, and I want Adrian to die. I want Adrian to die because he wants me to die. I want to live to spite him. I am not him, and that is worth living for. I want to live because my parents wanted me to live, and because they died so that I could continue living. I want to live for my own sake. I want to live and live and live. And live.*

The image of his father was petrified, its hand stuck in midair. Another hand had grabbed his wrist from behind. The hand that held him back was part of a soft arm. It led to a rolled-up sleeve, then a white apron, then a round chin and a corona of flyaway hair which sprung up without the restriction of her usual bandana. Her face was as stern and strong, and she held her husband's arm firmly in place. Dolly crept between their four legs as if her presence aided the effort, enchanting their tableau of struggle into permanence.

I want to live.

Suddenly, the spell broke, and Roy's body was free. Fighting his jellied muscles, he tore the bandana from his mouth and let it fall to the smoldering floor. He lifted his legs, causing his body to tip backwards off the window ledge, falling as he was used to falling backwards onto a bed of eiderdown.

As he let himself be taken into the massive void of space, he watched these twin figures and wondered whether the head of his father really did turn toward that of his mother or whether that was just a trick of the light.

Chapter Eleven

The goddess of automobiles is a fickle goddess. But today, as the dawn lifted the night, she smiled upon the war-torn property of the Mangers. The engine chugged to life through the magic of a little fresh oil. After the barn collapsed, but before all the ashes had a chance to smolder out, Woodrow, with a rag, had rid the vents of dust and got the car running again. At Woodrow's behest, Roy lay on the porch until his lungs felt better. He was on a diet of water and eye rinses and was not allowed to even offer Woodrow a lemonade. So he just watched him work as the day grew strong, letting his mind wander, occasionally turning to look at the smoking ash heap where the barn had been. Whenever he looked over there, he could not help but smile.

Roy's left arm was done up in a makeshift sling, and the pain came slowly, in aches instead of bursts, a tide instead of a hammer. They knew they had little time before the police came to retrieve Adrian. But they also worked with peace. No forces of man or goddess were so cruel as to end this adventure with an arrest, and they both enjoyed the aura of finality that came with the dawn, the solemn pleasure of a love sealed with blood. Woodrow fixed the car quickly, and when the time came for the few surviving bags to be loaded into the car, Roy contributed his meagre help and sat himself in the passenger's seat.

Woodrow told Roy to wait on one more thing. He rushed inside and brought out a small steel plaque and set it near the burned ruins of the barn. He slammed the car door behind him and turned on the ignition without a word. Roy knew this was the product of those hours and hours of secret metalworking. But he knew better than to press him for information.

Betty sat between them, one eye still open wider than the other. Looking at her more closely, Roy noticed a tiny triangle of green paper poking out from the joint in her neck. He pressed the piece back in and coughed, his lungs sore from the smoke but already breathing easier. He was lucky he had been holding his breath for so long. They agreed that he needed the sea air to recover. He smiled as the car lumbered into action, casting the lone farm building further and further behind them, the fields of dried corn shoving the site of the murder back beyond the vanishing point.

A mile later, Woodrow asked, "Feeling better?"

"I will in a moment," replied Roy.

After a moment, the beige sheriff's car shot past them on the way to the Manger property.

"*Now* I feel better," Roy said.

"Would you be offended if I said your voice sounded smoky?"

Roy smiled. "Do I sound like a man?"

Woodrow laughed. "Sometimes."

Roy smiled out the window. "Sometimes," he said. "I like that." *If I think of Roy and Raina like different places*, he thought, *then I am in two places at once.* Suddenly the smile fell off his face. *But only God can exist in two places at once. It's true,* he thought, shocked. *I read it in the Bible.* Then, a moment later, he laughed. *If that's the case, why, then I must be God.*

Woodrow turned and asked, "What's funny?"

"I'm God," said Roy.

"I thought God was omniscient," said Woodrow.

Roy smiled harder. "I *knew* you were going to say that."

Woodrow held his tongue between his teeth and whistled out a little laugh. The bags under Woodrow's eyes would go away eventually, Roy knew, and the burn he incurred on his hand would heal nicely. Roy's heart swelled with green as they sped further away from the Manger property.

Yes, he thought, the Manger property. *I am Roy Moore now*, he thought, *or Raina Moore; or Steven Wright or Carlos Ramon or Kelly Fineburg or anyone. I am Cleopatra*, Roy thought. *I am a miner. A scholar. Anything.*

The fingers flexed at the end of the broken arm. Though they hurt, at least they still worked. They were making out like thieves, Roy and Woodrow: their love, their health, some possessions, and Betty to boot. What more could they want?

"I wanted to thank you, Woodrow. You have saved my life one hundred different ways."

The smile that popped onto Woodrow's face at that moment

was fake. "Thanks," he said anyway. But five minutes later, Roy saw that Woodrow was smiling again—this time with a grin as true as the sun.

They passed the general store. The man on the porch waved at them. What was his name again? *John Hardt,* said a voice in his head. Roy sat back with the pleasure of knowledge and fatigue, feeling like an egg encased in warm felt or a marble in a baby's mouth.

Twenty miles later, he said, "Grover?"

"Yes?" said Woodrow.

"We should probably wait to eat until we're even further away, I think."

"I agree."

Roy sighed. He had known it. Who else could raze a building with such expertise? And could anyone love as strongly as Woodrow loved Roy if they had not first seen death? *But,* he thought over and over, *it will all come out in time. And if it doesn't...well then, I will still love him just as much.*

His shallow breaths steeped his mind in peace. No longer was anything dragging, no longer were the phantoms and shadows of his mind knocking about, forcing themselves into the realm of sight. They settled into their proper place. He lay in the tide of a shallow sea and basked in the blinding light.

"Roy?"

"Yes, dear Woodrow?"

"Can I ask you something?"

"Anything," he said slowly.

After a moment, Woodrow asked, "Why didn't you get out of the barn sooner? I was worried sick."

Roy smiled, watching the silken miles of fields pass by his window. Soon, he knew, there would be mountains to drive over, and then valley pastures, and then, like an epilogue, the Pacific. Roy decided then that it was not worth hiding anything. He would fill his life with the love he felt for himself and the love he felt for Woodrow; he would clear out the debris of the past and learn to build on a more stable foundation. He would fill his voracious mind's eye with a million visions of passion and fulfillment. Leaning back in his seat, he prepared to testify.

This is what he saw as he closed his eyes: a farm a hundred miles away now, where a police officer stood with one hand on his gun, inspecting the fields with a cool stare. Where the barn had stood, there was now a pile of ashes. It gave the officer the creeps. Or maybe it was the papered-over windows or the long tentacular nettles that sprung from the base of the house. Spooked by this sourceless malaise, he stepped off the porch and approached the smoldering lot, remarking that, on the north side, the ground heaved up twice. The only thing left standing, he realized, was a metal pole with a plaque on the top. Behind him, a bird called out and he jumped. This was too much for him. Roy watched as the policeman hopped in his car and drove off for backup.

Blazing across the landscape, Roy's visions melted into words. His eyes traced images of sleeping faces, of rivers, the movements of the planets; of the thoughts buzzing through the air and the secrets of the smallest bits of matter. He breathed. He watched lovers holding each other's hands thousands of miles away and hundreds of years in the future. He tasted the golden visions of love and the black ones of death, admiring the strength of compassion, the deep blue of grief. He passed his gaze over them as if he was passing his fingers over satin. They bloomed and dimmed, twisted and swelled, forming, at their center, the liquid, brilliant source from which flowed all wisdom. It was hidden and then peeked out. He could barely see it through the veils of time and space. *But there*, he thought, *right there: the very center of everything is there.*

He smiled and turned to Woodrow, thinking, *And here we are, lucky to be living within it.*

"I only ever had one cat," he started. "And I still have her to this day." Woodrow did not react right away. "And her name," said Roy, "is Dolly."

As he spoke he saw, on the empty property shrinking behind them, the police car speeding away, leaving behind it the two and a half mounds of earth and the plaque standing at their head which read:

The muffled drum's sad roll has beat
The soldier's last tattoo;
No more on life's parade shall meet
The brave and daring few.
On Fame's eternal camping-ground
Their silent tents are spread,
And Glory guards with solemn round
The bivouac of the dead.

About the Author

An author and lover of queer literature, Cameron Ramses lives in Virginia and has never set eyes on a straight person.

Email: avk8dw@virginia.edu

NineStar Press, LLC

www.ninestarpress.com

www.ingramcontent.com/pod-product-compliance
Lightning Source LLC
Chambersburg PA
CBHW050859250626
47155CB00001B/32